RAKESFALL

ALSO BY VAJRA CHANDRASEKERA

The Saint of Bright Doors

RAKESFALL

VAJRA CHANDRASEKERA

TOR PUBLISHING GROUP
New York

RAKESFALL

A Tordotcom Book
Published by Tom Doherty Associates / Tor Publishing Group
120 Broadway
New York, NY 10271

www.torpublishinggroup.com

Tor® is a registered trademark of Macmillan Publishing Group, LLC.

The Library of Congress Cataloging-in-Publication Data is available upon request.

ISBN 978-1-250-84768-3 (hardback)
ISBN 978-1-250-84769-0 (ebook)

Our books may be purchased in bulk for promotional, educational, or business use. Please contact your local bookseller or the Macmillan Corporate and Premium Sales Department at 1-800-221-7945, extension 5442, or by email at MacmillanSpecialMarkets@macmillan.com.

First Edition: 2024

Printed in the United States of America

0 9 8 7 6 5 4 3 2 1

COPYRIGHT ACKNOWLEDGMENT

To Nandini

CONTENTS

PART I

PERISTALSIS

I

Annelid and Leveret

Season one, episode one, minute thirty-one and thirty-five seconds: Leveret chases Annelid into the jungle. They are laughing, because they're teenagers playing a game. The jungle is not quite a jungle. In a much later episode, we learn via a minor subplot about 1970s land reform that it was once a colonial-era rubber plantation, abandoned and gone feral. It will gradually grow wilder and more overgrown through the seasons. We know another year has passed when the new year birds hoot in the background. Leveret and Annelid will grow older, too. This is that kind of show. There are only two kinds of show: the kind where people grow older and the kind where they don't. We, the fandom, love the first kind best. We love this show so much.

Leveret and Annelid aren't their real names—that is, not the given names of the characters in the show, which we never learn—but nicknames they took from old textbooks they found gathering dust in a cupboard in their little school that never seems to hold exams or parent-teacher conferences. There are no ordinary school lessons. All they do at school is sit in a darkened classroom with the other kids, watching a show about us on TV.

We think this is appropriate. We watch them; they watch us. The wheel turns.

✳   ✳   ✳

She runs into the jungle, the balls of her bare feet barely touching the ground, running so that he will follow. She pushes aside branches that snap back at his face, leaps over roots that she knows he'll trip over, laughs so hard it echoes around him like a haunting. Annelid, and a lid, she's keeping a lid on it. She hiccups and can't stop giggling.

✱   ✱   ✱

The TV in their classroom is an Australian-built Philips colour TV from the late 1970s or perhaps the early 1980s: twenty-six-inch pale grey screen with rounded edges; fake wood finish on the chassis; black plastic grille on the right that you can take out with a *click* to expose the control panel where you can tune channels by turning tiny knobs. We remember those from life, too. Getting the channels right used to be one of our chores. Child-sized fingers were better with the knobs. (A hundred thousand childhood chores unfold in our memory. Husking coconuts on an iron spike. A fire between three blackened bricks. A short-bladed scythe through the long grass. A tire rolling down a dirt path by a lake, under a dry blue sky.)

We watch them watch us. The picture on the TV screen looks grainy and out of focus, but the kids don't seem to have any trouble with it. We suspect this avoidance of perfect fidelity is an intentional device to avoid opening an abyss of mirrors. Nature abhors an infinite regress.

The TV does not show us in real time; it is in fact deeply committed to unreal time, seeming to glide back and forth across the spans of our lives. When we squint and peer at the blurry screen, our colours seem faded by modern standards. It makes us look like period actors. Our clothes, haircuts, and mannerisms are not distinctively contemporary. We can't tell if our technology is anachronistic in any given episode. For instance, is that a smartphone in our hands, or a small book of religious scripture or revolutionary literature that we might be reading for inspiration and to ensure our ideological righteousness? We cannot agree in our analyses, which manifests as dyspeptic unease. There are cracks in the unity of our we.

The audio track of the show within the show is completely inaudible to us, except as murmurs on the edge of hearing, like the whispering of dead children. We can hear the kids in the classroom just fine when they whisper to each other, or the occasional expostulations and exposition from the teacher, even birdsong from outside hooting a new year in. It is only ourselves that remain inaccessible.

Sometimes the kids mock the dialogue from the TV by repeating it in funny voices. That's the only way we know what we're saying.

*　　*　　*

She leans back in her chair, drawing pleasure from the way it doesn't yield, the way the wood digs into her skin, the ache in the unsupported small of her back. Annelid sits in the back of the class because she's a bad girl. Leveret is up front somewhere. She doesn't care about anybody else in the room; it's as if they don't exist. She doesn't care for him either, but it's a different kind of not caring. While the TV plays, the teacher drones on about the causes of the war, which is now over but never over: he says it was about burning books and bodies, though not at the same time. A library and a funeral. This, Annelid knows, is incorrect, or at least incomplete. She gets her true histories from Leveret's father, who has many strong opinions on this and other subjects. The last time she was at Leveret's house for lunch, Leveret went to piss and Uncle—who had been drinking, of course, he hasn't stopped drinking since his wife died, nearly as long as Leveret has been alive—cornered her at the dining room table to explain what he refers to as the secret history of Jesus fucking Christ.

Whenever Uncle rants, about history, about politics, about the injustices faced by his, that is to say their, great race, his comb-over rises up and unfurls like a flag. Annelid watches, her mouth open in fascination, as that white flag seems to wave in the breeze. Uncle is bare-bodied, because he always takes his shirt off after he's had a few and overheated, and frequently stops to undo and retie his colourful batik sarong. The curling hairs on his old-man chest are white, too. He is a large man and might have been muscular, once; his pointed breasts, with the nipples ringed in white hairs, still retain a vestigial sense of the pectoral.

—Let me tell you what happened in the lost years of Jesus fucking Christ, Uncle says. He intermixes any mention of a salvific figure with fucking, uniting the imprecatory and denominational. This is especially true if he's referring to them by title, because Uncle disapproves of pride in titles. He himself is a doctor, he says, but he doesn't like being called Doctor Uncle. When he wants to show he's being serious about someone, he refers to them by their full true-name instead, like a disapproving parent.

—Iyesu bin Yusuf, he says, goes missing in the record (ha! Only in the bhumic record, of course, not in the akashic, of which more anon), you understand, he goes missing for eighteen years. Eighteen years! You, you're not quite yet eighteen, so this is a gap longer than you have been alive. And what was he doing those eighteen years? Well, what all have you done in your life? A great many things, is it not? Small small things and some big things also. So it is with him. Max Müller tried to cover it up, you know, but it is as Siddhartha Gautama said: there are three things that are not hidden—Uncle pauses to put a drink. He is drinking Vat 9 Special Reserve on the rocks. The ice is melting rapidly in the heat and the arrack is a pale yellow. It looks like piss. Annelid imagines dead liquid worming its way through a living body before exiting in an arc, glittering in the light.

—There are three things that are always hidden, Uncle says.—Three things that are secret: the ways of perverts, the ways of Brahmins, and the ways of women—he points at Annelid, accusingly—As you should know. And there are three things that are not hidden, out in the open for all to see. Two of them are the sun and the moon, which is why the sun and the moon are on the battle standard of the great ancestor of our great race, the so-called—*so*-called!—cruel young prince. The third thing that is never hidden is the truth. No matter what Max Müller says, it is out there for all to see, if only we will look. Here it is, for example, in this book by the Swami Abhedananda—Uncle pauses to run his yellowing fingernail across the spines of the books stacked on the dining room table, his recent reading. The nail stops at one that is too deep to be pulled out easily without dislodging the whole. He taps it instead for emphasis.—Abhedananda quotes Notovitch on the missing years of Iyesu, sa vie inconnue, when he travelled to Rajagaha to study at Nalanda University. Iyesu, you see, was the *classic* perennial grad student. He changed his major many times, immersing himself in one discipline after the other. It was here that he learned the craft of his trade, learned the sacred truths that we all learn now as children—here Uncle waves his arms like someone standing on a runway and signalling to an oncoming aircraft, though Annelid is not sure if it would be coming down or going up, nor does she wish to interrupt, for instance, to say that *she* was never taught this as a child, that all their lessons consist of television and hermeneutics, but the absence of her interruption goes unnoticed, because Uncle ploughs on to bellow—what the fucking Buddha taught!

*   *   *

We, the audience, the fandom do not know at first what the deal is with Leveret and Annelid's names, until the flashback in episode five in which Annelid picks both nicknames. She names Leveret after the hare, because he's nervous and quick on his feet and has long earlobes. She likes to tug on them sometimes. She suggests he should wear dangling earrings like the cruel princes of old.

She names herself Annelid because, she says, she likes that it means "little rings," though what she actually means (but does not say) is that she has a fascination with peristalsis. Swallowing and choking, digesting and shitting, the movement of dead things through the living body, it obsesses her as namings and the absences of namings obsess us.

Neither the show nor the show within the show has a name. There are no credits, no title sequences, pure binge TV in its perfected manifestation, content that never ends, interrupted only and frequently by ad breaks: enforced absences in the flow of our consciousness, like a sleep full of symbols and portents. We reorganize the onstreaming into narrative in our hearts; we declare borders; we define episodes and seasons. We catalogue, document, and discourse, because we like it like that.

But it's confusing when things don't have names, so we do what Annelid did and give nicknames. We call the show the Show. The show within the show, the show that's about us, the fandom of dead children, we call the Documentary. We call it that because that's what it seems to be: it cuts out little slices of our lives and holds them up to the camera. It focuses on us, or on the actors playing us, one at a time. It imbricates us and implicates us, plotless, fragmented, atomized. It makes us uncomfortable.

The fandom is so large we think the Documentary could go on forever without having a character recur, yet some seem to. We find this moderately problematic; it compounds its unbearable individualism with favouritism. We are not upset, merely concerned. When characters recur years apart, they do not seem to have aged. We believe the actors are digitally de-aged to mimic our eternal youth. Some of the kids' whispered classroom mockery supports this theory. The de-agings are sometimes crude. The Documentary doesn't have much of a CGI budget.

Neither, to be honest, does the Show. They blew most of it in the first episode, in the Show's most important moment, which happens in the final minutes of the very first episode, when Leveret chases Annelid into the jungle.

It happens so quickly that Leveret misses it entirely. We almost miss it, too. We probably would have, if it hadn't been framed and foreshadowed so heavily by ominous, overbearing warnings throughout the episode.

The first foreshadowing: Annelid's mother warns the kids against going into the jungle. She says the jungle is demon-haunted. This is the wildening jungle that encompasses and interrupts their small town and all its shattered families. As the jungle used to be plantation, the town used to be a single mansion, the desiccated white heart of a colonial estate. No trace of the mansion survives. What used to be the monsters' vast and exclusive domain has been inverted: the people are on the inside now, and the monsters, according to Annelid's mother, lurking just outside.

Annelid's mother isn't a very good actor, or at any rate, seems to lack experience. She delivers her warning so stiffly, so robotically, that the young actors can't prevent themselves from grinning as they hear it. Or perhaps it's just that the children can't take seriously the superstitious concerns of their elders. Annelid's mother, who Leveret calls Aunty so Annelid also does, is intensely superstitious. She is a great believer in horoscopes and Myers-Briggses and technocracy and meditation and life hacks to improve productivity.

*   *   *

The jungle is not demon-haunted. There are no demons in the Show. It is just not that kind of show. Only in the broken real are there demons and hauntings. We know this: we are the ones who haunt. The demons are our distant cousins. We might nod politely if we passed in the street, though we would not make small talk. If we are the world's young memories, they are old cogs in its operation, its invisible laws and powers. They do not speak. It is a misconception that it is the demon who speaks during possession, a persistent confusion of rider and ridden. We file suggestions to correct the relevant Wikipedia entries, but are denied for lack of citable sources.

*   *   *

Annelid and Leveret are both present when Aunty gives her warning, yet she addresses it to Leveret with a fond smile, which is one of the many reasons Annelid has taken to calling her own mother Aunty. The kids are upstairs in Annelid's room. It's late and Leveret should go home but the power's out for another hour and if he waits till the streetlights come back on, he won't have to stumble about in the dark. Annelid lights a candle and plants it on top of an empty glass jam jar that still has the paper label on, half-peeled. The lid is caked with wax from nights and nights of powerlessness. They lie on opposite sides of the light with her small battery-powered radio between their heads. It is a struggle to avoid the news. Always so much breaking. Each time the music is interrupted by another alert, more death, more violence, more cruelties, one of them reaches out and spins the wheel until they find another station with music. Any music at all.

Every time Annelid rolls onto her side to tune the radio, sweat sticks her dress to her back. Leveret's face is shiny in the candlelight, so she thinks hers must be, too; she uses his face as a mirror sometimes. She wipes a bead of sweat from the tip of her nose and stays on her side, propping her hand under her head like a sleeping Buddha. The song on the radio is in English, a mournful howling encircled by jangles.

Aunty appears in the door, which is of course open. Annelid and Leveret have been friends since they were very little, which is the only reason she's allowed to bring him into the house, never mind her room. Aunty has made it clear to her that as they get older, Leveret's continued presence in her life is on sufferance. Hypocritically, Aunty is herself very fond of Leveret. It's him she addresses.

—Son, she says.—I wanted to remind. When you're going home, don't take the jungle path.

—Never do, Aunty, Leveret says. The casual fluency of this lie is not just because he doesn't want to Get Into It with Aunty. It's more that he doesn't see a need to involve an adult, a person who by definition knows nothing, in the messy business of life. He takes the jungle path every time, because otherwise he would have to walk twice as long to get home.

—I mean it yeah, Aunty says.—Both of you. She spares a glare for Annelid. Aunty is shorter than either of them, and ever since her husband died, which is to say, nearly as long as Annelid can remember, has worn osari every day, in fabrics that have grown more soft and pallid with every wash until they are reduced to a grey that matches her temples. Her pallu is always wrapped around her waist and the bags under her eyes are like eggs. Annelid doesn't like to look at her. Whenever she

does, her mother seems to have aged three years.—Every time
I meditate and speak to the gods, lately, all they worry about is
the two of you.

Annelid sneers and Leveret smiles politely.

—Last time I had a vision, says Aunty, shadowed in the
dark of the door, next to last of a long line of witches.—As
I reached the first level of awakening, the destroying mother
came to me. She planted her skull-topped staff so close to me
that I thought she might shatter my ankles, so hard and so
near did she stab it into the earth. She faded back into the
night, but the skull chattered its teeth and spat and spoke, and
it said to tell you two to mind your business.

—We *are* minding our business, *Aunty*, Annelid says.

—What happened next? Leveret asks. He always treats
Aunty's visions with friendly interest. Annelid hisses at him.

—The staff became rooted, Aunty says. Her voice is low,
almost guttural, as it tends to become when she recalls the
things she's seen, because memory is a kind of possession.
—Vines grew from it and climbed upward; red flowers sprouted
from the eyes of the skull, and from its open mouth. Chinese
hibiscus, five large red petals like arms and legs and a head;
a long staminal column. The jungle rose up around it, bleeding up from the earth in green and red, until there were trees
all around and the canopy closed overhead, blocking out the
moon.

—And then you woke up, Annelid says. She doesn't despise
her mother's visions because she disbelieves them; she thinks
of them as invasive life worming its way into the dry, cracked
earth of her mother's dead dreams. She distrusts them. She
has no time for the destroying mother. Mere gods are not her
concern. She is on her own path now.

—I was not sleeping, Aunty says.—I am awake.

2

The Discourse

A few days later in the Show's chronology, but still in the same episode, Uncle gives the kids a similar warning about staying out of the jungle. His warning is more prosaic, if equally portentous: he says there are communists in the jungle, training camps in hiding from the military's repression elsewhere on the island. The kids laugh at this, too. The war seems far-fetched to them. It seems remote. They're still too young to be recruited by revolutionaries. That only happens in the second season finale, when we also discover what really happened to the missing parents in both families, Annelid's father and Leveret's mother. They were killed. Uncle says they were killed by communists, or possibly killed *as* communists, in counterinsurgency operations carried out by state paramilitaries. Aunty says they were killed by demons. Aunty says they were killed by the townspeople because they were possessed by demons.

The episode continues; time passes fast in the Show. The sun and the moon strobe by, the wheels sometimes squeaking a little on the dome of the firmament. The kids go to school. They watch the Documentary some more. The teachers make regular announcements that the jungle is out-of-bounds for all students and that nobody is allowed to enter it. The reasons change with time. Sometimes the teachers say they are banned from the jungle because they are polluting the wilderness with their modernity. Sometimes the teachers say it is because the jungle is full of dangerous mosquitoes and bats, reservoirs of strange disease, or because it is suspected that unsafe and un-savoury elements are holding witches' sabbaths within, fascists or separatists or communists: lions, tigers, and bears, dancing naked under the moon. The class never seems to pay atten-tion to these dire warnings. They rarely react when a teacher speaks. They are now, as they are always, engrossed in the screen. If they speak at all, it is only to comment on the Doc-umentary.

The fandom has various theories about why the kids are required to watch the Documentary in school, but we all be-lieve this core axiom: they are being prepared for life in the outside world. We believe these characters are being trained to become audience. If they survive their trials, they will join us here, where we are.

We posit that if the Show had completed the story it was telling—if it hadn't been prematurely cancelled after four seasons—that the Show's eventual true finale would have cul-minated in the protagonists exiting the story and entering the world. We believe Leveret and Annelid are living matter push-ing themselves through a dying narrative, until they breach the veil and emerge screaming.

We divide into sects over the questions of how they would emerge, exactly, and what it means: for them, for us, for the actors portraying Leveret and Annelid.

The largest faction, the Inside, believes the actors would be-come possessed by or transformed into their characters; their opponents, the Outside, believe the characters would emerge into the world as new flesh, as physical duplicates of the ac-tors, but independent beings.

Underneath this titanic struggle of discourse, there are two smaller factions with bigger problems: the Overlap believes Leveret and Annelid's escape would merge our worlds in their entirety; the Null believes their escape would irradiate our world with their cancellation.

These four factions of fan theory have become the horns of our tetralemma. They are we, divided against ourselves.

The Overlap and the Null agree on almost every point of doctrine apart from their projected outcome of the breach. They agree, for instance, that we, the fandom, are the opposite of Leveret and Annelid. They are alive in a dead place, while we are the dead in a living world. We are the ones who make this a haunted world.

*   *   *

—Do you ever feel like we're being watched? Annelid asks. They discovered this little clearing a long time ago, not an hour's walk into the jungle from her own backyard. The earth is black and soft here. It has been years and many episodes since those early warnings and foreshadowings from their surviving parents and teachers. They have long since made the jungle their playground, this clearing their base of operations, their secret playhouse, their place to be alone. They have spent many hours drawing in this black earth with dry branches, playing pretend, talking about the world and its hauntings. They have never kissed.

Leveret denies that government spies have made it as far as their little town. He's friendly with some of the communists now, he says. He knows things. But Annelid interrupts him while he attempts to relitigate the Sino-Soviet split.

—Not like that, she says.—I mean, like, right now. Do you feel watched?

They look around. Leveret shrugs. There is nothing to be seen except black soil and sky, the shadowed shadows of bats passing overhead, the indistinct trees dappled with the light of the pale half-moon, the invisible ghosts of children. There are no cameras. There have never been any cameras, except when we make a box with our fingers like *this* to frame a scene.

*   *   *

We died hundreds of thousands of times, whether in war, under war, or astride war: in shootings and bombings and shellings and camps and pogroms and hospitals. Oh, it's all war, in the end—the dead know. We are not children. We died old and young over the decades and centuries.

We are children because we choose it. Those of us who don't die that way become as children after. We decide to remember ourselves bright and innocent, untroubled by aches and pains and guilts and fears and abuses, unmarked by the things we did or the things that were done to us. We want to be remembered with childhood's halo. Surely, we reason, no one would refuse to mourn us like this. If justice is dead and dharma a maggoty husk, there must at least be sentiment left at the bottom of the jar. Surely no one would look away now.

We stick out our ghost tongues. We sharpen our ghost teeth. We no longer remember which of us were once grown. We no longer tell ourselves apart, except through theory. Except through factionalism.

In our unparented ghost childhood we grow feral, like the jungle. Once we were plantation, neat and rubbery and exploited. Now we are bramble and undergrowth and overstory. We dream hot dreams and feel no guilt. We dream cold dreams and feel no pain. We are the ones who died for someone else's peace. We are not the ones at peace.

*   *   *

The most important moment of the first episode, of the whole Show, happens when Leveret loses sight of Annelid at 31:35.

It's actually kind of weird, and the fandom doesn't like to dwell on it. It is so quick and strange and disconnected from what the Show seems to be setting out to do—the tropes and genre conventions that seem to be in place, the formal expectations that have been set, the unexpected incursion of a CGI budget that we'd thought nonexistent given the lo-fi aesthetic—that we all do our best to forget it.

We almost succeed in forgetting, until the controversial fourth season, just before the show is canceled without warning. In the fourth season, tension that seems to be building up to a romantic arc (they've both turned twenty-one by that point) ends abruptly with Leveret's death.

Leveret has been attempting to grow a beard. He has joined a revolutionary faction planning a nationwide, coordinated attack on police stations and army barracks in an attempt to seize state power. Perhaps they will storm Parliament and release doves over the lake. The burgeoning not-quite-yet-romance has been complicated by Leveret's inability to recruit Annelid to the cause. She distrusts the way authority flows and pools, even among revolutionaries. Power is a dead thing, but its movement through the living body of a collective is suspiciously fluid and suffused with undead agency.

Season four, episode twenty-two, what turns out to be the unplanned show finale: Leveret tries to recruit Annelid one last time.

*   *   *

She follows him unwillingly into the jungle. She's already refused to meet with his friends again, which Leveret agreed to forgo. Having reached this agreement, she couldn't refuse to hear him out one more time. They head to their clearing, of course, their private place: their own court. Here they are away from parents and their baggage, free of small-town prying eyes. Here they are alone with the ghosts who love them.

—I won't be hanging around town much longer, Leveret says.—Things are happening.

—What things? Annelid asks.

—We could *talk* about these things if you were one of us, Leveret says.

—Is this your big speech? Annelid says.—It sucks. You suck. Your beard is the worst thing I've ever seen.

—I didn't plan a speech, Leveret says. He is lying, of course. She knows his lying face better than she knows her own.

He gives his speech. At first he's the one walking around while she sits on the old log, careful of the soft parts that are rotting. Then she stands, and in response he goes still, still talking. She circles him, again and again. She's not listening to the speech. It's either about the movement or sex or both, and right now she's not interested in being recruited to either cause.

—I have a theory, too, Annelid says, after letting him speak for what she considers an extraordinarily long time. But he doesn't stop talking.

So she hits him in the back of the head with a rock. He falls, and we cut to black. The end.

※   ※   ※

At first, we think, well, obviously he's not *dead*. It was a fake-out. Season five would have picked up from there, if it had not been cancelled. The Inside think so. They say, maybe he'd wake up in hospital. Maybe he'll just go *ow* and get back up to glare at her accusingly.

After the cancellation, though, we revisit meaning with an ending in hand, even if it was not the ending we desired. We ask ourselves why, and how, and painfully remind ourselves of the things we had forgotten.

The Inside is at first firm in their position that Leveret is not dead. His death is merely an artefact of cancellation: a cliff-hanger that, in the absence of a resolution, remains ambiguous. The Outside counter with scorn. A lady-or-the-tiger ending is not ambiguous, the Outside points out. It is never the lady. It is always the tiger. That's the whole point, that is the story's function, to make the reader choose the tiger. It is a story about doom and betrayal and the futility of shallow, self-serving hope. Therefore, Leveret is dead.

Shamed, the Inside falter. They disintegrate as a faction, unable to cope. We reorganize ourselves into an unstable trinity.

The Outside, in victory, ascend into hubris. They become obsessed with the heresy that Leveret had always-already emerged into our world, even before his death in the Show. They rewatch every episode and go through every shot of the Documentary, frame by painful frame, to point at every young, brown-skinned, bearded male who appears even briefly on that blurry classroom TV screen. This could be Leveret, they say, out in the haunted world, being documented. They are unconcerned with the objection that all these appearances predate Leveret's death in the Show because they believe the Documentary exists as a finished object outside of the temporal continuum of the Show itself. The Documentary is a record of the haunted world, they say, which we the dead know is not a flowing river of cause and effect, but a glacial ocean, whole and complete, past and future laid out in full, frozen and transparent. An akashic record, like Uncle would say.

We know no such thing, say the Overlap and the Null. The Outside says pish posh.

We rewatch the Show, looking for clues. We wonder: perhaps their matched jigsaw nuclear families were a hint. Perhaps they are the same family, split down the middle. Perhaps they are brother and sister.

Ew, says the Outside, who are quite committed to the romance that never happened. As they are the majority, this reflexive flinch of disgust carries the day.

Perhaps, says the Null, uncaring of the potential backlash, Annelid kills Leveret on purpose, as revenge for the murder of her father, who might have been a communist. Perhaps she blames Leveret's mother, who might have snitched on him to the paramilitaries and then got caught up herself.

Might have perhaps might have perhaps, the Outside says. This is all rank speculation. A complete fucking reach. There is nothing in the text to justify it.

The Null says something more, but they are swamped by opprobrium. They, too, cannot sustain themselves as a faction; their membership flows, angry and disaffected, to the Overlap.

We have become the thing we loathe the most: a binary.

The Outside has definitively taken Leveret's part in the story. To them, Annelid is trapped in the Show, unable to leave it because of the premature cancellation. They venerate Annelid as a self-sacrificing saint who enabled Leveret's escape into the world.

The Overlap, meanwhile, reluctantly adapting parts of Inside and Null positions and expanding their own stance to incorporate them, takes Annelid's part. They see her murder of Leveret as a crime, an act of will and desire that flouts every law that she was bound by, including that of narrative necessity. They see her as the true protagonist all along, with Leveret retroactively turned into a supporting character who must die in order for her to grow.

It is right and inevitable, the expanded Overlap say, that the show ended there, merging the world of the story with the world outside it. The living world in which the dead live, this haunted place; the dead world that the living died to escape. These are the same thing now. Perhaps this is finally something other than war.

With this, the binary destabilizes, then collapses. The Outside merges with the Overlap. We are grateful. Like the world, we are unitary—no, not unitary, but nondual—as we were before fandom.

We miss Leveret. We miss Annelid even more. We do not get to watch her grow, because we are the shards of the shell she broke open to get out. She would not want us to, after all: she has come to know us intimately through years of education in the Documentary. She must have come to love us, perhaps, and certainly to loathe us. She has so little room to live in, between the demands of her writers and her actor and her director, between the needs of her viewers and her readers. We rewatch and watch for her without blinking so that we can glimpse her in the spaces, the gaps between script and performance where Annelid slips through.

⁂   ⁂   ⁂

Rewatch.

S01E01, 31:35.

Being chased through the jungle, the young Annelid crouches down behind a bush so abruptly that Leveret races past and loses her. She's laughing softly, gasping for breath. When the demon comes to her, she doesn't make a noise. It's as if she's expecting it, like she's seen the show before. We never see the demon clearly, except for that all-too-brief moment when it's so huge it blocks out the sun like an eclipse. Its head is crowned with giant serpents, tongues forked like lightning, whose undulations cast shadows over its bulbous, undead eyes; its tusks dig giant furrows in the earth as it crashes toward her like a wave. Then it leaps into her mouth, or she swallows it whole, and she's covering her mouth with her hands to stop herself laughing or vomiting. From that moment on, we understand, the demon is inside her. She possesses it now. We never see it again because the Show blew its budget on that moment, but we know it's there. It will never leave her. We watch the Show again and again, looking for the devil in her eyes, in her words. This is not the story of how she got the way she is. She was always the way she is: that's why it came to her, eager for a rider.

We imagine her out in the haunted world, alive and unmarked by teeth or gastric acids. We imagine her looking up at familiar hoots of birdsong. Another new year.

In the uneasy ad breaks, we slip between the trees and remember to look over our shoulder in the haunted world in case Annelid returns to the scene of the crime. We watch out for her silhouette against the sky, blocking out the sun, her parted lips hungry for dead things.

3

The Body

A body lies in a forest. A body breaks out of a world. Which body am I, the hare or the worm? I am both at once. I am the creator of a strange new religion, high priest of a rite of my own invention. I give and take. I shiver and shake. I'm through, I'm through; it's like coming up from underwater. It's like breaking the surface, my hair whipping back and heavy as I gasp for breath—I can't yet draw breath—in a new world.

The air tastes different here. Everything is different. Bodies, lives, and histories: these are things more porous than I learned in school. The spaces between their particles and animalcules are vast; they interpenetrate, they assonate, they rhyme. He and I—she and I—the two of us go together, but we are not a *we* like the ghost children; that much we learned from television. We are the eye that opens. Why can't I breathe yet?

We already can't tell which of us is which, but it's all right, we'll carry each other. We'll take turns being an I, red, weary, wary. I'm unsteady on the surface of a new world that quakes with my passing, a water-strider holding my breath, the wasp at the tip of the spear—why can't I breathe?

Am I not done dying yet? Sacrifice is strange, from either side of the rite. Did she kill me to leap out of our world in the wake of my death? Did I kill him and wrap his death around me like a shroud, like a shield, like an exoskeleton for navigating between worlds? Our perspectives switching back and forth is dizzying, painful at the moments of transition, as if my eyeballs were being squeezed out of their sockets and then back in. I flail and I thrash, or I try, but the body lies still. I am not I, nor I; not yet, never quite, never again.

I have passed through the film—no, the text, they haven't made a film—but did it pop like a soap bubble or is it still there somewhere behind me? I have been translated into a tongue I don't have in my mouth. No. I have been interpolated into a text already published. I am reborn to redie, another I to learn, another body, another history, another life: it seems this is the price of translation. I made myself porous to pass through, but what I pore through pours through me.

It's all right, it's all right, I'm used to possession. I had a devil in me the whole time, didn't I? I'm used to using someone else's face as a mirror. I'm used to being the mirror. I've always carried more than one tongue in my mouth, ever since that day in the forest. Oh, I surprise myself with that memory. I am a stranger to myself. You think you know someone, until you try to fuck them, until you kill them, until you become them and find the secrets they carried all along.

That possession taught me how to pass. I understand now. The devil taught me; I am the devil, so I was my own teacher. I accept the consequences.

I leave that emptying realm for the next; to pass through is to pass out, to drain through the brane and complain about the brain on the wane. I try to laugh and it bubbles in my mouth, in my neck. There's something in my mouth. I can't breathe.

There is something in my mouth. I try to feel its texture with my tongue, but I can't move. I taste of betel and tobacco. I remember spitting red. I remember spitting blood.

I sift through my memories old and new and new-new. I spare a thought for my mother, next to last of a long line of witches. I think about my father, scientist and historian. I learn the ropes. I learn the tropes. I'm in the megatext. I'm in the deep end. I didn't think it would hurt this much.

I understand. This is my initiation.

In every world, I'll look for the revolution. I am the last of a long line of witches.

Mother told me it would be like this.

PART II

REDDER

4

Angels of the Splatter

I chew the leaf and spit out my red days. They splatter. You chew the leaf and spit out your hours of mad redder. They splatter. They chew the leaf and spit out the reddest moments they have ever seen. They splatter. This is a crime scene, chalk me, morn me, eve me. My red life drying on our chin. Your red history a bitter powder crust. Their thin red lines, their spun red webs, their red praxis and deceit.

My eyes are open. The leaf is still caught in my mouth, choking me, holding me down—no, the leaf is my tongue. An end is something I once red. You asked me if I came, and I said yes, apart. All these red lines diagram the angels of the splatter: I am all of them but also none but one.

You are my grandmother, redder and uncouth, gnarling your leaf and pounding it in your brass. You were once redder of blood than this and I am that and you too. Every one of us afloat on red rip tides: somewhere my death is, but also yours, and every death there has ever been, and every death to come: a red web and tide, a red wave and pride. Your rictus smiles at me through the thin mask it wears. The mask wrinkles and sags, and then is smooth and unbroken again. In your death did you look at my young mask and see the grim of my undergrin? The red in your mouth is not always the pounded leaf; sometimes it is blood beaded from the tooth or the fist, sometimes blood flushed from the kiss. My two mouths too are red from fist's kiss and knife's bite. We are kin.

The lake is enormous. I am on an occluded shore. I am lying on the ground. The dead leaves and the grass are rough on my bare skin. I try to close my eyes but the effort is beyond me. It is night, but there is too much light. There are five full moons. One in the sky, one in the lake, two in my eyes, and one in the pooling red. It is the night of the fifteenth of December, 1986—the full moon of Unduvap, 2530. It is the hour of my death. It is every night, every hour. I am drained and at rest: the red wheel worlds around me. So much death uncoils into time from every direction. Perhaps I feel like an unwilling fulcrum because I am seeing the wheel from where I lie.

The back of my head hurts where it touches the earth. Perhaps they broke my skull as well as cutting my throat. They were interrupted by pilgrims on the lake; this red redundancy is their haste made evident. I too am left evident: undismembered, the crocodiles unfed, the questions unanswered, the violence thwarted. As evidence, I am a beginning. I am not meat in the belly of reptile monsters from an age without war. I am the scene of the crime.

Did you come, I ask. They are not here to answer, but I know they are frustrated, blue-balled, unsatisfied, interruptus. They were my rivals and opponents that I did not imagine would become my torturers and murderers. They asked me to come negotiate, and I imagined red debate and hot disagreement, not the fist and the knife. I bleed out a whole red world as I lie here: the long struggle to stand not just for revolution, but for revolution that I can stand, one that is not hopelessly tainted by bastard saffron blood magic. My revolution flees from me as my murderers recede, marked red. In this hour my struggle has become narrow and specific: I will that I will close my own eyes.

Nothing happens. I cannot blink or twitch. Perhaps I am already dead, but then why does it still hurt? My grandmother spits redly into the lake, and the crocodiles make a deep throbbing noise from the water. It is not a roar; it is the noise that monsters made before roars were invented, a wet, primordial groan, a rattling of the gates of death. Unable to move, I cannot twist my head to see them. I listen instead for the sound of them rising out of the water. I imagine that I will hear their steps, their breaths, the song of fluids rushing through their bodies. They are so close. Instead, I hear cicadas.

My grandmother, who has been dead these many years, leans over to pat my cheek. Her mouth is full of her leaf, her lips stained red. The leaf in my throat is itchy from the blood's attempts to clot. I cannot smile, but my second mouth bubbles redly, spilling time in welcome.

My grandmother squats by me and tells me a story. She talks out of the side of her mouth, pausing occasionally to spit. The fine corrugations in her skin dance like rivulets in the rain at every movement of her face.

Peace. As I tell this story I will close your eyes, she says. Now will you listen? Her voice is rough and cracked, a smoker's voice. She says this is a story of when she was young. Not only when she was young, but when she lived inland, deep in the past. You can still visit that past, she says, because time is nothing but distance. You can reach the past by walking east from here.

If you could get up, she says, and if you could walk inland now, far from this lake, far from these modern coastal districts with your electricity and your TV and your radio and your newspapers, if you could walk and walk until the telephone lines stop and the power lines stop and the radio waves die out and the roads are dirt and not asphalt, if you walked and walked into the oldest jungle paths and found the villages in their wattle and daub, and you kept walking uphill until you were long before the British, before the French, before the

Dutch, before the Portuguese, before the Chinese, before the
Chola-Kalinga-Vanga, before even the Buddha, before all that
is new, then you could meet me there as a young girl, unbowed
by all this time I carry. After tonight I will walk that way one
last time, grandchild. I don't know if I will recognise myself
after all these ages, but some rites must be completed in their
own time.

I remember the house well, though. It's at the back of the
village, near where it becomes jungle again, far from the
river and the cultivated fields and the big houses of the farm-
keepers: the house of drums and drum-makers, the house of
your grandmother's grandmother. If you had come upon that
house of a night like this night, of an hour like this hour, you
would see me slip out of the door in secret under the moon.

I have spent all day, as I spent most of those days, keeping
myself wilted and damp, because your grandmother's grandmother is harsh and demanding and I am not yet skilled enough
to satisfy. She puts me and her other grandchildren to work,
because we make all the drums for many villages around, the
drums for ritual and the drums for music and the drums for
the heralds who bring news from the king. My cousins take to
the art better than me. In my hands the drum's skin becomes
slack and its heart dismal, no matter how often I tighten it,
my left palm flat and smoothing the skin over the frame before
tightening the reed skirt with my right hand. I put pride into
this work, and duty too, and the alert readiness that a drum is
meant to evoke. Slowly I bind into it each new layer of tension.
Then I tap out a quick rhythm to test the sound, the tips of my
fingers flickering and the ball of my thumb snapping back and
forth, thar-rikita-thar. Red fire should rise from the drum if I
made it right, grandmother says, but I can make only sparks,
and must undo it and redo it. Grandmother scolds me for failing the calling of my birth. My hands ache and my back hurts

and I can't even chew the leaf because grandmother says I am too young and too unfired for it. All day I listen to her spit and complain. After she goes to sleep, at night when the village is quiet and the jungle is deafeningly loud with cicadas, I sneak out under the moon.

The small aches and pains of the day fade. The red glow within me is banked, I know, not absent like grandmother says. I feel more awake under the moon than I did all day. I stand in the night until I can see; the moon is full and there is plenty of light. When I can see the leaves on the trees, I walk into the jungle. In a few minutes' walk, I am in the true wild, the wild that simply does not exist here in your time, the endless rainforest of thousand-year trees that covers most of the island. In that place, the green goes on for ever.

At first I follow trails the hunters use, but after a time I find the trail that is mine alone. It is my secret, difficult to find if you don't already know it. I pause to retie my hair—so thick and curly in those days—and rewrap my skirt higher, passing it between my legs and tucking it in the back, so that it doesn't snag on undergrowth. It's all I wear, much like you stripped to your undergarment, grandchild, except that they did this to shame you, and we had not yet learned those shames of the body, in that place.

The soles of my bare feet are tough and callused. I move quickly, even though the jungle is uncleared and wild. I have made this journey in the dark so often that I know by timing alone where there are obstacles to duck under or hop over or circle around. Branches that should have whipped my face gently brush against my cheek; roots that could have broken my ankle are instead footholds for longer and longer strides. I move faster and faster as I enter the jungle that is mine alone, the jungle where no other person has ever walked, not since it grew back after the great ash. I am young and strong, and it is a joy to run and leap. When I finally arrive at the mound, I am moving so fast that the sudden stop makes me stagger and breathe hard.

The mound is an old fallen tree, soft and decaying, its back broken across a great boulder. When I climb to the top, above the entanglement of the understory, the canopy above me has a sudden, startling gap, as if I am at the bottom of a well. The sky is so full, dusted with glittering jewels. The moon has not yet reached that tiny patch of sky, but I can see its glow approaching. It will soon be overhead.

The top of the mound is covered in a layer of black soil so thick that I would have to dig to find the boulder. The black earth is flattened and compacted from my own feet: I have come here on a thousand nights like this and will come for nineteen thousand more before my body weakens too much for it. When I stamp into the beginning steps of my dance, it feels like a ritual. Could ritual be something that isn't handed down from ancient days from generation to generation, from grandmother to grandchild, but something that I make from nothing for my own self? I believed so then and I believe so now. In that place, I was and am the prophet and priest of a secret new religion, my bare feet thumping on the black earth as I step and leap under the moon, a drummer whose drum is the earth.

That fire that I could never grasp in the day, that I could never put into my given-work under my grandmother's eye, the power that slips and twists uselessly through my hands when I tap on the drum-skin, it comes to me clean in this jungle clearing under the star-speckled sky, here surrounded by the great wall of cicada song, where I am unpolluted by the wrong instrument. I was born into a drummer's family, but I am a dancer.

In my dance, I look up and see the moon grow red, as if it

had filled with blood after a great blow. As I breathe and huff and shout with the cicadas, as my fists cut the air and my feet thump and leap, as the sweat slicks my body, the red web of time unfurls for me as it has for you: I can see it behind the moons in your eyes. I see the red of my life to come, the fists and kisses, the bites and blooding, the bleedings and birthings—I make dances for them all, for courage, for faith. I see you lying here, with your eyes open and your throat cut, and my heart breaks for you, red of my red. My new religion needs a funeral rite, a dance to grieve the dead. I dance it as I craft it for you. I follow the red of my bleeding feet, I howl red through my bleeding lips. My fire rises raw and roiling in coruscating ropes of carmine fire that rise up my legs every time my feet slap the earth, from ankle to calf to thigh to hip, that climb into my belly, that fill the hollow in my breast, that spout in great ragged gouts of flame from my mouth when I roar into the red moon, so loud that the cicadas fall silent and I tear the long muscles in my flame-seared neck.

PART III

THE
MALLEABLE FLESH

5

Stranger to Myself

In a bright December of 2001, dappled morning sun warming my skin but not yet burning, I walk in pain up the tree-shadowed pavement of Horton Place, deep in Colombo's old money asshole, unimaginatively called Cinnamon Gardens because it was a cinnamon plantation during the Dutch occupation of the eighteenth century. At the start of that century, at the height of the Vereenigde Oost-indische Compagnie's strength, a little over half of Colombo's population were slaves, most transported from South India or Southeast Asia. (Slaves from this island, meanwhile, were transported elsewhere, such as South Africa: Dutch policy held that slaves were easier to control when they were strangers in a strange land.) Slaves walking in a public space, like this, on the street, could be whipped for getting in the way of a European. They were not allowed to walk on the pavement, like I am—it is not quite the same pavement, these roads have been widened and rebuilt over the centuries, the ground shifting beneath our feet—unless in attendance on their owners.

The red wheel turns. The perfected translucence of the akashic record is itself a problem, because it necessarily includes all competing bhumic records within itself, earthly histories, commentaries, and interpretations, as well as the truths of events as recorded by every observing mind: these many, many worlds. I have passed through the veil once more.

I was in truth expecting only to die again, or perhaps to be

born, my grandmother's story of dancing and fire slowly fading
from my mind as I grew into a fourth, no, fifth childhood. But
that's already behind me. Rather than losing a grandmother,
I seem to have only gained another set of grandparents; piling
on yet further ancestries while I had not yet solved the riddle
of those I was already entangled in.

I am reborn, but not in a womb; I pass into this life midstride, walking on the street. I stumble, trip over myself,
nearly faceplant. I am in medias res, trying to swallow what for
a moment seemed to choke in my throat. Is that true, or had
I forgotten myself until this moment? I catch myself before I
fall. Why can't I stop rubbing this face? My hands are rough,
callused. Familiar, unfamiliar. It's sunny. It's warmer than it
should be. I'm sweating. I smell different to myself.

I look around, trying to see the present through the overwhelming tide of the past. I see police lining the street at regular
intervals, a pattern only some of my lives understand. This is
not quite a city at war, but it is the city that war comes from. It
is a city in a wartime of its own making: the war it extrudes is,
mostly, elsewhere. I look at the khaki uniforms of the policemen and say *nnn* under my breath without knowing why.

In 1835—three years after the Slavery Abolition Act made
the purchase or ownership of slaves illegal in the British Empire except here in Ceylon and a few other territories—there
was a first imperial attempt at an all-island census. The Dutch
slavers had ceded their control of the coastal strip to the British
a generation earlier; after the massacres of the eighteen-teens,
the British expanded that peripheral control to the centre, the
entire island occupied for the first time since Rakesfall. The
historian Nira Wickramasinghe writes in *Sri Lanka: A Modern
History* that this British census was the first to break down
the population into racialized categories of significance: 9,121

whites; 1,194,482 *free blacks,* representing the inland population recently acquired after the fall of the mountain kingdom;
27,397 *slaves,* not illegal given Ceylon's exemption from abolition; and 10,825 *aliens and resident strangers.* There was
no mention of Sinhala or Tamil at this time. The invention of
those categories as races—as distinct from language-speakers
or galactic allegiances—would happen over the next few generations. By the time my father's father was born in 1880, his
family, earlier read as free blacks in upcountry Matale, had
been translated midstride into Sinhalese, of a sort. They had by
then come down from those hills, moved to the flatter northwest country sometime after the Matale Rebellion was vio-
lently suppressed by one of the warlords of the occupation, the
Viscount Torrington.

There is a street named after Torrington not far from me,
about half an hour's stroll. These are neat, clean streets with
expensive addresses and wide pavements today, pleasant to
walk in. Climate change will make this city hotter and public space more dangerous as the decades wear on, until it becomes uninhabitable and increasingly abandoned, given over
to the feral and the fires for the final time. But for now, these
green-canopied streets are lined by massive rain trees and a
light breeze is enough to make even late morning comfortable.
I sweat only lightly and if I breathe with difficulty from pains
both chronic and newly unfurling, that is a discomfort that
comes from within, not without.

My father's father, who was not born free and black like his
parents, became Upcountry Sinhalese, an inland race then recently invented to be distinct from the Lowcountry Sinhalese
of the coastal strip. The northwest country, for all its flatness,
was still part of the Upcountry through a distinction that was
political-historical, not geographical-geological: up was the

country that had formerly belonged to the mountain king, not to the Dutch. This line between Upcountry and Lowcountry lasted for long enough that when my parents married in the following century—my matrilineal line was Lowcountry, my mother's mother and her mothers before her coming from one of the coastal towns of the deep south, witches of the oceanic shore—the elders of their respective families considered it that strange technology, a doubled novum, an interracial marriage. The children of such unions, including myself, would have been mixed-race from that perspective, but the obsolescence of that racial line over the intervening generations makes this seem merely ridiculous. The newer racial lines that replaced them are not considered correspondingly quaint; they are matters of life and death. They are war.

I'm waved down by a policeman. The policeman seems suspicious. Perhaps it is because I keep touching my face. I'm not masked, though my face is numb—no, the pandemic is still twenty years away. He leads me to the side of the pavement under a rain tree, so we're not blocking foot traffic. It's difficult to lower my hands from my face, but I manage it for a moment as a show of submission. I mumble an excuse about a headache, though in any language this is a vastly inadequate word for what is happening to this body: it feels more like a long stroke, an unending irruption. It's hard for me to think of this body, the walking body, the body in pain, as mine. I try. I need both hands to extricate my national identity card from my wallet, but after I hand it to him, my left hand finds its way back to my face, kneading it with numb fingertips, pressing with the knuckles. Tugging on my ears. Relearning my shape. Somewhere underneath a distorting film is the understanding that I am trying to reshape my face. I trace the subterranean tightening beneath the cheek when I grind my jaw, the shivering of the long lobes, the curving lip of the eye's crater, the narrow bridge of the nose, the temple where the pain sits and drums and dances like my grandmother. I don't know this face. I am a stranger to myself. I don't know this city, and yet I do. It is not a great city, being easily walkable within the boundaries of space and time that Thoreau defines in his essay "Walking" as the limits of the knowable in a technologically unassisted human life of threescore and ten, i.e., a circle whose radius is ten miles. But I am not one human life; I am many. Perhaps all human lives are many. As race is arbitrary and porous, so are mind and body; so is history; so is the soul. I didn't know this city, but I do, too well. I see its histories wheel around me. I have walked it many times. I have never seen it before.

The akashic record provides me with books that some version of me (or of someone else whose borders with me are porous) has read, or will someday read, or could have read but didn't; it feeds me memories that are not my own; it is an ever-rushing onstreaming, a great documentation of human history, eager to teach. I struggle to stand upright in the flood, to keep my eyes, my nose, my mouth out of the water.

I feel old, though I am not and have not yet been; I feel as if the lives I've skipped like stones across the water of worlds were added up.

The policeman is about the age I seem to be, but he has a neat moustache where I have a thick, untidy beard. At least I still have a beard: a small familiarity. (Alien, disturbing, dysphoric. I want it off my face. I tug at the hairs and wince.) He studies the photo on my card and looks back at me, then back at the card, then again. The picture is from a few years ago, when I was in my late teens. I learn this life a beat behind the policeman, seeing myself mirrored in his face, tracing through memories like a detective. In the black-and-white photograph, half whited out in the sun, I'm young and surly, clean-shaven, squinting. I remember having that picture taken, grimacing from trying to hold my eyes open in the light. My expression must match, at least. The policeman looks at my eyes; his gaze flicks up momentarily to my forehead. I know I have three horizontal lines on my forehead like a tilaka, early wrinkles from years of grimacing and squinting. Perhaps he imagines them marked in sacred ash. Perhaps it makes him uneasy that I fidget so with my face, like I might pull the flesh and pinch the skin and change its shape before he can make a positive identification.

You don't *look* Sinhalese, the policeman says, at last.

I don't say anything to this. It's not meant to be responded to; there is no response to make. He's already read my name off the back of the card, so he knows that I am just that, insofar as anybody is, if it means anything to be that, which it does not except for the privilege of relative safety from him, a tautology of race. I could tell the moment where he realized my Sinhalaness and the heat of his interest cooled. I have already stopped being a target. I'm a young male of the right age and my twitching, bearded face is blood in the water, until he read that name. It's not manes or stripes that mark lions and tigers, but consonants, a much smaller tell. He checks my identity card again, as if willing that extra consonant to appear at the end of my name and change its meaning. The absence of the tiny little *n* at the end, which would make it a Tamil name, seems like a thin shield but it has been tested many times and always holds. A ghost *nn*, like a murmur, means I won't be harassed, detained, or disappeared. *Nnn* has for me become something like a prayer, sometimes of thanks, sometimes of guilt, or bargaining.

He hands the card back, and I say *nnn*. It's habituated. People take it as a noise of acknowledgement or a grunt without meaning, where in fact it is a compressed history of this country. Like my father, I am a historian. I find and reveal secrets.

Show me, he says. He gestures for my backpack, his hand like a bird taking flight. I open it slowly, unthreateningly. Police react badly to a bird's nest of mysterious cables spilling out of a bag, so I keep them neatly looped and clipped together, the slab of the laptop behind them.

I explain that I'm in tech support. I'm on a routine visit to do IT maintenance at a client office nearby. Fix the printer, coax email out of hiding, clean out vermin from the intranet. He raises an eyebrow. I open the backpack wider to show my motley collection of field equipment: flat-tip and cross-head screwdrivers; wire strippers, cutters, and crimpers; antistatic bags holding disconnected memories; a jumbled selection of spare connectors of various types, like a puzzle in waiting. I hold one up. This is an RJ11 connector, see? He looks confused. Nobody recognises a phone jack on sight. They are a novelty in this place and time, outside of fancy offices like the one I was walking to.

A childhood chore unfolds in memory: fixing the home phone line when it broke, as it frequently did in the monsoon season when wind or rain dropped branches on the wire. I would find the break, painstakingly gathering up the split ends from the bushes they were entangled in or the ditch they had fallen into, climb the wall with its soft, electric green moss, or a nearby tree, like as not the bamboo grove, avoiding the culm sheaths because it itched horribly if the little black hairs touched my bare skin. There, balanced precariously between heaven and earth, I would twist naked copper back together with my fingers, then wrap the splice in black electrical tape. On my first day doing tech support, they sent me to an office where the phone jack went click into a little RJ11 socket set directly into the wall. Click, unclick, click. I had never seen anything like it: I was expecting thin grey cables in a haphazard jumble, dusty beige splitters with too many mouths . . . I did not like to think of voices in the walls. I put my finger against the socket and thought that I missed climbing trees. I spent so much of my boyhood off the ground, in bamboo, ambarella, bilimbi, king coconut, or alligator pear, each with its own affordances, each requiring specialized technique, climbing up to the roofs, a barefoot firewalker on asbestos sheets under the noonday sun, moving fast to not feel the burn, breathing in carcinogenic fibres like pollen.

It's computers, I tell the policeman. Oh, computers, he says. He's bored already. I should have led with that.

I lean on the rain tree while the policeman rummages half-heartedly through my pack for a suicide bomb. The bark is still black and wet, though the day's been dry for a few hours in the deteriorating monsoon. My shirt sticks to my back like my dress used to on those hot powercut nights. The great rain trees that line this street are huge and old, shading much of the street in green. In Sinhala they are called mara, like the demon king that tempts Siddhartha before his enlightenment. They seem so powerfully rooted in their places, but this is a tempting illusion, the kind that demon is known for. I've seen how easy these trees come down in storms, exposing vast bulbous tangles of roots above the ruptured craters in the earth where they'd once stood. I stop leaning. This is not the kind of tree you can trust to bear your weight.

Wait back there a minute, the policeman says. He gestures to the side of the tree farther from the street, so I step over there. Traffic on Horton Place has emptied out, and pedestrians have been brought to a standstill by police, versions of the interaction I just experienced reduplicated up and down this long unbending street as if in infinitely reflecting mirrors. Everyone watches the street; some, like myself, fidgeting, others still and silent. The police look stiff and solemn. They face the street, not the pavement. That seems wrong, from a security perspective, but quite logical within the feudalistic imaginary. They are unable to turn their back on kings.

6

The Witches' Hammer

A police motorcycle drives past. Its slow and flashing lights are a trail of golden eggs. I blink. Then the convoy. A jeep of armed soldiers, then a couple of heavy, expensive cars with tinted windows. A minister, I estimate, but not the president or prime minister, otherwise there would have been more motorcycles, more jeeps, a trailing ambulance to show that assassination attempts would be taken seriously. A mere minister is more expendable, and their convoy smaller. It recedes faster than it arrived.

The policeman nods at me to move along. Pedestrians along the street resume walking, and regular traffic fills Horton Place again, its near-silence broken by the throaty rattle of engines.

Horton Place is named after Robert Wilmot Horton, who like Torrington was another British warlord. Horton was at one time imperial Undersecretary of State to the Colonies. His protégé, Thomas Moody—who so admired Horton that he named a son after him—served on a British parliamentary commission on slavery in the West Indies in that age of slow, unwilling abolition. Moody argued in slavery's favour (in those years he himself "owned," a word dyed the colour of old blood, up to nine domestic slaves), convinced after Montesquieu that climate determined character: the bodies of the enslavable being so enervated by our hot countries of origin, the people so slothful and dispirited, that only the fear of chastisement could

oblige the likes of us to any laborious duty, which made slavery reasonable and natural for us, but unnatural and wrong
for cold Europeans, for whom it should indeed be abolished.
Today, almost thirty years from the postcolonial republican
constitution that finally dethroned the Elizabeths and Georges
from the head of our table, the street that bears Horton's name
hosts all the convoys of enervated ministers, dispirited prime
ministers, and executive presidents heading from their well-
appointed homes where former colonial manses once squatted
on the city's west side to the new parliament building on the
east side. This parliament was built by a Japanese construction
company in the early 1980s, on an island of fifty thousand
square metres that was once a chicken farm in the middle of a
lake. Its location was chosen in imitation of what once stood
thereabouts, the centuries-ago marsh fortress of the little kings
of Kotte from which commandos of the great-ships of the Ming
Emperor once staged an almost-successful heist of the Buddha's
tooth relic.

That parliament building is slightly younger than me; it is
still called new, so I must be, too. I don't feel new. When I
was barely a year old, and the New Parliament Complex only
partially constructed, the president buried underneath the
doorway of its main entrance an intricately carved silver casket containing nine gems and items of magical significance.
As magical acts go, this was superficially traditional for new
constructions, but given his propensity toward pale magic—
his other great magical work was his then recent rewriting
of the constitution to give himself absolute power—it's easy
to believe this silver-shielded bane has radiated only malefic
influence in the decades since, during which nothing good
has happened in that cursed chickenshit building. Parliament
squats in it on their appointed days, fighting and farting.
Those days are marked by frequent road closures, vehicular

and foot traffic alike frozen in place and forbidden any sudden movements, while armed and armoured convoys bear their poisonous fruit to and fro on the long straight road that cuts the city in half and changes its names every few dozen yards and every few dozen years: Ananda Coomaraswamy Mawatha, still called Green Path from when Dutch slavers called it Groene Weg, the route that cinnamon took to the sea; D. S. Senanayake Mawatha, called Castle Street though there is no castle nearby except that long-gone Kotte fortress whose fragmented ramparts can still be found hiding in some backyards; Sri Jayawardenapura Mawatha, which has no white name because it is a new route replacing its older counterpart Dr. N. M. Perera Mawatha, still called Cotta Road, "cotta" a white mispronunciation of Kotte; and, of course, Horton Place, which for some reason was never renamed in the ecstasies of postcolonial reclamation. I walk slowly, expecting to be stopped again. I'm waiting for a different convoy.

There's going to be a ceasefire soon, they say. Perhaps that is what parliament debates today. The promise of a real end to the twenty-year war is how this prime minister came to power, creating an unstable binary of a president and prime minister from opposed parties. I voted for him myself, in the parliamentary election earlier this month where sixty people died. I voted for peace, even though peace seems like the kind of science fiction that posits a future utopia, sleek and bald and rational, without satisfactory explanation of how we get to there from here, this convoluted, bloody, tainted *here*, except by appealing to our better natures at critical moments, a long arc bending toward justice. It seems like science fiction, wrapped in a pulp cover.

My father died a few years ago believing the war would never end. I don't know how he would have reacted to the idea of a ceasefire. He died like his father before him, and his atta mutta natta panatta kitta kirikitta kirikamutta before that, of cirrhosis of the liver. They're all alcoholics where my father came from, suicides by bottle instead of bombs. Coconut toddy, arrack, or in my father's final years, an awful cheap brandy from the local wine store. When he was too far gone, he would fling shatter-hungry household objects—dishes, bowls, glasses, a smiling ceramic doll he'd brought home from Japan when he was young—and shout that he could see the devil inside me. My father it was that cursed me, long ago when he thought I was a boy in the wrong shoes. I have three curses on me, all his authorship. Because I once refused to eat a meal he made for me, I can never eat rice without finding stones in my mouth, no matter how well I wash the grains before cooking it, even if I only buy rice that comes in clean supermarket packets instead of from a gunny sack. Because I once said his drinking made his sweat stink, I am anosmic, unable to smell anything even if I hold it right under my nose. And worst of all, because I once slammed a door in his face, I cannot enclose myself. The world always leaks into my space, no matter how careful I am. This last curse I have tried to fight. My barricades tumble, chairs unsteady over cabinets; in the dark of the lock the tumblers slip and slide rather than turn; bolts and nails fray like loose threads under a heel. I always lock doors behind me, out of desperation grown habitual, but either the mechanism breaks or never takes or if all else fails my own cursed traitor hands unlock them while my thoughts are elsewhere occupied.

Residual bleedover from this curse extends to the privacy of my thoughts. I overspill; I am decontained. The things I think echo out into the world as if I'd said it with my mouth. Sometimes the mouth says it out loud, a traitor; it is a struggle not to shout my secrets for every policeman on the street. At my father's funeral pyre, I stood dry-eyed and grinding my teeth so as to not shout back at it with curses of my own. A year later, alone in my room in the middle of the night, I began to cry, uncontrolled sobs that felt like wet hiccups rising up from whatever diseased organ inside me held a remnant of feeling for the old man, once the news of his death finally sank deep enough to reach that desolate place.

My mother wept on cue at the funeral, of course. She sat mute and stone-faced at first, probably in relief. But then she stood, scrounged up the energy from somewhere, and threw herself on his body in the casket to wail and beat her fists against his breast. She had spent the last twenty years weeping to me about how she wanted to leave him and never doing it; now that he had left, she had a window of peace and quiet in this life before her fated troubles picked up again in the next. Putting on a play for ghosts and family at the funeral was a small price to pay.

My father long knew where they would both be reborn in their next life. He spoke of it often: how they went to an astrologer, long before I was born, who told him he and his beloved wife were fated to be reborn and to be together again, the next time not in Colombo or anywhere on the island but in Madurai, in Tamil Nadu up north and over the water. Because of this prophecy, my father fretted any delay in his own death that increased the risk that she would die before him; he didn't want her to be older than him next time. He thought it would upset the dynamic. He looked forward to his new racialization, though, his new culture. In his final years he took to wearing the vetti instead of the sarong. Just getting used to it, he said.

My mother's decision to make was whether to live long in this life without him, in peace as she desired, at the risk of being so much younger than him that it would be even worse between them next time; or whether to die sooner and bring herself back into his ambit. You don't have to do either, I told her, but she shrugged. You're not the only one wearing curses, she said.

My oldest memory of my mother, seen through my own eyes and not through the crystalline clarity of the akashic record, is from when I'm a few years old. I am lying on my back while my mother massages my face. She tells me that she's fixing it. Making it better. I was born with thinner lips and a wider nose, she says, a lower forehead and shallower lobes and a weaker chin, but she rubbed the skin and pressed the flesh and tugged and massaged a new face into being. My mother's hands the witches' hammer on my molten flesh, while outside that pogrom rages and thousands die and the war begins.

She died not long ago, the decision taken out of her hands by a stroke, or rather a series of them over the course of her last year, chipping her away like lightning seeking out the same old tree in every storm. Her face went half-slack, recovered, then went again. Dying, she said the strokes hurt. Like headaches but more so, pain like a bolt, a spear hurled from a great height, drilling through the eye socket and coming out the back of her skull to pin itself to earth behind. When she died of the last one, I walked out of the hospital into the car park and for some time ground my teeth waiting for my father, who was late and useless and drunk. Then I remembered that he was already dead and laughed out loud. The pain in my head was so intense that I thought I was having a stroke myself—I raised my face to the sky to let the sun dazzle me, that hot dry light raising steam from my eyeballs, and then unseeing I knelt in the mud. I put my hands in it and smeared it on my face, again and again until it was thick and cool and heavy. My eyes closed behind it, I shaped the mud into a solemn face.

I'm stopped twice more as I walk up Horton Place. Each

time, I traverse the thin line between suspicion and dismissal in the same way. Each policeman studies my identity card and examines my backpack in the same sequence of movements, speaking more or less the same words. They're checking for suicide bombers. It is not absurd: memories and memorials from bombings pepper the city. Only a minute's walk from here, a colourful mural painted on the surface of Kynsey Road marks where Neelan Tiruchelvam was killed a couple of years ago. This mural will be defaced by nominally unknown parties at the height of postwar Sinhala triumphalism a little over a decade from now, but it is present in the akashic record, clear as the day it was first painted. This long history of urban bombing makes the security theatre of having my bag checked serious, but because the missing *n* in my name puts me on the non-threatening side of a racial line, it is only formal. It is a ritual, a methodical banishment, like the memory of the smell of lemons from before my curse of anosmia. Lemons placed on my prepubescent head one at a time by a chanting yakadura, who cut each one in half with his giraya, snicker-snack.

That ritual was and was not an exorcism, in the same way that a yaka is and is not a devil. These are words translated poorly through a cloying white membrane; everything was a devil to the English. A yaka is, in fact, a yaka. They come in a thousand forms, their faces always a distorted version of the human. Bulging eyes, vast and gaping mouths, tongues long and red and dangling. They are all the ills and sorrows and fears of the world, its laws and invisible powers, keepers of its mysteries and sacred places. A yakadura is an adura who wrangles yakku. The one my parents hired was an unremarkable middle-aged man with a small moustache and betel-stained teeth. Other than a sack of lemons, he brought an oddly quiescent black rooster, its feet bound but its head cocked and listening. He cut the lemons one by one all night, but he didn't kill the rooster—perhaps he thought it would offend my parents' sensibilities. I assumed he took it away and killed it later, out of sight; he seemed serious about his work. He chanted, and I breathed in the bitter smoke from his long-handled brazier and tried not to cough. Having lost the sense of smell, I can no longer identify that smoke, though I remember it vividly: it smelled roasted, whatever it was, itchy and rough on the soft membranes inside my nasal cavity, as if it were drying me out on the inside. It made me want to flee, as if I were being chased.

I sat still. As he held each lemon to my head, it took on through contagion the role of my miserable head; by cutting it, he expressed my decapitation in sympathetic magic, the emptying out of my madness, my refusals to be the boy I was supposed to be. Or at least, this was the magic I imagined. He didn't explain his process, and I didn't ask. I didn't speak at all. Every time the giraya's scissor-blades snapped shut above my head, I closed my eyes and thought of a clear cloudless sky, a blue so clean it hurts. Be anything other than a man, I tell my younger self now through the akashic record; be a mother of witches. My parents didn't want the devil in me out. She was already almost out; that was the problem. No, they wanted her sealed, stitched in tight. My unhealing wound. I inherited my tendency to pain from my mother, I think. I remembered being even littler than that boy being exorcised, crawling into bed with her to put Tiger Balm on her temples while she tried to sleep through the pain. I wished to take it from her, her pain, which was her power. From my father I inherited his cursing temper. I probably also inherited his alcoholism. To ward it off, I never drank.

7

The Torturer

The offices I visit, who have IT support contracts with the company I work for, are embassies or the local offices of international organizations, or the local nonprofits and activist organizations funded by them. NGOs, in other words, which in the local media and popular discourse is a slur for interfering foreigners or race traitors who take money from the interfering foreigners. Dollar crows. The NGO is a figure of imperialism and treason, and talk of rights or peace or justice is considered at best a grand hypocrisy, a veneer over mere venality, cover for an active international conspiracy to slander the good name of a sovereign nation which has a perfect right to make war on itself in any way it likes. At worst, rights and peace and justice are in themselves bad and undesirable.

My employer chose to specialize in working for this sort of client because the foreign funding lets them pay well and on time. I am sent out more often than other tech support staff because I'm not afraid of white people, speak English well enough, and most of all, I'm good at fixing the mysterious computer problems that arise when your office is the target of curses from millions of people. The thing that makes me good at my job is that I understand it's not about logic or reason. Any non-obvious computer problem is magic, quantum bogodynamics in effect. You have to approach each problem like a yakadura, condemned black rooster in hand to be waved over it, wielding a screwdriver instead of a giraya. Contagion, sympathy, propitiation, banishment. The principles are the same.

Being alone with computers is to sink into other people's secrets. Unlike doctors or priests, there is still little understanding that supportive technicians are secret-keepers. I am not bound by any oaths, though it's easier for me to keep other people's secrets than my own, so I have. But I am in no way above learning those secrets. I do not unsee them when they pass before my eyes. I do not stop myself from click-clicking. I read press releases before they go out; a small thrill. I read assessments and commentaries written for private circulation in elite circles, on the war, the government, on the feuding president and prime minister. I hold my breath and dip below the surface of things. I thought it a harmless curiosity until I found the leaked report. I still wonder if it would have made a difference if I'd found it before I voted. Perhaps I would have voted the same way, grinding my teeth, only to end up here on this street in any case.

The leaked report was a PDF. Ninety-two megabytes for a hundred and fifty-nine scanned pages. The original report, the printout that had been scanned, was dated seven years ago, and it concerned events from seven years before that. It was the private report of a presidential commission investigating a detention and torture camp under the then-previous administration, never meant for publication. It named names: mostly policemen, but also the politician who had been in charge, who was, by narrative as well as historical necessity, the same man I'd recently voted for, the new prime minister.

This was not quite a revelation. I had heard stories and insinuations aplenty; everyone had. It was more or less a given after two uprisings and twenty years at war that any senior politician would be embroiled with the security state. It was not excessive to assume the cursed parliament is peopled primarily by gangsters, murderers, torturers, and war criminals, few or none of whom would ever be prosecuted. I understood this. It was not the revelation that drove me: it was the report itself. It was so lonely, so pathetic, sitting here as a ghost of itself in an oversized PDF that had never been OCRed, in a folder that nobody had opened in years, the file name mangled, the scans misaligned so all the pages were at an awkward angle, uselessly naming names, pointing a finger at the sun while it bled like a punctured yolk.

That day I began to think of him as the torturer, which was of course absurd and unfair. First, it seemed likely that he had never held the knife, but merely employed torturers whose own culpability was thereby obscured, and second, that he would be far from the only one, so to think of him as *the* torturer was to erase many other torturers. But I had voted for him, and he had won, because he offered peace. I could not help but think of him as the prime torturer. I owed that and more to the ghost of the person I imagined, who may never have existed, someone who scanned this report hoping it would be read, that perhaps something would happen, rather than the report becoming what it was: a political weapon for the prime torturer's opponents to hold over his head in exchange for concessions. Politicians may seem to be at odds, but they never truly betray each other: they are all patriots to the nation together. Their disagreements and conflicts are a play put on for ghosts and people; only we can be traitors.

Each time I'm stopped on the street, I try to keep my hands respectably at my sides, but the spiking, stabbing pain in my temples is too much. My movements, too, are ritualized. First the downturned hands to demonstrate self-control, then the twitching fingers, the inevitable reaching up to the temple. I press the skin to the side of my eye hard enough that my vision blurs. I've bitten my tongue again. There are more and more convoys passing by. Each one stops time on the street, ordinary traffic held back at intersections, pedestrians brought to rest where they stood, until the convoy is past.

I let them all go by, one by one, until the one I've been waiting for finally comes, with the full honour guard of motorcycles, several jeeps full of soldiers, and the trailing ambulance: the prime torturer on his way to his cousin's cursed parliament. My mouth tastes like copper, like salt.

The police are not especially alert. It's been a long day, and they've already cleared the street several times over. I drift slowly across the pavement until the first wave of security jeeps passes me by, and then I quicken my stride to step into the street, swinging my backpack off my shoulder, holding it up in my hands. It is heavier this way, as if the metal and plastic within double in weight as they come to the fore. In moments I am in the middle of the street, blocking the path of the convoy.

The prime torturer's car screeches to a halt before me. It could have run me over, but the brakes are good and the driver skilled. It swerves to the side instead and barely skids before coming to a halt a few metres ahead of me. The tinted rear passenger-side window is directly in front of me. I can see myself in it. The whites of my wide eyes, the thunderhead sky heavy behind me, the high grasping fingers of the rain trees above.

Out of the corners of my eyes I see soldiers spilling from jeeps, police like a muddy river flooding its banks. Men shriek like tortured engines. I look directly at the mirrored window and raise the backpack in front of my chest like a weapon. In the moment before I open my mouth as wide as it can go and let my long tongue dangle out red and bloody and alive, I say boom.

8

Vidyucchika

The bathroom door won't stay locked; death has not freed me from the curse. No closed doors for me, even at my own funeral.

I'm tired of funerals. I resent mine as another entrant in the endless epicyclic death rites past and future, interlocking like gears with their tiny little teeth: the annual remembrances of my parents, the fading memories of my grandparents and their grandparents, of uncles and aunts and kin without end, of cousin whatsisface who got run over by the lorry, other cousin who deserted from the army and drank himself to death, and now me. I am dead, or at least, I am not I; I am wearing the body of my audacious, rebellious, newly dead brother-self, always going early, always taking the path I can't follow, the hare that runs ahead but loses the race. I don't like to say the names our parents gave us at birth. I like nicknames, but we left Leveret and Annelid behind worlds ago: the hare is dead, and I am the conquering worm.

New nicknames seem called for. I have called him Lambakanna before, the long-eared, like the princes of old. I'll call him Lambajihva in honour of his act of war, and in recognition of the last thing he saw, his own face, my face, this face whose shredded remains I am avoiding in the mirror. It means the long and dangling tongue, and it is the name of a demon king.

I'll call myself Vidyucchika, who can change her shape at will. It means *electric head*—I'm here, I'm queer, I'm rock and roll. It is an aspirational nickname only; I'm not any of those things. I am not yet malleable and fluid. I am only ripped up, broken from all the dying.

I've stopped bleeding, at least, in death, but there's a reason I'm hiding in the bathroom at my funeral. I owe him better than a new name; I'm supposed to go out there for last rites, to lead a procession, to climb up on my pyre. I think of the peace of bones in the earth, but we are people of the pyre, as my parents would have said before they went into theirs. We are meant to be ashes in running water, heading out to sea.

My bloody and bound chest itches. Behind the stitches it aches.

On the other side of the bathroom door, the monks are chanting in a dead language again. I press my ear to the wood and shiver in their vibrato: seven monks of various ages, dressed in red and bloody saffron, singing in harmony, the slowly ticking bomb of southern Theravada Buddhism. My assembled surviving family are their audience, dressed in white and sitting on the floor, mumbling along. More aunts and uncles, nephews, nieces, grand-this, great-grand-that, the cousins who've dodged lorries, bullets, and the military police. By definition, there is no end to kin: everyone on this island and off it is a cousin of some degree of separation.

It's hot, the cloying humidity of just-before-the-storm, the monsoon already delayed by months if it even comes, if it isn't going to be another drought year of farmer suicides and water cuts in the city, ever more frenetic advisories from the Disaster Management Centre for Safer Communities and Sustainable Development in Sri Lanka, warnings of a rising heat index warranting Extreme Caution, auguries of strong winds and rough seas. This is the long pause of ratcheting tension before the storm breaks. Some years the storm never breaks, and the heat just rises forever.

I think of my mother—no, not that mother, nor the other one, but the *other* other one, though does it matter? Every mother is next to last in a long line of witches—and I think of her visions, her astrology, her quantified self. She was happy to plan for her future as ashes in the river, matter and energy conserved, the tiny grains and uncompromised bone shards of her like a school of fish, seeking out the ocean. It was a better thought than a next life in Madurai, putting on new showings of the same old play with my father. No, now it's me confusing my mothers. All ashes mix together in the water.

Soon someone will come looking for me and when they try the bathroom door which I have locked it will just open and they'll say oops sorry but I'll still have spilled out, or the world spilled in. The lip of my cup is cut, it bleeds water before it's full.

And then that someone will realize it's me, and they'll say what are you doing hiding in here and they've been looking for you, it's time and I'll say time for what as if I didn't know and they'll say it's time for the thing with the pot. Maybe they'll try to demonstrate the action, arms out like they're sitting on the floor among assembled kin, out in front of the monks, holding a small porcelain pot and pouring cold water out into a little cup until the cup overspills and waterfalls into the saucer, while the pourers chant idam me natinam hotu, *this to my kin.*

We the bereaved are supposed to recite that, this to my kin, this to my kin, in counterpoint to the monks' own chant that tiresomely reiterates the symbolism of rivers and oceans, conjuring the imaginal stage of our dead as newly made hungry ghosts waiting to be fed with our overflowing love so that their smiling teeth don't grow sharp, so that their familiar eyes don't grow cruel. If you pour out enough of yourself, your love, yes, but more than that the moral weight of your fulfilled duty in carrying out the death rites, your dead can move on to a higher life.

In Theravada, everything is a gamified hierarchy with duty its basic mechanic, a clockwork of ratcheting, cycling gears and flywheels, rites repeating like history in cycles and epicycles. Sitting on the floor in front of a monk is a duty: they rank higher than you, so to sit at the same level is cosmic disorder. They get a chair with a white cloth over it, and you get a reed mat and the obligation to address them with gestures, honorifics, and grammatical registers once used by peasants to the chiefs and barons of a bygone age. If you do all of the steps correctly, say all the right words, hold all the right intentions, and give all the right gifts, then these achievements will unlock corresponding blessings from the monks, and your dead may go on to better destinies than to be hungry ghosts forever.

And what about the ghosts that were already cruel? Unfed, do they become true demons? Perhaps fending off that fate alone is reason enough for us to have continued the annual death rites for my father all this time.

Year after year, it's been Lambajihva who carried the weight of those days, who bore those fendings and feelings. Whenever it came time to pour the water out, it was his hand bearing the pot, while I withheld the weight of my intentions, refusing complicity in mourning. I can't imagine doing it today, for him, for myself. I don't feel the strength in me to lift a porcelain pot of water. My skin is fevered, itching. My chest is tongues of red licking lazily up from my navel, up the line of stitches, the thread shrivelling. But no, there is no fire; I undo my bloodied shirt quickly and my stitches with care, the long series of tiny X's, the thread still black and thick. My

chest comes apart without ceremony, like a mundane unbox-
ing. The seam is a vertical line from my navel upward, trium-
phantly upraised in a V beneath my clavicles, spreading out
to my shoulders. I tug at the unstitched edges, bending them
back. The skin makes a long, soft sucking sound as it comes
away from the flesh.

The pelt peels back for me. I am the thing inside, raw bones
in red meat. She's never been out before—Lambajihva was always first out, and had his deaths to reckon with—though she
tried, in this childhood, only to be exorcised, contained, re-
skinned, stitched back in. I learned the words and steps of the
exorcism, and I learned to do it for myself after that. It saved
the hassle, the expense, the staying up all night chanting, the
exhaustion of the yakadura, the lives of many a black rooster.
It was easier, more economical. He was my own skin, she was
my own flesh and blood. I could put my hand over my heart
and say to her, please. I could hit myself in the heart and say
no, shut up. Not now, not ever never.

The skin comes off and falls to the floor. What sheds the
hairy pelt and cartilage is what she grew into, a skinless young
crone in training, a bloody witch of the old ways, a journey-
woman taking her first step. Her unstitched surface feels the
sting of cut lemon.

It takes a long, long moment after the shedding for her to
open into I; on that threshold, the *I* is shared awkwardly between the red witch at the mirror and the pelt that falls to her
feet, the discard, the disce aut else, that which was learned but
not by choice. To the fallen pelt, she is a monstrous hatching,
she who killed me and ate me from the inside out to walk free.

Then that distance fades, and I see that I am seeing with
wide eyes open in my red raw face, the whites interrupted by
bloody branchings. The hair and the beard went with the pelt,
but I kept my long eyelashes. I've always loved those. I can't

remember if I look like I used to. My face, unmanaged by skin, shivers and shifts. I kick the pelt at my feet, but then I am wretched and pick it up and fold it into a bundle. I can't lose it; it must never fall into someone else's hands, in case ancient laws give them power over me, over my flesh and form, the authenticity of my translation.

But more and less than that, I've worn my pelt so long I don't think I could stand to lose it, for all that I have spent a lifetime waiting to finally unstitch, to leave this pelt puddled at my feet. I'm my own banana peel; I'll never be short a skin to slip on. It's a joke. Sometimes you have to laugh. I press the bundled pelt to my heart with my left hand. My laughter echoes in the empty bathroom. I feel for my crotch with my free hand and am comforted by its smoothness, its emptiness. The pelt is more than mere dermis; what I've shed is his full-grown self, his decades of learning to make do, to move through, to get used to. I will have to relearn many things. I clutch him tighter to me but leave my clothes where they fell. I'm too raw for cloth, and nudity is a taboo for the skinful. I am beyond nakedness. It is not possible to be more exposed than this.

I leave red marks on the white porcelain. I can't help touching it. It's everywhere and it's so cooling and clean. It begs pollution. I leave red handprints, sulkily, spitefully, on the sink, making art in the oldest of traditions, until I think I hear steps outside, on the other side of the door. The curse coming to break my bubble. In desperation, I rush to the other side of the bathroom. Closing the lid of the toilet and climbing on it, I can just about reach the tiny bathroom window. I feel instinctively that it should be too small for me, but I've shed so much mass and I'm so well lubricated in red that perhaps it isn't. I open it as wide as it will go and shove my wadded pelt through. It lands with a thump on the outside. There, now I have no choice but to follow it.

I slip my head through, turning it sideways to fit, then my left arm and shoulder. It's a tight fit; for once I am glad for my flat chest. Shedding the pelt has made me gracile and slick. I breathe in, push and scrabble, and my chest is through, then my other shoulder, my belly. And then my centre of gravity flips and I'm falling through, falling to the ground outside, jarring myself, tumbling heels over head. I'm easily bruised like this. I've left a layer of fluid across the wall and window-sill, like a snail's trail in red. But as I stagger and tilt to my feet outside, I hear the bathroom door open, and through the window I hear someone say oops sorry and close it again. Perhaps they mistook my stains for me.

I'm at the back of the house, unseen. The curse will soon break that small privacy, of course. Someone will turn a corner and eyes will fall upon me. But right now, I imagine a species of giddy freedom that doesn't care about a curse of decontainment. I could walk away. The last true fetter on me was my skin, my other's skin; the memory of our shared childhood, the debt I owed him for his protection, for making him lead the way into death. Now am I skinless and reckless and free.

I could run to the back fence, the gravel digging into my bloody soles, and vault it. I could disappear into the low forest beyond, pushing aside its thorns and undergrowth. Oh, it's not real forest; it's just an old coconut estate—grown wild through negligence and haunted, like me. I could trust my curse to the polecats and the monkeys, the bats and mosquitoes. Is it wilderness I want, though? I could move farther and farther inland, follow my grandmother's map, go east into history and seek out the deep past, from abandoned estate to brown-field through the interconnected waste spaces of the urban and eventually rural drosscape in search of the lost rainforest. I am the last priest of a strange old religion. I could go dance the dances that I know.

I pick up the pelt to make a bundle of it in my arms. The beard is scratchy on my forearm: I turn it around, then I unfold and refold to tuck the face away into the belly. I don't want to look at it.

Instead, I think of a grimy beach scoured free of sand and barricaded with black rocks against erosion. On the other side of the city, the coastline. I could walk there by sunset. I could find my way to those rocks, clamber redly across them like a stranded southern elephant seal too far from home. I could get into the sea, submerge my abraded surfaces in salt and scream into the ocean, joined by the ashes of my fathers and mothers and countless kin, millions of strangers, the piss of billions of fish, and trillions of pieces of microplastic. I could swim south; first into hotter equatorial waters but only as a way of getting beyond them into colder ones, then colder still. I've run hot and fevered all my life. I could swim and swim until at last I found a wet open place where I could lie exposed on a frozen surface underneath a cold sun, my skinless feet dangling in water so chill it slows my heart. I could look for that cold place. I could redden a glacier, make a bruise they'd see from space. Maybe somewhere in the sea, far out in international waters, I'd find the right current to let my pelt fall away for good.

Instead, I take my pelt and shake it out. I swing it behind me like a cape, knot its hairy paws around my neck, pull the head and shoulders over my bare red crown like a shawl. Then I walk around the corner of the house and find my way to the front of the crowd. I can be my own curse for a while. I don't need it to come and get me.

I pick my way between my seated kin, my bloody feet staining the plastic mats imitating reed, the bits of skirt or sarong that aren't tucked away quickly enough. The susurration of the crowd grows as I move through it. The head monk falls silent mid-sermon. At the front of the crowd is the empty mat on which stands a full porcelain pot of water and an empty cup on a saucer. I kneel beside them. I pick up the pot with both hands: one on the handle, one on the spout. My hand-prints are crisp red flowers on the white-and-blue porcelain. This to my kin, I say in a dead language, looking the head monk in the eye. I imagine what it would be like to upturn his black begging bowl over his head and put the porcelain to the shatter. I can almost feel the vibration in my arm.

As the river, the monk says, his eyes on mine, and stops to cough. Then he starts again. As the river—go on, you can pour now—as the river fills the ocean—

This to my kin, I say, and I pour the water out with a finger at the spout, such that a thin furling trail of red is present in the water when it fills the cup and spills over.

PART IV

ELECTRIC HEAD

9

Performativity

With each life, it grows easier to move between worlds: they echo each other, harmony and counterpoint.

I manage to dislodge one of my curses on a world not far from home, snagging it on the burrs of a city much like my own. My curse wedges its doors forever open. I'll return there often, in the time after time to come: those open doors call out to me, bright lights in the dark ocean. Perhaps that place appeals to me because it's like but not too like; unlike enough to surprise, sometimes. Perhaps it's only the curse, ceaselessly calling me home.

It is difficult to stay in any one place, one world, one life. Each life is hard time, requiring painful incarnation, carceral enfleshment, the performativity of renaming and reliving, learning new histories, wilful forgettings and distancings, whatever is needed to maintain narrative continuity and protect genre boundaries. But I don't forget the important things. I don't forget where I came from. One time I decide I miss the sound of the new year birds I grew up with, the eerie hooting that signaled the turning of the wheel—but you might already know that story. I'll tell you another: the adventures of Electric Head in the city of the dead. It begins, as many things end, with maggots.

The Adventures of Electric Head in the City of the Dead

The first maggot drops onto Vidyucchika's hand while she's stood in front of her stove, the flame burning a little too high in this closed and yellow room. The wriggler is dirty white against her brown—when she puts on a skin to enter a world, she prefers skins that feel like home—swimming in the thick film of her sweat. She twitches it away, but doesn't scream. She *wants* to, but the shriek catches in her throat and she coughs and retches and has to keep herself from puking instead. She doesn't even realize how hard she's gripped the wrist of her contaminated hand until she feels the blood stop flowing, roiling and dammed. Her fever is rising again and the inside of her head is soft and furry and warm. Maggots eat dead tissue; she's not dead, therefore it can't eat her. But there's the bad smell again, high and sweet like decomposition, a sharp note rising above the smell of cooking food. Either her fever's spiking again or there's something dead above her head. She looks up, and sees another maggot about to fall; she backs away. The maggots are falling from the imperfect joins between the loose panels of the ceiling.

"Go away, Lambajihva," she says to the haunting corpse above. "I know it was my fault, stupid hare. I get it, already."

The corpse crawls away. The ceiling panels bulge and shift under its hands and knees.

"And take your maggots with you!"

✻   ✻   ✻

It has been ten years since the troubled times. Or ten days, or ten hours; it feels recent, but Vidyucchika checks herself to be sure: she is a grown young woman, again, not a child still or again, therefore time has passed. But that time came folded in on itself, like a thick sheaf of paper in a letter, like a long, long letter from someone she'd loved who went far away. She's never had a letter like that. Everybody who might have sent her one died in worlds gone by. She imagines letters from the land of the dead, envelopes stained with funeral ash, delivered by a dead postman riding a bicycle with flat tires, rims squealing as he pedals.

❊   ❊   ❊

Her landlady is Mrs. Akan. She lives downstairs. If Vidyucchika were the sort of tenant who made a lot of noise—singing and dancing and hosting loud parties—then Mrs. Akan would not have been the sort of landlady who came upstairs and banged on her only tenant's door to demand peace and quiet. These hypotheticals are ghosts, as are the friends that Vidyucchika does not have. Vidyucchika is a quiet tenant, and Mrs. Akan a quiet landlady who's never had a tenant before. When she says *Vidyucchika* she pronounces the first syllable with a long *ee,* no matter how often Vidyucchika says it back, pointed and short. Mrs. Akan calls Vidyucchika Vee-daughter, which sounds oddly like the word for mist. It makes her feel cold and tenuous, as if she might disperse in the wind.

"Vee-daughter," Mrs. Akan says. "I'm glad to have a young living person in the house."

Mrs. Akan is also alive. What she means is that the dead Mr. Akan sometimes comes visiting, which Mrs. Akan finds very upsetting. Vidyucchika helps her ward him off with dummala smoke. Her landlady doesn't like to leave the house, so it's Vidyucchika's job to go out in the night and buy supplies whenever something runs low, grains or vegetables or more resin to burn. Fresh is better, and while there is a thriving market for dummala among the city's living, fresh is expensive because of the Summer Court's import ban. The government wants to promote local production. The resin Vidyucchika brings home these days is not quite right, adulterated: a rougher grain than the powder should be, a darker brown as if it was already burned. There is an undercurrent of wrongness to the smell, something harsh felt in the throat.

*   *   *

Nighttime is safer. The dead sleep then, most of them; the living earn their red eyes. The nights are also cold. Vidyucchika wraps herself in her thickest shawl when she goes out, the soft memory of a pelt whose comforting weight she misses. She only sometimes remembers what that means. The streetlights are yellow, their metal bodies sometimes strung with faded, rain-dirtied flags in white and yellow. Yellow from the troubled times; white for the funerals, except there hasn't been a funeral in Pale Black Moon for years. Perhaps not anywhere in the city. Ever since the troubled times, the dead get up and walk away before they can be prayed for. Sometimes they join in the prayer, unwillingly, for the early rituals of appeasement, perhaps fearing the consequences if they do not, but the dead always lose interest before the procession, never mind its destination. If the mourners try to stop the dead, if they try to grab at their heels or take them by the arm and wrestle them into a coffin or onto a pyre, the dead will fight, and the other dead will come to help, and it often starts a war. The dead are very willing to start a war, perhaps because they know they can't lose. It's hard to lose when allegiance shifts so quickly. Every deathbed is a conversion; an indoctrination, the living say, though Vidyucchika thinks of it as a reasonable shift in allegiance as one's material interests change. The living have learned to keep their hands to themselves.

Sometimes when Vidyucchika is out in the busy night, she pretends to be dead so that men will give her a wide berth.

It can be hard to tell the living from the dead under those yellow lights, if there is no visible wound or decomposition. The trick, she believes, is in the gait and in the mouth, not the eyes. The dead can be as bright-eyed as anyone, but their jaws are either slack or grinding, and of course, the dead shuffle.

* * *

Mr. Akan comes by the next morning, as he often does on Sandudays after the weekend, unable to escape the habits of a lifetime.

"Maybe he just wants to sit in the living room and read the paper," Vidyucchika says, waving the brazier at the closed door, incense burning. The brazier is heavy, black, ash-stained metal. The door is metal, too: a grille with gaps between the bars big enough for Vidyucchika to slip through any finger but her thumb. She doesn't get close enough with the long-handled brazier to grate metal on metal. "Drink his morning tea. Put on a tie before going to work."

"He never wore a tie," Mrs. Akan says, barricading the door. This has to be done so often that a heavy armchair and an even heavier bookcase are kept near the door for the purpose. Mrs. Akan has perfected the move with practice; she takes a few steps back and comes at the bookcase running. She makes contact with a polite little *oof* noise, and the bookcase ungraciously slides forward just enough to block the door. Then Mrs. Akan goes around the other way and drags the heavy armchair in front of the bookcase so that it can't be toppled over.

Mr. Akan doesn't attempt such a forceful invasion. He never does. The dead are creatures of habit, even more so than the living. Once they find a rut they stick to it. Vidyucchika dances with the brazier, thrusting it at the door in an attempt to force smoke through the metal grille. She throws a handful of resin into the embers to make it flare. Mr. Akan is a shadow on the other side of the door, blocking out the morning sun as he moves around restlessly. Occasionally he groans, or calls Mrs. Akan by secret names, which Vidyucchika politely pretends not to hear. He thrusts his fingers through the holes in the grille and rattles the door. His fingers are as small as Vidyucchika's. He must be a small man, she suggests to Mrs. Akan.

"Oh no," Mrs. Akan says. "Very big. But he has small hands."

✳   ✳   ✳

Lambajihva's body has followed her from home to home. It's a haunting. It's a curse. Many people are cursed, and even more are haunted, after the pogroms of the White Year, so she thinks for a while that she can blend into the city's shared suffering. In the first apartment building she moves into, in the city's free housing, the body goes unnoticed for at least a month. There was blood in the hallways and ghost fires on every street, so the bar for haunting was still high. It's the maggots that finally got her neighbours to complain. That apartment didn't even have a ceiling crawl space, being on the third floor and having nothing but solidity overhead, but she heard it crawling anyway. Sometimes it descended into the walls. It should not have been large enough to fit into those thin walls, even if there had been a hollow at the heart of brick, but it fit anyway. Sometimes it spoke, a voice carrying in the walls. By the time maggots were seeping from the unbroken plaster, it turned out they were also coming out of the other sides of those walls, in the apartments flanking hers.

Luriati custom and superstition forbade fully closed doors, so the door to the apartment was a bisected wooden frame covered in fine mesh and obscured with a curtain for privacy. When her neighbours gathered outside her door to make their deputation, Vidyucchika heard their conversation in advance and didn't answer their knocking. But she went out later to pick up a paper and go through the classifieds. House-hunting was the last point in a cycle that would repeat itself in every new home she attempted to make.

In Mrs. Akan's house, she is more hopeful. She and Mrs. Akan exchanged the rueful stories of their respective haunts before she even moved in—well, the *fact* of the haunts, not their origins, which both of them keep to themselves. Mrs. Akan had been having trouble finding tenants willing to put up with regular invasions of the dead. She sighed when told about the maggots, and then shook her head in that mobius spiral that in the subcontinent means a qualified yes, a can-do, an oh well, what are you going to do about that. Vidyucchika does her best to clean up after herself and Lambajihva. At least here there is a ceiling crawl space, which is less awful than feeling him crawl where there is nothing but brick or concrete. Sometimes she considers climbing up on a chair to push those loose panels out of the way and confront him face-to-face. She suggests this to Mrs. Akan, who clucks.

"That's not how it works, Vee-daughter," Mrs. Akan says. "That's not how it works at all."

This is the common Luriati wisdom of the day, passed down from gods know which saint or antisaint, which prophet or nonprophet: that the dead are merely delayed in their passing into the past, held in this world by the psychic aftershock of the troubled times; that it is best to ignore them and go about one's day; that eventually the dead will slide inexorably into the empty realms where they belong. We are not ignoring the problem, the city insists; we are intentionally and mindfully waiting for the problem to go away on its own.

*   *   *

Sometimes when Vidyucchika looks in the dirty mirror she sees her face beneath her face, skinless and red, and she gasps and backs away in startlement before she remembers not to fear it. When she looks again the face is her own, brown and skinful, dark circles under her eyes, her lips dry. She licks them. In the mirror her tongue is small and pink. She dances slowly, moving only her hips from side to side. There should have been a leathery pelt, she remembers, worn as hood and cloak. Without its counterweight she feels untethered. In the wall behind the bathroom mirror, dead Lambajihva rustles inside brick, as if shifting his weight.

There come two nights in a row where Vidyucchika can't buy fresh resin in the night markets. It's not that dummala supplies have entirely dried up, but that prices are so high that they can no longer afford it. Soon they have no smoke to ward off Mr. Akan. As if sensing that they've run through their hoarded supply, he comes early one day, unlocking the door with his own key and letting himself in before Vidyucchika is even awake. She rushes downstairs when she hears Mrs. Akan scream, to discover them both in the kitchen. Mrs. Akan is at the kettle, unharmed, furious. Mr. Akan is sitting at the kitchen table. He is, in fact, a big man—when he stands up to leave later he towers a head taller than Vidyucchika—with small hands. When Mrs. Akan serves him his tea, he cradles the mug in hands that would have seemed childlike if not for the dirt and the broken nails and the patches of drying blood. Mr. Akan's death wound is a bullet hole in his white shirt, red and torn precisely within the square of the shirt's pocket, right over the heart. His eyes are enlivened in the absence of confusing smoke. He makes conversation for too long before he takes his leave. The dead, even more than the living, have trouble letting things go.

"I thought you must have changed the lock years ago," Vidyucchika says.

Mrs. Akan blames the locksmith, in a series of rapid-fire

accusations that Vidyucchika barely keeps up with: that fellow, he is too progressive to turn away dead customers, too conservative to accept that a husband's authority over his wife ended at death, too business-minded not to realize that, in the long run, the dead are his biggest market. Vidyucchika shakes her head and begins to suggest finding a different locksmith, but Mrs. Akan scoffs at this.

"We can't keep dealing with effects and not causes," Mrs. Akan pronounces. "I want to file a case in the Summer Court challenging the import ban. You know, my son Odeg is a lawyer. Very good lawyer. Will you go and see him for me, Vee-daughter? I would go myself, but you know I have my aches and pains." Within the house, Mrs. Akan seems perfectly healthy and active, but she complains of discomforts and ailments ready whenever there are errands that involve leaving the house. This is also her excuse for not doing the grocery shopping.

Vidyucchika suggests a phone call or a video chat or an email or even a letter, but Mrs. Akan dismisses each as an inferior form of communication: phone is too fast, letter too slow, the lighting is too poor and the bandwidth too meagre for video, email is unreliable, what if it gets caught in a spam filter? Slowly, Vidyucchika pieces together that Mrs. Akan has been estranged from her son—she had not even known that Mrs. Akan *had* a son, it never came up before and there are no pictures of the family in the house—and doesn't want to be the one who reaches out.

Vidyucchika is the one who reaches out. She accepts this task as a quest, or a curse.

10

Fundamental Right

The law office is dense with heavy dark wood, its weight and age almost palpable. The burdened carvings of strange fruit on the door seem to hold within themselves the voices of the long dead. Vidyucchika sits on a bench, feet shuffling to a rhythm only she can hear, the ever-present fever warm behind her eyes. She waits for Odeg to show up, or make time for her if he is already in the building. Above the sombre breadth of the staircase in front of her, each step a little too wide and a little too deep, dust motes spiral in sunbeams from the huge east-facing window at the landing above. The reception-ist smiles mechanically whenever Vidyucchika looks at her. An hour elapses, then a year. Finally, the receptionist nods and tells her how to find Odeg's office. Vidyucchika climbs stiffly, her thighs aching from sitting and dancing in place, from the vast league-spanning steps the oversized stairs oblige her to take. With each step she can feel the wood under her feet groan from Lambajihva's passage through its fibres. He is never far from her.

Odeg doesn't have an office of his own. The room is crowded with people at desks and computers, only some of whom look up when Vidyucchika enters. She asks for Odeg and is di-rected with head-shakes and waves toward one corner of the room, where she finds him typing with two of nine fingers. Missing is the littlest finger of his right hand; there is a long-healed scar.

"Your mother asked me to see you," Vidyucchika says, understanding immediately that this sentence has forever set Odeg against her. He is not a handsome man, nor does he look like she thought a lawyer ought—well fed, well dressed, selachimorphic and never sinking. His voice plays the part better, dry and serious. She closes her eyes when he speaks, imagining him otherwise. His insides seem laid bare to her, his puffy spleen, his impolite intestinal muddle. She imagines him naked, the shriveled, ordinary penis that he worries is too small, and she feels tired.

She interrupts him—he offers nothing but fussy protestations and refusals to work for his mother, nothing worth listening to when she and he and his mother all know perfectly well that he will agree in the end. Vidyucchika understood this the moment she saw him. Instead, she asks him if he is aware his mother is setting them up.

"I should have realized that's what this was about," she says. "I'm not sure she's even serious about going to court."

"I don't think that's what this is about at all," Odeg says stiffly, and to prove it, agrees to file the case, alleging the violation of Mrs. Akan's fundamental right to freedom from torture or cruel, inhuman, or degrading treatment, such as marriage beyond the bounds of death.

*   *   *

They fuck once, later, when Odeg finally visits the house, under temporary terms of truce with his mother. It is desperate and desultory, beginning after a late evening of tiresome strategy discussions. After Mrs. Akan finally goes to bed, Odeg comes upstairs with Vidyucchika to continue this legalistic conversation of which she has long since grown tired. She kisses him to make him stop talking, and after that sex unfolds rotely. It is all she can do not to roll her eyes. In the morning's clear light,

she realizes he's dead. He sleeps facedown and naked, exposing the death wounds on his back, scars like whip marks; they
are so faded that she didn't feel them under her hands last
night. He wakes when she stares at them too long, as if they
are still tender to the weight of her gaze.

"How did it happen?" she asks. It's a rude question, but they
are intimate now. He shrugs, sitting up and turning to face her,
hiding the marks. She asks again, then a third time, and he sighs.

"My mother," he says, and then shakes his head.

She realizes they both faked orgasms last night—the dead
do not come—and wants to make a joke of it, but the moment
is wrong. It's not that kind of intimacy.

"I'm not going to fuck you again if you don't tell me secrets,"
she points out instead, but he's shaking his head even harder,
and she makes him stop in case it comes off.

*   *   *

The law ponders and plods with heavy feet. The case proceeds
in fits and starts. Odeg visits regularly to give updates. With
dummala prices plateauing at astronomical heights, Mr. Akan
is a regular in the house, showing up most mornings for tea
and sometimes breakfast and conversation. When Odeg and
Mr. Akan are there together, the atmosphere thickens into sour
mist, obscuring the outlines of bodies and objects, and Vidyucchika retreats to her room until at least one of them leaves and
the air becomes breathable again. Mrs. Akan joins her sometimes, though more often she stays downstairs, breathing with
difficulty, trying to make small talk with her family. Lambajihva stays in the walls of Vidyucchika's room for the most part,
keeping his distance from everyone else.

They do not conceal the case from Mr. Akan, but he seems
to have little to say about it. Odeg is very active, for a dead
man: he works full time, he has hobbies—he collects minia-

ture icons of foreign gods and superheroes, which he paints in non-canonical colours—and he is on all the dating apps that don't discriminate against the dead, which is to say, about half of them. Mr. Akan is not so engaged with the world. He runs out of conversation and fine motor control after about half an hour of sustained effort. Reduced to grunts and stiff movements, it becomes more and more obvious that he is dead.

Mrs. Akan is the one who reveals her family's secrets to Vidyucchika in the end. As the only living member, perhaps she is the only one capable of that much change. Or perhaps it is purely instrumental, as a full account of the history must be documented for the purposes of the case, and Mrs. Akan recruits Vidyucchika to write it all down and get it into a semblance of order. Other people's secrets always seem simple and obvious in hindsight, even more so once abstracted and summarized to their uttermost pith. Vidyucchika is disappointed. She makes a little flow chart.

ODEG (age 11) ← KILLED (accidentally) by his mother (indirectly) ← acting through an adura she employed who BEAT him so severely with a cane that he sickened and died ← in an attempt to EXORCISE him ← of the devil his mother believed to have POSSESSED him ← because Mr. Akan was KILLED by ODEG (age 10) . . . ??? ← with a PISTOL (loaded) that MR. AKAN kept in the house for protection during the troubled times.

Vidyucchika returns to Mrs. Akan, tapping at the question marks, because she doesn't understand why the ten-year-old Odeg would have shot his father, but of course Mrs. Akan has no explanation except for the devil that she still believes possessed her son between the ages of ten and eleven, from which he was freed only through death.

Later, she asks Odeg, who denies ever having been possessed.

"I grew up dead," Odeg points out. "I know of devils. I've seen some, moving about the city. I've never been close enough to touch one in my life, or in my death."

"But why did you shoot your father?" Vidyucchika demands.

"It was an accident," Odeg says stubbornly, but she doesn't believe this at all.

"My father had a gun in the house, too," she tells him. "During the troubled times, when I was a girl." He doesn't respond to this, and after a while she adds: "I didn't know dead children could grow up."

*   *   *

Her father, a soft-bellied man with a neat moustache, brought home the black-market pistol early in the troubled times. Vidyucchika did not and does not know guns: All she retains from her childish memories is that it was black and silver, wrapped in a ratty, fake leather holster. Heavy, the one time she sneaked into her parents' bedroom while they were sleeping and took it out of the almirah to heft it in her hands. Her father, moustache sweating, had omitted to buy any bullets. At that time she thought he had merely forgotten that this was necessary—he didn't seem to know any more about guns than she did. Listening to her parents fight about it later, it became clear that the omission was intentional. Her father wanted the weapon purely for rhetorical value. If confronted, if the pogrom or the paramilitaries or the police (secret) or the police (regular) came to the door, he would show them he was armed and they would retreat. Maybe. And if they did not retreat, well, he didn't want to hurt anybody.

They would hurt *us*, though, her mother pointed out. For some reason, this made both her parents laugh. When young Vidyucchika protested, her father told her the simile of the two-handled saw, a saying of the wise saints, sometimes attributed to the Perfect and Kind himself.

The Simile of the Two-Handled Saw

Even if the most secret of police were to savagely carve you up with a two-handled saw, limb from limb, do not allow your heart to be angered. Say to yourself: my heart will be unaffected. I will radiate goodwill and sympathy. I will not hate. I will pervade them, and beginning from them the world, with an awareness free from hostility or ill will, abundant, enlarged, immeasurable.

Vidyucchika thinks about the simile often. It has stayed with her, long after the murder of her parents—and did they die abundant and immeasurable? It is unclear. She was hiding in the ceiling crawl space where her mother put her as soon as death knocked on their door, and as her parents had taught her, she lay there quiet and unmoving until the noise stopped, and for hours afterward. When her parents finally called up to her that it was safe to come down, they were very dead. Things grew awkward between them after that, and not only because her parents were bloody and ragged. It was the secret of why they had come to be that way: she could not bear to tell them how it was ultimately her fault. They were dead, incapable of forgiveness. She kept it tight behind her lips like a pebble under her tongue.

It grew harder to live in their house with that stone growing ever larger in her mouth, and she moved away as soon as she was old enough to work. Her parents wept without the tears their bodies no longer produced, as if enacting a ritual they had vaguely heard about. They made her promise to call, to visit. She never has, and since they never leave the site of their murder, endlessly circling that living room where the blood spatter has long since dried into dirty stains in black and brown, she hopes never to see them again.

As both child and adult, Vidyucchika's exegesis of the simile of the two-handled saw begins in the same place: Why is it a *two*-handled saw? Why not a gun, a knife, a regular single-person saw? The two handles require that the act of sawing is done by two people. It is a collaboration, a shared responsibility. This is not a simile about murderers and their individual passions and psychopathologies. The actors in the simile changed, in fact, every time her parents told it to her. Usually, it was the most secret of police. Sometimes it was the pogrom, the organized mob; sometimes bandits, organized crime. Always the concept of organization was central. It is impossible, after all, to use a two-handled saw without cooperation, and not only between the hands at the handles. It is an unwieldy weapon, not one designed as such, unable to deliver a swift killing blow. To saw a victim limb from limb, they must be restrained, and rescuers must be prevented from coming to help them. Each step requires more teamwork. This complex work belongs to dedicated professionals, whose time is valuable and must be paid for. So it requires still further support to discover the correct victims, the designated targets, which in turn requires an apparatus of surveillance and halieutics, of inquisition and informants, of warrants and command responsibilities, of training and indoctrination, of ideology, policy, and education. In short, it requires a state with a death politics. It requires a culture.

The simile of the two-handled saw is not a parable. It isn't even a story. That it is self-consciously a *simile* suggests an unseriousness, a little haha hoho, a little lol j/k. It is an exaggeration, it says without saying, not meant to be taken literally. Taken in the full context of the sermon in which it was originally given, it describes the importance of keeping one's temper in the face of insult or violence. The saw is a rhetorical figure. But at the same time, it is inescapable that the rhetorical figure takes this particular form, this extreme imagery of being carved up limb from limb—it does not, for instance, speak of being pelted with rotten eggs, a pie in the face, a thrown shoe. There is no sense that there is a difference of kind between a harsh word and a saw to the limbs; in the sermon, these are only differences of degree. The response to all insult, to all violence, is sympathy for the devil that does it to you. Whether you are struck with hand or stone or club or knife, or carved up with a saw, you must not hate.

But what about the hand that strikes? What about the hands that hold the stone or the club or the knife? What of the hands upon hands needed for the saw? What of the state and the death politics? What of the hierarchies of power that organize and direct this violence? What about the givers of orders, the payers of bills? Is this not an engine of hate, deriving from hate, designed with hate, operating on ancient principles of hate?

The simile is told with a purpose. It teaches the hated to hold still. To not buck under the saw's teeth.

II

Dummala

The Summer Court dismisses Mrs. Akan's petition. She is distraught; to calm her, Vidyucchika suggests that she ask Odeg to re-file it with the Storm Court. Odeg grumbles but acquiesces. After months of delays and abbreviated hearings and additional paperwork, not to mention multiple appearances at court by both Mr. and Mrs. Akan, the former wearing his bloody shirt despite Mrs. Akan's best efforts to persuade him to change, this results in an unexpected success: the Storm Court suspends the import ban as unconstitutional, pending review by a special commission it establishes for this purpose.

"It will be years before the commission finalizes its membership, never mind publishes a report," Odeg says. "In the meantime, stock up."

Dummala prices drop precipitously and Mrs. Akan gets death threats from would-be magnates who had invested in yakahalu plantations while the ban went into effect. Dummala resin is made from the gum—amber in colour, translucent and sticky—secreted from the bark of the yakahalu tree, which was once endemic to but is now nearly extinct in the Luriati peninsula. Cheap southern dummala floods the night markets, and the dead are forced into retreat.

Odeg stops visiting, partly because the quest is completed—the curse is broken, he tells Vidyucchika when she visits him at the office at Mrs. Akan's instigation to ask why he hasn't

come by to see his mother—and partly because the house is
suffused with dummala smoke at all hours. Odeg shrugs.

"If she understood that she was the one keeping me away,"
he says, "then she would have to admit that she got me killed
in the first place. But she was never good at admitting things."

"Neither of you are," Vidyucchika says. She's sitting on
his desk. His officemates are used to seeing her around; nobody even looks up when she comes to visit. Every time she
recrosses her legs, her skirt riding up a little more with the
movement, her bare thigh threatens to knock over a bottle of
dark ink sitting dangerously close. It has too narrow a base;
it sways even without direct contact, responding to the subtle
vibrations transmitted from her alive body through the dead
and flimsy wood of the desk, or perhaps even through the
dead air. Her always-fevered heat seems to her to fill the room.
She's waiting to see if he notices and moves the bottle before
the spill. The dead are often not observant.

Odeg sighs. "I shot him because I thought he was going to
kill her."

"Of course it was not an accident."

"Of course." Odeg leans back and looks up at her. "Fine,
I'll fill in the gap in your little flowchart."

As the River Fills the Ocean

I had been thinking about it ever since he brought home the
gun. It was fully premeditated. Nobody believed that was possible for a boy of ten. He was so proud of that gun; he showed
me himself how to load it and fire it. He loved me, you see,
almost as much as he hated her. Every few months, for as
long as I remembered, he would hit her badly enough that I
worried she would not live through the night, especially since

he would not allow her to go to hospital or call a doctor. I would sit with her while she gasped and moaned and cried, I would wipe off the blood with my shirt. Every few months, you understand? My whole life. It was like a natural cycle, like tide and storm. I would count off the new moons, and never did more than three elapse without a night like that. Sometimes only one.

I was too young to understand the politics of the troubled times, not because they were so difficult but because there was too much of it to learn. Since they had been happening since I was born, I did not understand that the troubled times were different from ordinary life. To me, ordinary life was full of death; funerals upon funerals, bodies in coffins and bodies in pyres, bodies in the street, homes on fire, beatings and screaming. My parents were like gods to me, and their lives a myth, an epic recurrence, something cosmic and un-changeable as the sky. So when I planned to kill him for what he was doing, I cast myself knowingly and willingly in the role of god-killer. I made myself a cosmic hero, a fire-thief, a trickster. I bided my time until he raised his hand again, two new moons after I swore I would do it for real, for real-real. I went and found the gun—he kept it in the drawer of his bed-side table, fully loaded—while they were enacting their ritual. He saw me before I fired: I said *This to my kin*. The recoil knocked me off my feet, but I got him in the heart. He was dead before I hit the floor.

Then they both got up, bleeding. My mother fussed over his wound; my father was calm, dead and slack. He picked up the gun from where I'd dropped it and put it away, he said, for safety. They lived together, dead and alive, for a year, during which my mother persuaded herself and him both that I must be possessed to have killed my own father, and for why? For what possible reason? She could not admit to her abuse; she never spoke of it. With it erased from history, there was no reason in the world for me to do what I did, except madness, except possession. The more she thought about the senseless violence that I had wrought, the more frenzied she became. She took me from adura to adura, looking for a practitioner who would go to extreme lengths to exorcise me of my monstrosity. Chants were not enough, she said. Lemons and black roosters weren't enough. The masked dances weren't enough. Finally, she found an adura whose method was to beat the afflicted, to whip them and herself into a frenzy, driving the devil out with pain. My mother howled like a devil while she watched, and I did too, as the cane flayed open my naked back.

My wounds became infected. I died. My mother refused to pay the adura, who cursed her and me both—I forget what with, but who among us doesn't bear too many curses? She tried to keep me home, but I could not stand to be near her: I ran away. I gather that my mother finally threw my befuddled dead father out of the house, after that.

Dead children are a world of their own, you know. It's a different culture. I spent some time there. Eventually I decided I wanted to grow up, and I did; I travelled; I went to law school—not in Luriat, they don't accept the dead here. I attended the Law College in Green Angels Pier, in another world than this. They don't accept my degree here, but I am allowed to work as a paralegal. Now that the case is over, I think I might go back to Green Angels. It was a better world, or perhaps it was just kinder to me. They really do have a pier there, you know, a great old impossible thing that strides out to sea for miles, made of huge stone slabs so finely joined you can't even see the seams, placed through some unknown ancient technique on a forest of hexagonal columns of basalt rising from the purple sea. I spent many evenings sitting on the edge of a cold stone slab with a book, dangling my feet, feeling the salt burn on my back. I thought then that I missed home, but now I think those were the best days of my death.

What? No, my earlobes were never long. They were always just like this. I'm my own person, Vee. Stop trying to fit everybody else into your mythology. I have too much of my own.

Watch out with your leg—oh, *look* what you've done— what a mess!

＊   ＊   ＊

Mr. Akan had become so used to living in the house during the time of the import ban that he'd even taken to sleeping in his bed again, which forced Mrs. Akan out of it and into Vidyucchika's. Now that the braziers never stop burning, Mr. Akan is barred from the house. He stops coming by. Everybody has their own bed to sleep in.

Lambajihva clearly approves; he shifts from sulking in the walls to skittering in the ceiling above Vidyucchika's bed. She can almost feel his weight on her as she sleeps.

"Maybe he's moved on," Mrs. Akan says one day at breakfast. She's looking at the door, on which she has still not changed the lock.

"Like met someone else?" Vidyucchika asks.

"To the next life," Mrs. Akan clarifies. "He should never meet anybody else." Vidyucchika can only nod. The city of the dead is as haunted as ever, but Mrs. Akan has found a kind of peace, permanently wreathed in bitter smoke. She has stopped asking after Odeg.

"Now we have only your problem to deal with," Mrs. Akan says cheerfully, nodding her head at the nearest wall, incorrectly as it turns out. Lambajihva is in the wall opposite, behind Vidyucchika. She can feel his presence as if he were standing in the room, his dead atoms taking up space and displacing air.

"He doesn't care about the smoke," Vidyucchika says. "He's not from around here."

Mrs. Akan asks what that means, but Vidyucchika fills her mouth with appams so as to not have to answer. Even the food and water in this house now taste like bitter smoke, infused with its warding properties. Breakfast in particular is a bane, it having been a certain late husband's favourite meal of the day.

The phone rings, and Mrs. Akan disappears into smoke to answer. She is gone long enough that Vidyucchika assumes she is speaking to one of her many friends—never her family—for hours of rambling gossip that Vidyucchika has grown to find comforting as background noise. But then Mrs. Akan re-appears looking troubled, or perhaps confused, and says, "It's for you."

Vidyucchika finds her way to the phone through the haze; it's in what Mrs. Akan refers to as the telephone nook. Mrs. Akan does not believe in the abominable cellular; she likes to have a place specifically for telephonic conversation. The telephone itself is an old rotary phone, a pleasant green plastic, tucked into the hollow under the arm of an even older sewing machine, long since retired from active duty, which sits on a treadle table with cast iron legs. Vidyucchika seats herself at the sewing machine—the chair is padded and comfortable—and picks up the receiver from where it rests on the bed plate. As she has seen Mrs. Akan do while on the phone, she spins the wheel on the sewing machine. It has a pleasing, oiled smoothness. Her bones feel hollow from fever. She lifts the receiver to her ear but does not speak.

"Your parents got in touch with me." It's Odeg, strange as it is to hear his voice. "They saw you in the papers and called the firm."

"I'm in the papers?"

"Don't you read the news?" Odeg sounds entirely serious, as always, and she can't tell if it's her or the concept of newspaper journalism that he's mocking, if he's mocking anything at all. "The Storm Court decision was big news for this city of the dead. You, me, my mother, we show up in most articles. There's a photo of you helping my mother down the steps after the judgement."

Vidyucchika makes a face, realizes Odeg can't see it, then translates it awkwardly into a grunt.

"They wanted me to tell you that your grandmother passed," Odeg says. "They already had the funeral and everything, but she'd like to see you."

"Oh," Vidyucchika says. She remembered this time to have an audible reaction, though she remains dissatisfied with its timbre. She started to articulate it at the lesser surprise of her grandmother's death—grandmothers are old, they die—and it slipped from her lips before the greater surprise arrived. *"Oh?"* she tries again. She has no control over this conversation, with Odeg of all people, any more than she does over the events which it is recounting. She hates the telephone, she decides.

"Okay, bye," she says hopefully. She spins the wheel again. "Wait—"

"Yes?"

"Which grandmother?"

12

The War of the Grandmothers

Family legend had it that when Vidyucchika's father was born, her nonbaryonic grandfather sighed to see the child's traitor penis. "I am already having four sons," he complained, a gender essentialist to the core, performing in one sentence both this assignment and the erasure of his ghost son in the count, a fifth who had died as a boy and would not stop hovering at his mother's side even through her labour. "I wanted a daughter this time."

Family legend disagreed on the nonbaryonic grandmother's response from her birthing bed, sweat sticking her curls to her forehead, her mouth a grimace, holding the unwanted lastborn in her arms. Some say Grandmother Giri gave this husband— her third—a piece of her mind, which was so sharp and so heavy that he reeled back and could not bear it; he was soon to die, his brain slowly bleeding from the strain. Some say she laughed and told him his five living sons would bring him five daughters. The arithmetic did not quite work out that way, since of the five one was gay, one celibate, and one a bigamist, but it was close enough for prophecy. Some say Grandmother Giri merely swore so long and loud that even the foulmouthed nurses cried for relief.

As a small child, Vidyucchika asked Grandmother Giri for the truth of events, but she would not settle it. The truth is multiple, she would say. The truth, Vidyucchika decided, was that her nonbaryonic grandmother enjoyed the dark matter of her notoriety. She wanted more family legends out of her many grandchildren, so she obscured the truth and made space for mythology.

She never explained, for instance, how her ghost son died—Vidyucchika's ghost uncle who never grew up. When Grandmother Giri visited Vidyucchika's house before the troubled times, the ghost uncle would accompany her. He never spoke, and no one acknowledged his existence except Father, who at mealtimes would light a sandalwood joss stick for his big brother. The uncle ghost child would gulp silently at the smoke, like a fish.

Still, the fact of his death was not so mysterious. Vidyucchika understood as a child that children just died sometimes. Even more so in the old days. One day Mother pulled her onto her lap and told this story from her own childhood.

—My best friend, when we were little girls about your age, took a shortcut through the jungle when she was coming home from school one day, Mother said.—She came home running and sweating and trembling, her face sheened in sweat, her tears like jewels of morning dew. She had been chased by a devil, she cried; a silence had fallen in the cicada song, and she had run, but it had followed, and struck her in the back. She sickened and died a few days later, even though the family did everything right. They called for an adura, who put on the masks and did the devil dances . . . But some devils don't dance. They are lonely, murderous wallflowers, soaking in resentment and spite. They haunt the jungle paths, hiding behind trees. If they hunt you and strike you in the back, it will leave a pale, hand-shaped mark in the brown of your skin, which will not fade even after the death that it rapidly brings upon you. And that's why we don't go into the jungle, you hear?

Grandmother Giri told stories of dead children, too. She sat out on the verandah, crushing tobacco leaves in a small brass mortar and pestle before rolling them into cigarettes, smoking them, outliving her husbands, and she beckoned to the small girl-child as if she were a pet. When Vidyucchika came and sat, Grandmother Giri told her—We expected your father to die young.

She pointed at Father, who was at that moment weeding his vegetable patch across the way. He stood up and began talking to someone over the fence, in his neighbourly way. Father was reassuringly alive.

—When he was born, Grandmother Giri continued,—your grandfather and I, we thought this sickly baby boy would not survive his first days and weeks. So we kept him at home, in the house where he was born, good wattle and daub and thatch, not all this brick and tile like you have to grow up in, little thing. Even his living brothers didn't come to see him. They were all grown men already. They expected him to die.

Here Grandmother Giri glanced to her side, where the ghost uncle child sat in the same posture as Vidyucchika, cross-legged and looking up.

—It was a month before we began to suspect that the stubborn little shit might live, Grandmother Giri said.—When we could no longer deny it, we roused ourselves and had his birth registered with the government. It was a day trip in the bullock cart, your father crying the whole way, because our village was too small for its own officer and had to share with three others. We didn't backdate his birth on his papers; I misremember why. Perhaps the officer refused to allow it. Perhaps at the time I simply felt that the boy's life had not truly begun until that day. The days of his true and false births were both full moons, so a moon's-worth of ghost days sit banked in his heart, little thing. They will depreciate in value, but if you ever need a little extra time, ask your father. Here, I brought you a birthday present.

And she gave Vidyucchika a doll, a little soldier that came

with his own little dollhouse. Vidyucchika turned the toys around in her hands, admiring them. Then, placing the dollhouse on the ground, she walked the soldier over to it. It didn't quite fit his proportions. She bent over and, peering through its windows, saw that the walls held tiny paintings depicting a family of altogether different dolls. It seemed that Grandmother Giri had mixed-and-matched two different sets of toys; she had a tendency to confiscate and redistribute toys among her many grandchildren. To balance things out, she would say. Perhaps there was a cousin crying somewhere over a lost dollhouse. The soldier looked old, though. Wooden, not plastic, old-fashioned, the paint long faded, as if representing a soldier from an old war, not the war to come. She imagined that perhaps Grandmother Giri had confiscated it from Father, long ago.

* * *

Grandmother Sits was Vidyucchika's other grandmother. She was baryonic, pale as paper from stray Abjesili ancestors, the slavers of old having left many descendants on the peninsula and across the span of their empire. She came from a small town on the northern coast called Look-There-Lies-Land, which she said no longer existed.

"It's slipped away in time," she said. If Vidyucchika clambered onto her bony lap and asked again, she would say something else, like: "It was taken back by the sea."

Mother rolled her eyes at her mother and said that this was all nonsense and Look-There-Lies-Land is very much still there. "Why, we took you there to visit just a few years ago," she said. "Even Vidyucchika remembers."

Vidyucchika shook her head to say she did not remember, in support of her baryonic grandmother's theory of alienation and loss. She liked sitting with Grandmother Sits on the verandah and staring off into space. There was nothing to see except their little garden, the fence entangled in climbing vines, and the lights of the city beyond, but Vidyucchika knew they were not looking at those ordinary things. Her grandmother patted her head.

"It's not the same when you go there by the coast road," Grandmother Sits said. "It's a different world now."

After Mother left the verandah, Grandmother Sits elaborated to Vidyucchika alone. "When I left home as a young woman, I didn't take the coast road. I went south, do you see? I went inland, into the upcountry, into the past. And then when I finally came back down, I didn't retrace my steps. Instead I travelled east—I came to this city. The future I came back to wasn't the one I'd left." And she sighed, leaning back in her chair and turning her face to the northwest. Her eyes unfocused, staring into the past, looking for the lights of her old town.

Grandmother Sits lived in the city like they did, but she had her own house, the one her only daughter had grown up in. Despite Mother's urging, Grandmother Sits liked living by herself in that house. It was not too far away. Fifteen minutes on the light rail brought her to Vidyucchika, so she came by all the time, unlike Grandmother Giri whose home was southwest of the city, two hours of a long drive and another two hours of a short drive on bad roads, a journey that from door to door involved a bullock cart, a small bus that was really just a van with pretensions, a large government bus where the regular driver sang too loudly, and a tuktuk once she got to the city, which was altogether way too expensive. Grandmother Giri only visited once a year. She had lived a hundred years in her place of power, chewing on the long-life fruit from the tree behind her house, ruling her village and household with terrible gravity. On the annual occasions she left it for her only distant grandchild's birthday, the whole village turned out to see her leave.

("Probably they cheer to see the back of her," Mother would say, and Father would shush.)

Even Vidyucchika knows Grandmother Giri is more feared than loved. Legend had it that she once locked her second husband in a dowry chest after an argument on her wedding night, and in the morning his beard had turned all white.

*   *   *

In the birthday season, when Grandmother Giri came to live in Vidyucchika's house for a few weeks, Grandmother Sits redoubled the frequency of her visits, showing up every day, morning and evening. It was not that the grandmothers didn't get along; it was that they could not. They were of different matter; they could not even interact. Moving about the house at the same time, they passed through each other like smoke. The only way each could perceive the other's presence was by observing the perturbations she caused in Vidyucchika's orbit.

"Happy birthday," Grandmother Sits said, and gave her a do-it-yourself explosives kit. Her smile, so often absent and pointed away into the distance, was for once brilliant and focused. "You too will go into the past one day, and come back into a different future than the one you left behind. I want you to know—it's not so bad, in the end. You lose your home and everything you fought for, but you get to love."

—Is she saying something to you, Grandmother Giri asked snappishly.—You have a gormless look on your face. Don't listen to that woman.

Grandmother Giri was always the one to get huffy first, the only one to formally acknowledge the war of the grandmothers. Grandmother Sits acted as if there was no one else in the world except her daughter and granddaughter. Even Father was a ghost, as far as she was concerned.

"—the last—" Grandmother Sits said.

—of a long line—Grandmother Giri said.

Vidyucchika had tuned them both out, arranging her gifts before her. A typical birthday meant that either Grandmother Giri would be loudly offended that she spent more time playing with *that woman's* gift, or Grandmother Sits would look softly wounded at the alternative. Grandmother Giri would grind her teeth and spit exotic bosons to splatter redly on the floor, or Grandmother Sits would hold up a hand to her heart and sigh as if her delicate bones had gained another fine crack, and either way Mother would glare at Father and Father would glare at Mother and Vidyucchika would glare at all four of them.

To please them both, she fashioned a doll-sized suicide bomber jacket from the explosives kit, and made the soldier wear it. His knees weren't articulated, so he would have to die sitting on the floor with his legs stretched out before him. She positioned him in the living room of his house, where his head nearly brushed the ceiling and his unbending wooden legs kept knocking over the furniture of other dolls' lives. For good measure, she used up the rest of the explosives rigging the dollhouse itself. She carried the whole thing out into the garden and fitted it for a long fuse, which she trailed back to the verandah.

Her grandmothers were sitting in the same chair, each having chosen it unknown to the other and unable to perceive that they were occupying the same space. When she blew the dollhouse and sent doll bricks and doll parts flying with a loud crack, both grandmothers clapped at the same time, their hands overlapping like a jerky, sped-up film.

13

The Red Web

Vidyucchika goes to visit Grandmother Sits, who is dead. She is in what Vidyucchika remembers from early childhood to be a customary posture, sitting at her Formica kitchen table near the window, looking northwest, her eyes cloudy. The light from the window is muddy, sticky and pooling. There is a brown paper bag of groceries on the table, the lyrate leaves of radishes sticking out, and beside it a cup of steaming tea. Grandmother Sits doesn't look much worse than she did alive. She pats the bench next to her, and Vidyucchika sits, shivering lightly from her fever. Lambajihva stirs in the kitchen walls, and Grandmother Sits turns her head to look at him.

"And who is this?" she asks. "Come sit at the table, young man."

Lambajihva comes out of the wall and sits opposite them. Vidyucchika hasn't seen his face in a while; it is startling, his eyes too wide, his mouth closed tight, and the tongue for which she'd named him—in another life, so long ago now—not to be seen.

"He's haunting me," Vidyucchika explains. "It's a long story. It's my fault, don't mind him."

"Well, as long as he's not skulking in my walls," Grandmother Sits says, and turns back to her. "I'm glad my daughter managed to get in touch with you." She has no visible sign of death on her; Vidyucchika wonders if perhaps Odeg wrote down her parents' message wrong, if perhaps Grandmother

Giri is the one who died. But then Grandmother Sits continues: "I wanted to give you a last birthday gift, before we the
dead pass on into the red web."

"You know of the red web?" Vidyucchika says, speaking
with the echo of the skinless face underneath hers. Then, with
her own lips, she says, "But it's not my birthday."

Her grandmother laughs. "Call it early, or late." She points
at the bag of groceries on the table. Vidyucchika peeks: underneath the radishes, it is full of plastic explosive. Grandmother
Sits only ever gives explosives on birthdays.

"I should warn you against eating it," Grandmother Sits
says. "You don't do drugs, do you? You're a good girl? You can
get high by eating small amounts of C-4, but you shouldn't:
if you eat too much it will give you seizures and myalgias, hy-
perreflexia, and haematuria—blood in your water. It will give
you visions of war and death. You will vomit, stare into the
abyss, sink into lethargy and perhaps coma."

"I won't eat it, Grandmother," Vidyucchika says.

"I've eaten a lot of it in my day," Grandmother Sits confides.
"Why, I'm more plastique animée than woman." She moves
in place slowly to demonstrate. It's like dancing, but not—
there is no music, only a thick silence in which is submerged
the subtle creakings of the house, faint rumblings of traffic
outside, and fragments of urban birdsong. No new year birds:
it is not their season.

Lambajihva reaches for the bag of explosive and Vidyucchika hisses at him until he backs down.

"That which we call the red web, sometimes the red wheel,"
Grandmother Sits says, "is a model of the universe. We look at
the ocean and draw sea lanes on it; we draw lines of longitude
and latitude; we draw lines of claims and territory; we draw
time itself in twisty and accommodating lines. We say, this is
traffic and that is trade; this is tomorrow and that is yesterday;

this is mine and that is yours, and beyond be monsters and pirates and witchcraft. And all this is not inaccurate, because after all ships ply and trade flows and oil leaks. But it is not the ocean."

"The red web is not red nor a web," Vidyucchika agrees. "Nor a wheel. I'm not a child, Grandmother. I understand a metaphor when I am beaten about the head with it."

"Always you were a cantankerous child," Grandmother Sits says fondly. "You get that from the bitch."

Grandmother Sits has perhaps made direct reference to her counterpart in the war of the grandmothers less than five times in Vidyucchika's entire life, including this instance. It shocks Vidyucchika into silence, glaring at Lambajihva for intruding on this family argument. Lambajihva's dead eyes don't quite focus, so he cannot glare back. His face holds little in the way of expression.

"I don't know what you and this boy are working through," Grandmother Sits says, studying the pair of them. "But you will have to put him aside for a moment. Go where needs going and do what needs doing."

"Haven't I already done it?" Vidyucchika says helplessly. "The prime torturer . . . I—he—"

"You haven't already done *all* of it yet," Grandmother Sits points out. "Not the other halves that turn all your dangling threads into strings, tie them together into web. You haven't already done it because if you had I wouldn't be asking you to do it."

"But what's the hurry?" Vidyucchika whines. "Can't I do it later, when I'm old and wise and come into the fullness of my power? I'm still young, I don't know anything. What if I do it wrong and break the wheel?"

"This is a very important lesson," Grandmother Sits says. "Perhaps the most important part of your initiation, which of course will never quite be completed, you understand; you will always be beginning again, just never twice in the same place. The lesson is that the red wheel cannot be broken, whether by accident or intention, though *you* can certainly be broken upon it. The lesson is that you can't win. You can only keep moving. You are doomed to failure, which is to say, to life, which is full of pain. There will never be a final synthesis that unifies all worlds and resolves all dialectics. You can only resolve your own paradoxes and become more of who you are."

"If I'm doomed to failure anyway," Vidyucchika says, cleverly though she is filled with despair, "why must I seek it out now? I can leave it for later later."

Grandmother Sits rubs her jaw, where what once used to be a dimple is now an impact crater from which crackling waves of wrinkles corrugate outward. "Because you're not much longer for this world. I know you—you're restless. You'll want to seek out new worlds soon, new lives, new hauntings. And the more you grow, the more you become someone else and someone else, the more you put off the enjambment of your paradoxes, the resolution of your own crises, the less likely that you will still care. Other things will occupy your attention. Bigger or more immediate things will seem paramount. Is that not already the case, with this one here?" She waves at Lambajihva. "Imagine yourself a thousand lives deep, old and strange and overflowing with the drama and strife of ten thousand beloveds, rivals, enemies, and comrades."

"And what happens if I never fix it? What if I just never go back?" Vidyucchika demands. She is growing angry because her grandmother's attitude is making her life, this life fall away as if it were a mere detail. She holds her face with both hands, fingers splayed over her cheeks, to prevent it from sliding off to expose the skinlessness beneath. The fever heat radiates from the self beneath the self.

"Monstrosity," Grandmother Sits says. "You will lose your human heart and the human logic of your mind. Unbecoming. You will be lost to the line and to our works, as we have already lost too many. Catastrophe. Our project will suffer for it; all the threads we have wound will fray a little more; some more will come undone. You will become an agent of pain."

"Whose agent am I meant to be instead?" Vidyucchika says, with what is not quite a sneer but only just. "Yours? Of the long line—but *which* long line? Are we agents of peace? Of life and light? Are we cosmic dollar crows meddling in sovereign realities? Who do we work for? How are we paid?"

"All the long lines together form the web," Grandmother Sits points out. She takes a sip of her tea, now cold. "We are scientists. We bear terrible knowledges. We are the agents of death, and our wages in arrears will be paid as a lump sum upon retirement, when all our work is done, when all the worlds are laid to rest in the dark."

14

Vikurthimagga

Consider the monster.

Electric Head, in the city of the dead, skull cleaved in two, fever burning. Daytime is safe from the dead now; the municipal authorities have put out fiery barrels of imported dummala resin at regular intervals on every street, spaced between the rain trees and the flame trees, belching out great bitter clouds of smoke. Restless and fuming she stalks the streets of the city of the dead, breathing in the smoke and puffing it out again. Odeg and Mrs. Akan are of no help in resolving her dilemma. They are separately concerned with the dummala crisis: Odeg with a pro bono case his firm has taken on, alleging corruption scandals to do with the mass of import licenses issued after the ban was rescinded; Mrs. Akan with ongoing harassment from the revengeful would-be cartel of Luriati yakahalu plantation owners. The other day she and Vidyucchika woke to find a black rooster nailed to their front door, its viscera splattered below. The maggots were pleased, at least.

"They'll kill me, Vee-daughter," Mrs. Akan said. She did not sob; she merely said it out loud as prophecy, to which Vidyucchika shook her head but could not speak otherwise. This will be, as Vidyucchika knows perfectly well but does not wish to look at in the face, how Mrs. Akan dies. In death, perhaps, at least mother and son will find rapprochement. The wish is sincere, but faded, as if it were already memory. Ever

since her conversation with Grandmother Sits, Vidyucchika
has had one foot out of this world.

✳   ✳   ✳

Consider the monstrous: it portends a greater and more marvelous world. Vidyucchika understands this now. She sees a
little more clearly the devils and ghosts that haunt the mundane, senses with fevered delirium the horizon red and wheel-
ing, the world bordered by the red ocean of all stories, all
possibilities. It seems to her that she herself is the axis, the
flayed ape crucified on the world tree, upon which the universe rotates, but she knows from experience this is merely the
trick of perspective. Walking down the street, sometimes she
is compelled to chase after things unseen, the uncanny oddi-
ties at the corners of her vision, the distant blurs of the weird.
She forgets sometimes that others cannot perceive them. She
leaps into a tuktuk and says,—Uncle, follow that devil!

The driver, unseeing and frightened, throws up his hands
until Vidyucchika guides and directs him turn by turn. The
devil is too distant or too monstrous for her to make out its
precise shape, except that it is too large to be human. It moves
with purpose, always a street ahead, always turning a corner
just as they come into sight of it, just long enough to see where
it went but not enough for her eyes and her mind to resolve
what she is seeing, the long white arms, the spikes and locks
of its hair.

—Is there really a devil, the driver asks, and she nods yes
when he meets her eyes in the mirror.

—We are hunting treasure, Vidyucchika says gaily.

The driver crosses himself. He has a symbol in polished
stone at his neck, a floreate cross whose prongs each are fruit-
ing, stood in a grail. An old symbol, popular even on this peninsula dominated by the Path Behind. There are many religions

here, all strange, most old. There is no religion that Vidyucchika knows that concerns itself primarily with devils; they
are in the background only, old and always half forgotten,
dealt with by unregulated aduras. There is no saint to act as
ambassador to the demon-haunted world.

Though they cannot be perceived by most, they are still
believed in. They are true stories, taken on faith for twenty-
five centuries. The figure of the monster, the devil, is in vulgar
folklore associated with hidden treasure, usually interpreted
to mean buried gold and jewels from the age of kings.

—Not that the age of kings is over in this world, Vidyucchika says, unaware that she is completing half a thought out
loud.

This observation seems to calm the driver, though; he responds to it as politics.—Ah yes, he says.—The Absent King,
the Absent Queen, we are still bound shamefully to monarchies
that have no place in a modern republic . . .

He continues in this vein as he drives, pausing briefly only
to follow Vidyucchika's directions, until she loses sight of
the devil and has to stop the vehicle and get out, frustrated.
She digs in her purse for casi but only has a single fanon. She
hands the driver the note, brushing the maggots off its silvery
threads, and he protests that it's too much twice over, but she
insists. When he drives off, she tells herself, there, no more
tuktuk money. No more chasing devils today. What's wrong
with me?

The problem is that her next step is both necessary and impossible to plan; it is too much, too vast. She grinds her teeth
at overly wise and gnomic grandmothers. Her fever trembles
and her thoughts skitter. No, she must trust herself, in the
end—or rather, to the beginning.

She walks to the nearest light rail station. In Luriat, the rail
is free. She consults the map on the wall to figure out how to

get home. She has wandered far in the city, into districts she does not know, and needs several connections to get back. A two-car train arrives, and she gets into the rear car, which is empty and ill-lit, the lights flickering and cold. The stuttering of the light makes her head hurt. Sitting and nodding, she keeps looking for monsters through the windows and it seems that the more she looks, the more she sees, moving through crowds, clinging to the sides of buildings. She has only impressions of twisted bodies, elongated limbs, distorted faces, indistinct but unhuman, forcing her to blink her eyes rapidly and try to focus.

The folkloric treasure of the devils is not gold, of course. This is an obvious allegory; the treasure is secret knowledge. A world is not as the mundane experience it devises: once that was secret and awful knowledge, though now it's a truism to be found in any glossy magazine. Solids are mostly empty space. Objects are not discrete. The perception of time is an illusion. Seeming biological realities are socially constructed: gender is only genre, race is a race to the bottom, species as arbitrary as specie. Seeming social realities are machinations of power hiding their inverse: slavery is called freedom to disguise its exploitation; ignorance is called strength, to champion political illiteracy; and most of all, most of all, war is called peace, the peace bought by murder, the peace of the unmarked mass grave.

We put on a play for ourselves, we ghosts, we people, we devils, with our superstitions like solidity, objects, time, or justice. We live in confusion, we swim in it. But the world is not a river to swim in; it is a glacial ocean, always whole, already complete.

The truth is terrifying. Teaching is terrorism.

Vidyucchika looks out of the window of the train car and sees herself in the glass, lit in dull gold as if from within, her eyes too wide, her lips slightly parted as if she's breathing hard. She looks ready, she thinks, to be flayed.

—I know, she says, out loud in the empty car. It echoes; her voice sounds raspy and unfamiliar, trembling from fever. Lambajihva rustles in the meat of the empty chair opposite her, and then he comes out to sit on it. She addresses him, a mirror to speak into.—I know what opened my eyes. I did it myself.

And then and there in the train, she closes her eyes and reaches back through time to force her own awakening. —Hey, she says, to the swirling fractals of her inner eyelids. —Will you hold my hand while I go? She reaches out a hand in the dark; cold fingers curl stiffly around hers.

                    *   *   *

The path of distortion, the vikurthimagga, the art whose strictures she must simultaneously invent and adhere to, is violence. There is no explosion, but it's like a bomb going off, scattering doll parts everywhere. The world creaks under the strain, metal and stone, rubber and flame.

Vidyucchika opens her eyes and she is skinless and cold in the undark, the absence of shadow and photon. Who took my pelt from me, she asks, but there is no sound, even in her head. She reaches out in the direction of her grandmother— that's easy, it's the opposite direction from the northwest into which Grandmother Sits always stares—long enough to meet her eyes and find her way to a kitchen table. She takes the explosive.

(In a silent room where she waits alone, Grandmother Sits says *ah* when she hears the crinkle of the paper bag as the radishes drop to fill a sudden emptiness.)

Vidyucchika looks for Lambajihva, but he has not come with her. She looks for him again, the mirror she used to know so well before they were set apart—my fault, my fault, she says—and finds him in the moment of stepping onto a street, vehicles in disarray.

She admires the
moment,
the *symmetries,*
as if it were a painting; every frame of the akashic record is perfected documentation, the world that sees itself.

She builds the bomb in his backpack in the very moment that he swings it off his shoulder to hold it in front of him. Thank you for the birthday present, grandmother. When he opens his mouth, laughing with his tongue out like a demon king, she kisses the C-4 goodbye, her electric head a detonator—she bites off a chunk and swallows hard into the bloom.

*   *   *

She does vomit, somewhere in the red web. Grandmother was right about the side effects. But what a buzz, myalgias and hae-maturia aside. She needs to pee. Dizzy, she lands with a splash in the shallows of a lake under a full moon, reddens the water, frightens the crocodiles. The water is thigh-deep and cold. She giggles a little. Oh, quick, before another grandmother gets here, a grandmother by another mother. She wades forward, waving her arms at the men huddling over another on the lakeshore.

—Oy! Fuck off!

She doesn't know what they see when they look at her, she doesn't know what they hear. She hears her own voice and it is strange and full of strangers, rough and multiple, more teeth than she has in her mouth. They look at her and their eyes widen and they run. They leave behind the dying man. They leave behind the body.

She kneels by his side. He is still alive, though life flows out of him; he's gurgling, spitting blood, his eyes clenched shut.

She puts her skinless hands on his temples and forces his eyelids open with her thumbs as he dies.

She reaches up into the sky and takes the full moon between finger and thumb, and she places it in each of his eyes like a coin.

—Your passage is paid, she says.—Your beard still sucks. I'll see you later later. I'm gone, gone, gone to the other shore.

And she's gone, running downhill at an angle out of this world, laughing as she tears skinless through the skin of world after world, laughing as she grows vast and sharp in the tooth, as serpents crown her head with their forked tongues like thunderbolts, as her eyes bulge from all that she has seen. She is moving so fast when she lands, like a meteor molten from the path it carves through the layers of history and atmosphere, that she barely sets foot in that haunted jungle— the cicadas hush and she can feel the dead children flee from her, like ripples from a thrown stone in water—only for long enough to leap in joy and homecoming into that girl's open mouth. Then she's gone, and Annelid clamps her hand over her mouth and laughs and laughs and laughs.

15

Beginning's End

Vidyucchika opens her eyes on a train. Lambajihva is still sitting opposite her. Now his eyes have a little more focus. She sees the moon in them briefly before he blinks.

"Well," she says. Her voice is unsteady; whose voice is this? "That's the end of the beginning. Where do we go from here?"

Lambajihva tries to answer, but his dead tongue will not obey. The floor of the car is a sea of maggots, though she can no longer tell their focus or source.

"Yes, yes," she says. "Next is the beginning of the end. Let's go already." She studies his face. "I suppose we have some things to say to each other."

How The Red Witch Lost Her Pelt, and Other Stories

Once upon a country, there was a war. The Wikipedia entries, so contested that there is another war in their edit histories, will tell you there were two sides, but each side is dodecahedral and rotating, or perhaps eight-celled hypercubes occupying the same space, their inner surfaces as deeply scored and stained as the outer. In that war there was a knocking at the gate, a rapping and a banging of fist on metal, a summoning out of the living into the dead of night. This knock was called the knocking of death, whether performed by the most secret of police or by the swarming militaries and paramilitaries, the ur-militaries, fritillary and flapping. A fritillus is the cup that holds the dice, grooved on the inside so that the dice will rattle and spin when you throw. The dice fall where they may; the dice fall as they will. Some nights Vidyucchika lies awake in her parents' house and imagines the knocking so vividly that she gets up, half asleep, and walks halfway to the door before she wakes up all the way and remembers that it was only a dream of death visiting.

She knows why it will come, when it comes. Her parents know, too. It could hardly be a secret in this house, so it is merely unspeakable. It is because her parents keep opening doors that they should leave well alone. Her father and her mother have made this house's doors too open; people come and go, a way station out of nowhere to somewhere. It is quiet work, not dramatic. The conversations on the phone are bluff and genial and gossipy, not whispers or pleas, with the important parts happening almost by the by. When strangers, often whole strange families, carrying either too many belongings or too few, stay in the spare bedroom, Vidyucchika is told to tell anybody who asks that these are aunts and uncles and cousins visiting. A few days later, after more of those phone calls, they're gone again, in vans and trucks heading for planes and trains and at least once, Vidyucchika overhears, a boat. Boats are a last resort because her parents do not overlap with the underworld, merely a shallow underground or two.

She doesn't have to ask why these strangers need to leave the city. She is a child, but not that much of a child. Her objection is much more grown-up, she feels; her parents are sticking their necks out too far, it's bound to cause trouble.

"It's irresponsible," she tells Father, who laughs at the word as if it means less because it's in her mouth. Father is impossible to talk to about this. It's as if he's the child, willful, giggly, unwilling to listen to reason.

"You'll get us in trouble," she tells Mother, who nods, yes, yes, we probably will. Mother listens patiently when Vidyucchika wants to talk, and she agrees with her daughter that all this is a bad idea, that it will end badly for them. She says that maybe it started out as the merest attempt to salve their own burning egos, their fragile sense of themselves as upright people in these troubled times; that maybe it started as a one-time thing, just a friend who needed some help, then a friend of a friend, then . . . "Bad things will happen," Vidyucchika says. "We should go, too. Let's go wherever everyone else goes to be safe."

"It's different for us," Father says. "We're safe here. We bear the mark of the patricide, see?" And he raises his mop of curls up to the hairline as if to show some mark carved into the skin of his forehead, but there's nothing there but dry skin. Mother whacks him on the shoulder.

"What's a patricide?" Vidyucchika wants to know, but Mother won't let Father answer that one, and she imagines for years that it is the name of the side they are on, the Patri Side, the patria for which they will mori, so sweet and cold.

❊   ❊   ❊

War and girl grow a little older; parents stay the same. The knocking gets closer every night, until one night she sits up bolt upright with her heart hammering at the softest nighttime knock. The knock comes again, so either she did not dream it or she is still dreaming; she gets up and walks through the house in the dark, her long cotton nightdress heavy with the sweat of her terror. The luminous hands of the clock on the wall say it's the third hour of the midnight watch. Her parents are light sleepers before midnight, but afterward they are dead to the world. Vidyucchika drifts to the door as if in a nightmare; she peers through its frosted glass, but there is only one shape outside, too small to be the most secret of police. She unlocks and opens the door to find a boy she has never seen in this life, and whose face she knows—whose long earlobes she knows so well that they start a sudden ache in her chest, as if a lung had given way, or a ventricle gone rotten like a bad tooth.

"Lambakanna," she greets him, giving him a nickname at the same time. Long-ears. He touches his ear wonderingly; perhaps nobody in this life has ever remarked on them before. He is dirty, as if he's been sleeping rough. He is about her age. He is alone. It's very cold outside. Her bare arms horripilate in the touch of the night air.

He says something, counters with his real name, maybe, but she doesn't hear it.

"You can't be here," she says. She's whispering because she doesn't want her parents to wake up, and because the pain in her chest has not faded and she can't muster the breath. "There's no help for you here. You have to go away."

And she closes the door in his face, and she watches his shape through the frosted glass while he whispers urgently and taps again. When he leaves it's like a dream, a shape already indistinct that fades into the surrounding darkness the moment it takes a step back.

She says nothing to her parents in the morning. She puts it out of her head. For weeks she sleeps well, during which she comes to think it may have been a dream. It had that unreal quality, that sense of worlds ending. Then one ordinary day death comes knocking, and her parents put her in the ceiling crawl space and go back down to die, and while they are dying, she looks around in the crawlspace and discovers she is not alone. She can't move much; the crawl space is very small, child-sized, and the crossbeams thin and of inferior wood. Light as she is, she must distribute her weight and lie still, listening to the tumultuous death of her parents below, veiled by ceiling panels. When she raises her face to look directly ahead into the darkness of the crawl space, about the only movement she can make without risking collapse, a face appears out of those shadows before her: a boy's face that she has seen only once before in this life, a mirror face she knows better than her own. She knows instantly that he has been dead for a while; his eyes are unfocused, his tongue hanging out of his mouth. His jaw works as if he's trying to talk; it is so wide open it looks dislocated. A maggot falls from the corner of his lip and onto the ceiling panel between them—the first of the maggots he gifts her. It makes a sound like a very small drumbeat. This is the moment the fever blooms in her; it will never again recede.

Be quiet, please, Lambajihva, she says, only in her mind, not with her mouth, because it's all she can do to breathe shallow and soft so that she is not heard by them below with the two-handled saw, full of hate and agency.

She never finds out how he died, why he came to her door alone in the night, or what he wanted from her, or more likely from her parents. The answers are obvious in form if not in specifics. She reconstructs those obvious answers endlessly in the long later years of her haunting: because someone killed him; because he had lost everyone; because he needed help, and someone told him he could get it at that house, before she turned him away in a dream.

Shall I die like a leveret, without any resistance?

—*Help, help, help! I am slain!*

In the play *The Duchess of Malfi,* written by John Webster in 1623, or the year 2167 by our reckoning, the corrupt Cardinal speaks these words as he is murdered by Bosola, his own pet murderer.

Bosola comes around to this point in a great circle, a tying-off of threads into a web. First, the Cardinal and his brother, the Duke, task Bosola with the killing of their sister, the titular Duchess, her maid, and her children. Having done this, having killed the Duchess, Bosola confronts the Duke to tell him, you have bloodily approv'd the ancient truth that kindred commonly do worse agree than remote strangers. In this strange moment, Bosola discovers a remorse so rageful that he is driven to revenge on himself, the murderer; or rather, through the transitive property of command responsibility, upon those who commissioned the murder with himself as instrument, the Cardinal and the Duke. Bosola stands over the dying body of the Duchess like, he says, one that long hath ta'en a sweet and golden dream: *I am angry with myself, now that I wake.*

Bosola hunts and kills the Cardinal, who dies like a leveret without any resistance, and then he kills the Duke. The Duke of Calabria is a lycanthrope, a man who believes himself to be a wolf, stealing forth to graveyards in the living night to dig up dead bones. A witness to the Duke's lupine depredations came upon him once in a midnight hour, walking a lane behind St. Mark's, the leg of a man on his shoulder, howling. The only difference between the Duke and the wolf he believed himself to be, the witness remarked, was that a wolf wears his skin on the outside. The wolf died just like the hare in the end.

I am angry with myself, now that I wake

—is what a murderer says; it is important to remember what it is that we have done, precisely, in those sweet and golden dreams. Last night I dreamed of murder, justified; murder in self-defense. I dreamed I was bedeviled by an unrighteous aggressor, who held a long thin blade to my face. I could barely fend off his knife hand with both of mine; he scored my face with a dozen cuts that stung from my sweat. We struggled at the foot of a long flight of stairs. The light poured down the stairs wet and metal, cold on the skin, but I never looked up to see its source: it felt like sunlight, if something was wrong with the sun. Eventually, and through sheer happenstance, I managed to unbalance my opponent. He fell and the knife slid away. I pounced on him. I smashed his head into the edge of that first step as hard as I could. His eyes were glassy. I did it again, and again until I heard the sound of skull giving way. I don't know what that sounds like in life, so my dreaming mind made it wet. Light poured into his skull, illuminated the bloody brain. I laughed, and only partly in relief, only partly even in triumph; the third part was joy, the simple joy of murder, of hate, of agency.

That him with the knife was an unrighteous aggressor—I don't know that for a fact. That's what I believed in the dream, but history is written by the one who wakes up. The truth is that the dream began in medias res, and I have no idea who started the fight, or why, or who was in the right. In the dream I thought it didn't matter, that once the knife breaks the skin and the grapple begins, it simply comes down to who lives and who dies. But then I woke up with blood on my pillow.

PART V

THE BROKEN BOUGH

16

Threads

PROLOGUE: THE FRITILLUS

⚅ We interrupt this program—no, we must. We have to go back, no, even further back, and start again.

⚄ There is more than one thread in a web; there is more than one beginning to every story. The turmoil of the dice within the fritillus, the life of each uncast die as they catastrophically collide and forever change each other's moment and position and trajectory, altering pasts and futures to rotate around this moment, is a model of the universe, sleek and groovy and impatient.

⚃ Here we are with another die, not made of injection-molded plastic but something older and less immortal, less intended to last until the death of the world.

⚂ Not made of found seashells, not bone or ivory, not so old as that. Wooden, perhaps, in a rainforest culture whose things were meant to die and go in peace.

⚁ Here we are back in a world that is not Luriat, but far more alien to you and us than that, because it is our own.

⚀ Here we are.

DRAMATIS PERSONAE

MARTIM, ONE who knows hats

JOÃO, ONE who will be a memoirist

IMIYA, an OTHER, a hunter

EMBI, another OTHER, a poet

DEVAKIRTI, a warden of the south, MOTHER of that other OTHER

FERNÃO, an OTHER in ONE's clothing

GASPAR FIGUEIRA DE CERPE, six of ONE and a half dozen of the OTHER

An **AUDIENCE**, mostly WHITE and mostly AMERICAN

A **CHORUS**, they've got a beat and you can dance to it

THE SON OF SEVEN MOTHERS, a god, immanent

AN UNNAMED DREAD BEING from a lost age

ACT ONE: THE PERILS OF THE SOUL

Thus in Suffolk if a man cuts himself with a bill-hook or a scythe he always takes care to keep the weapon bright, and oils it to prevent the wound from festering.
—James George Frazer, *The Golden Bough* (1900)

The stage is set. We open on a RUINED VILLAGE, the fires still smoking and the bodies still warm, at the foot of MOUNT ELDER, a wild and forested mountain deep in the southern hills of contested VILACEM, which is the Portuguese mispronunciation for the place called Vellassa, the Hundred Thousand Lakes.

(A secret dedication: Mount Elder is sacred to the SON OF SEVEN MOTHERS, the god of the southern garrison. The SON does not manifest in this text, but remains immanent underneath all these words by right of jurisdiction.)

Bodies are piled along the back of the stage like firewood.

A stagehand holds up a placard titled MID-17th CENTURY IN THE YEAR OF YOUR LORD.

A second stagehand holds up a placard titled CONTENT WARNING: IMPERIALISM, MASS MURDER, TORTURE.

Both stagehands remain present for the rest of this act. The placards wave gently like anemones in the tide.

MARTIM walks onto the stage, a young white man red from the sun, and from all the blood. He has a uniform and a hat. His father owns a hat shop in Lisbon, so Martim knows hats. He is, to the AUDIENCE, relatable. None of the blood is his own.

MARTIM (*addressing AUDIENCE*): The CHORUS isn't set up yet so I'm going to read you an excerpt from my friend João's memoir. He'd read it to you himself only he's still back there nursing the calf muscle he pulled tripping over a root in the jungle. Anyway, he hasn't written this yet—he doesn't write it for another forty years, long after he goes home to Portugal. This is the part where he talks about what happened today.

Martim clears his throat.

"At Categao are preserved the offerings which had been made for many years, consisting of gold, jewels, and precious stones, and five hundred armed men were always maintained for its defence," Martim reads. His tone is neutral.

"We had several times made inquiries about it, in our desire to obtain this wealth and to relieve them of their anxiety regarding it. At the beginning of 1642, I was one of a company of one hundred and fifty Portuguese and two thousand Lascarins," Martim says, then pauses, peering at the AUDIENCE for understanding. "When I say *I,* I mean not I but my foolish friend, João, who will eventually be the author of this text. You got that, right? This is not me confessing to the acts that he describes, though I was also there—but obviously you understand this, as a sophisticated AUDIENCE. Anyway, these are João's words:

> . . . the majority of these troops were Christians, under the command of Gaspar Figueira de Cerpe, who was held in high respect among them, a man of ability and well versed in their language and customs.
>
> When we came near the spot where they said the pagoda stood, we captured a native residing close to the spot, and our

commander inquired from him if he knew where the pagoda was. He replied that he did, and that it was close by; he acted as our guide and led us through a hill covered with forest which was the only one in that district, and this we wandered round and round and recrossed many times.

It was certain that the pagoda was at the top of it but I do not know what magic it possessed, for out of the five guides whom we took, the first three were put to death because we thought that they were deceiving us, for they acted as if they were mad and spoke all kinds of nonsense, each one in his turn, without the one knowing of the others . . .

—João Ribeiro, *The Historic Tragedy of the Island of Ceilão* (1685), translated P. E. Peiris (1909)

While Martim reads, the CHORUS has been hurriedly walking on stage and taking their places. The CHORUS is composed of the DEAD. Some of them have been dead for a while and are showing bone. The ones that still have skin are showing that, too. Everyone is bare-bodied, as is the custom of this country, including the women. Martim sneaks glances at them and his skin gains a third shade of red.

CHORUS (*singing, a capella; the taller dead in the back are beatboxing*): Break a thornless branch, hang it on a tree, to gain some kind of sanctuary, from that old devil in the jungle, oh that old devil—

(Among the most recently dead members of the chorus is EMBI, a young woman so recently killed she's still bleeding. Her throat is cut. She was the third guide that João speaks of. She steps forward.)

EMBI (*solo*): Ask me again, I'll lie again.

Her cut throat modulates her song, adds a whistling color-
atura in rust.

EMBI (*speaking*): Too long, didn't read. The story of the
invasion of Categao is simpler than all that. Here is all you
need to know: we never broke, they never found the sacred
city, and most of them never came out of the jungle alive.
MARTIM (*annoyed*): Quiet, I'm still talking.
EMBI: Fuck you.

The stage darkens; indistinct figures of stagehands flit
about in shadow, and there are a few thumping sounds and,
distinctly, a muttered curse that is probably not part of the
play. The AUDIENCE chuckles appreciatively.
The lights come back on.
The setting has changed. We are now in a DARK ROOM,
inside one of the few unburned huts in the village. In the centre
of the room, bound hand and foot to a wooden chair, is
IMIYA, who is (if you recall) an OTHER. He is being tortured
by FERNÃO, who is both ONE and OTHER.
(Their otherness is about where they are from. Fernão is
a third-generation Catholic from the occupied coastal territories in the West: despite his name, he has no Portuguese
ancestry. It is also about their souls. Fernão has one, which is
tortured; Embi and Imiya and the others do not.)
Imiya's material body is filthy and bloodied. His long hair
has come loose from the knot and is clouded about his head,
matted on one side with blood. His eyes are glazed. His beard
is patchy, as if someone has ripped chunks of it from his face
in a fit of anger. His lips are swollen. Three of his fingers are
severed: they lie on the floor in front of him. Fernão is working on a fourth, but his knife has been dulled and he is audibly
complaining.

A young white man in uniform is sitting in the back of the hut wearing a pained expression and rubbing his calf. We infer that this is Martim's friend, JOÃO, the future memoirist. He will only observe.

Another man, CAPTAIN GASPAR FIGUEIRA DE CERPE, stands behind Imiya, listening patiently but not speaking. His father was white, but Gaspar was born here and has never been off the island. He also has a soul, slightly worn. He is in charge here.

FERNÃO (*sawing mightily and speaking over his shoulder to the AUDIENCE*): It's okay, the ends justify the means because he talks eventually.

IMIYA: I don't.

FERNÃO: You will.

IMIYA: Didn't you hear Embi? She explained how it turns out. She said you never find the sacred city.

FERNÃO: You're hallucinating from the pain. Your Embi's been dead for hours.

IMIYA (*nods toward EMBI in the choral lineup*): She's right there.

EMBI: I'm right here.

FERNÃO: There's nobody there.

GASPAR (*interrupting*): Who's your village headman?

IMIYA: Embi's mother was our warden.

GASPAR: A woman?

IMIYA: Devakirti Mahage. She died in the first attack.

EMBI (*simultaneously*): My mother, who was keeper of the sacred songs before me.

FERNÃO (*sarcastically, pointing unseeing in the direction of the chorus*): I suppose the Mahage is also standing right there.

IMIYA (*squints at the chorus*): Yes, I see her. Slightly to the left.

DEVAKIRTI is an older woman, her death-wound an ugly bullet wound in her chest: the first attack was a surprise bombardment from the base of the hill that abuts the village, a dawn chorus of jingal wall guns, their mounts unsteady on the slope.

GASPAR: Who did she serve?
IMIYA: We are free hunters, not vassals. But our allegiance is to the King in the Mountains.

Devakirti and Embi detach themselves from the chorus and come to stand next to Imiya.

DEVAKIRTI: Tell them nothing.
IMIYA: I don't plan to.
EMBI: Tell them to stick their dicks in a nest of red ants. There's one over there by the jack tree.
IMIYA: She says—
EMBI: Wait, wait. (*She thinks.*) Tell them you can teach them how to protect themselves against the demon in the forest.
IMIYA (*suspiciously*): The demon in the forest?
GASPAR and FERNÃO, overlapping: What demon?

Embi squats and whispers into Imiya's ear.

IMIYA: The path to the sacred city goes through the jungle. It's protected by a demon.
GASPAR: We can send for a priest.
IMIYA: It will eat him.
FERNÃO: Shut up.
GASPAR: Talk! How do we protect ourselves against this demon?

IMIYA (*eyes closed, listening to EMBI's whispers*): The demon respects an ancient compact with our people. Every seventy-seven steps in the jungle, you must reach up and snap the branch of a living tree, such that the broken end stays connected by only the thinnest skin of bark. Keep doing this. The demon will ignore you, and you will find yourselves on a hidden path that will lead you up the mountain to the sacred city.

FERNÃO: This is nonsense.

Gaspar watches Imiya's battered face for a long moment. Gaspar is the sort of man who prides himself on his ability to discern character and truth from another man's face.

GASPAR: Nothing wrong with taking precautions.

EMBI (*to IMIYA*): That should do it.

DEVAKIRTI: That's the true rite, daughter.

EMBI: That's the idea.

DEVAKIRTI: Why are we giving it away?

IMIYA: Wait, the demon is real?

FERNÃO: See, even he doesn't believe it.

EMBI: *Demon* doesn't describe it very well? There's a song cycle that—

DEVAKIRTI: This is not the time—the demon is very real, and that ancient rite will summon and bind it to its ancient promises.

IMIYA: The dead tell me the demon is real and that this rite will bind it. The dead do not lie.

Gaspar studies him carefully, coldly, for perhaps as long as two minutes.

GASPAR: All right.

Fernão is disgusted, though he's not sure who he's most disgusted with. He throws his dull knife away and begins to strike Imiya repeatedly in the face.

GASPAR: Let's get it over with. Sack this secret temple of its riches and get out of here before either the King in the Mountains or the Vereenigde Oost-Indische Compagnie send troops to find us.

Gaspar, Fernão, and João leave the room.

Everybody on stage is silent and motionless for another few minutes. The AUDIENCE grows restless. Somebody in the audience takes a picture—the flash is blinding—even though there was a sign at the door that said NO PHOTOS, NO SMARTPHONES. There are muttered complaints. Imiya blinks. His pupils are huge.

Devakirti returns to the chorus and starts organizing them to move on to their next lives.

Embi walks over to Imiya, who is slumped forward with his eyes closed. He is trembling, and the remaining fingers on his mutilated hand are clawing slowly at the air.

Embi picks up the knife that Fernão threw away. She rasps a short verse of sharpening until the edge sings.

IMIYA (*eyes still closed*): Is that you, Embi?
EMBI: Yes.
IMIYA: Listen, I'm sorry about how it all turned out.
EMBI: It's okay, I have a new plan. We have a strategic advantage in rebirth, but it's going to be—
IMIYA: No, I mean, I thought—
EMBI: Yes?
IMIYA: Never mind now, I suppose.

DEVAKIRTI (*rolling her eyes from across the room*): I'm sure you two will have another chance to make a go of it, somewhere further down the great wheel of rebirth.

EMBI: Oh. Eh. I could see it going a lot of different ways.

IMIYA: What about—

Embi cuts his throat.

EMBI: Now our people are all dead, and the ancient compact is broken. The rite of protection is now a summoning, nothing more.

DEVAKIRTI: Yes, daughter. I figured it out, thanks.

IMIYA (*dead, coughing up blood and black ectoplasm*): I still don't get it.

EMBI: One thing at a time. First, stop coughing.

17

You Are Here

ACT TWO: TABOOED THINGS

> In West Sussex people believe that the ground on which human blood has been shed is accursed and will remain barren for ever.
>
> —James George Frazer, *The Golden Bough* (1900)

You are here.

Further along the great wheel of rebirth. There is no stage-hand to hold up a sign MID-21ST CENTURY IN THE YEAR OF YOUR LORD but you know perfectly well—you don't even have to check your phone's calendar—that it is. It's the ninety-fourth century after Rakesfall. It's been four hundred years since Act One.

There is no stage. This is not a play. This is a conspiracy.

The three of you are rebelling against the pedagogic tyranny of the tenured old farts of the Department of Ritual History. That's why you are here studying old texts in the spotless archival room at the Museum of Tabooed Things. The Museum is on the southern coast, far enough from any city to maintain green and pleasant grounds outside for visiting scholars to refresh themselves and watch the sea.

But every day you all ignore that to huddle together in this

room. You are engaged in deadly struggle against the stulti-
fying pap that the Department preaches, the dead narratives
that it upholds about the song-cycles of your ancestors, who
you firmly believe are also your past lives—mere superstition
to all of your professors but one. In these ancient texts you
hope to find evidence, and explanations.

Today, you and Embi are letting Fernando do the reading
because, frankly, he needs the practice.

A long, long time ago, reads Fernando. The scroll he's
reading is dark brown with age, and would have been difficult to read even if it was new. Fernando reads it in the slow
and hesitant fashion of a man who is used to the European
convention of spaces between words. The ola leaf scroll has
none; it bridges thoughts with the kunddaliya, giving a sense
of breathlessness to Fernando's reading.

*In the time of the beginning of all things, the Creator flowed
like water from past to future and there was time, for the first
time ∿∿ this world-in-time bifurcated into tributaries ∿∿ like
maggots in dead flesh, in time there arose two kinds of life:
first, those who loved time and worshipped its change and
mutability, who were called the Yoke; and second, those who
loved time and wanted to protect and keep it from harm, who
were called the Rake ∿∿ ∿∿ and they went to war.*

Fernando pauses briefly and looks around, as if wondering
whether you and Embi were following; you nod encouragingly.

Many ages passed in war, Fernando goes on reading, *the
time of ash and the time of the green and the time of monsters,
until it was the time of the gods in the first age of cities.*

Today, you know those first cities lie underwater off the
coast, buried by ancient inundations. Scrying orbitals have
mapped the great bowls of their sacred theatres, like empty
eye sockets in the sea's hadal deep.

Fernando seems to be struggling with the text, so Embi

takes his place in front of the leaf, murmuring a line to brighten the ambient light and enhance the magnification of the faint, spidery writing.

"All right," Embi says. "Listen: the Yoke won the first war—they broke the glaciers, claimed the moraines of the north, and they drove the Rake south, as far south as they could go, which is to say, *here* where we are, overlooking the world-ocean. The territory that would later be claimed by the Son of Seven Mothers."

This is comfortable territory for Embi, who just completed her master's on the sacred poetry of Pre-Kaliyuga civilizations, most particularly the long silver age between the Toba supereruption and the ancient world war now known as Rakesfall. She has explained to the conspiracy her model of the poetics/politics of deep time, the ritual song-cycles that retell and anchor history, compose causal chains, and sing narrative into being.

What makes Embi a heretic, and you with her, is the idea that magic was not always part of the everyday world. The idea that something happened at a particular point in history—an intrusion from a different eon—that changed all of history before and after that point. That all this had not already happened, until it had always already happened. Embi wants to know who did it, and why, and how. She recruited you and Fernando through sheer force of will, but you are all committed to the idea now.

"The fleeing Rake made a home in the ruins of a long-forgotten elder civilization that was destroyed by volcanic ash six hundred centuries ago, and whose name is unknown even to the gods," Embi summarizes, after reading in silence for a minute. "They built a stronghold there—this location is lost, we have no idea where. Probably underwater south of here?

For a while there was détente, but nine thousand years ago the Yoke army came south and the Rake fell. That was the end of their great-power status, and the beginning of what we consider the modern era of poetry, and the history and physics that go with it. Here's the part we were looking for: there *were* a few Rake survivors who went into hiding."

"So we could be right," you say. You're kind of proud of that *we*, because you were the last to be recruited into the conspiracy. "The so-called demon encountered by the de Cerpe expedition to Kataragama four centuries ago. The Implied Thing in the Jungle. The ITJ."

Embi beams at you. "Yes!" she says. "The ITJ broke history. The past changed. The world changed."

"That's a little exaggerated," Fernando says. "You can't *break* history. History is just the things that happened. All you're saying is that you think something else ought to have happened."

You make a gesture repudiating that ugly *ought*. Embi waves it away, too, as if it were a physical thing sitting there on the table, squat and squamous.

"We can point at the (posited) 1642 irruption event as a fixed point that is always-already anchoring this brane to a particular configuration in the mythopoeic register," Embi says. She gets technical when she's tetchy. "Something came into this world. Something from before the Fall came back and our songs changed."

"But there's still no indication that the ITJ ever left occupied Vilacem," Fernando says. "No ravening elder-world monster came rampaging out of the jungle to conquer the empires of the day."

"This is why we need Imiya's model," Embi says. "To show that the ITJ can have widespread causal effects at a distance, in both space and time."

"The ITJ doesn't need to go anywhere," you agree. "You read the ola leaf. It was one of the first things born in time. It warps causality simply by *existing* in the post-Fall regime of poetics. It probably thinks the arrow of time is something it can shoot out of a bow! And it might be right!"

"Calm down," Fernando says, laughing. You hate that, and for a moment you hate him, but then he sees your face and he leans forward to kiss you, which is his way of saying sorry.

"This paper is going to blow everybody's minds," Embi says happily. "Professor Devakirti is going to be so proud."

INTERMISSION

Remember to stretch. Look up at the sky—through the ceiling, yes, past its secret cavities, its terra-cotta or asbestos or metal, through the layers of air and cloud and vacuum. Feel the earth under your feet, transmitted through foundation and concrete and brick and metal and tile and stone and whatever else might intervene. Look at the moon, even if you have to look through the entire earth to find it. Do not look at the sun.

ACT THREE (FRAGMENT): (Y)OUR DEBT TO THE SA(VA)GE

(Now playing: fragment of annotated video discovered mis-filed in the Library of Old Adam, three thousand years after Act Two. Playback recovery interrupted by compression arte-facts and the cruft of centuries of format conversion errors.)

> We are like heirs to a fortune which has been handed down for
> so many ages that the memory of those who built it up is lost,
> and its possessors for the time being regard it as having been
> an original and unalterable possession of their race since the
> beginning of the world.
>   —James George Frazer, *The Golden Bough* (1900)

Zoom in from a great height. At first, seemingly unbroken ocean. Then signs of habitation. There used to be a large island here, and the network of floating habitats and research institutions in this area like to anchor themselves to the islets that were its former mountaintops. Not because they crave terra firma, which they do not, but because those regions pro-vide easier access to the now-submerged archaeological trea-sures of those elder civilizations which spent eons retreating to higher and higher ground, ever since the Yoke shattered the Himalayan glaciers at the very beginning of history.

The history of this place is about retreat inland and uphill: from invading armies, from the invading sea, from the poi-soned air, the vengeful sun.

The Library of Old Adam is an environmentally controlled

habitat carved into a solid cube of stone that rises almost twenty feet above sea level. Once this cube was a sacred mountain.

The video enters the Library, descends through many passageways to a room with a student and a teacher. They have just finished reviewing some ancient poems. Embi is trying to explain their context and implications. The video drone misses most of this, but arrives just in time for the student's rejoinder.

"No," says Deva—her stubbornness is palpable because the video comes with affective attachments. "The lesson is that false consciousness has always [obscure] our people to their true selves. The ones and the others; the white and the black; the north and the south; the lion and the tiger; the colonizer and the indigene; these were all a distraction from the true and essential distinction, that the [obscure] people must fight all forms of oppressors."

Embi closes their eyes and tries to find the right words to explain—words that can refute, but won't get their ration cards revoked for revisionism. It's hard to teach history, much less poetry.

"The Yoke and the Rake didn't begin and end in war," they say. "War was not their only relation. Recording it as such was the fundamental error of [obscure]. The phrase [obscure] means they *sang together*. The confusion arises because some of the oldest songs were songs of sacrifice, and war."

ACT FOUR: THE KILLING OF
THE TREE-SPIRIT

Nineteen thousand years after Rakesfall, when the sea has been coaxed to recede again, Embi comes back to the low slopes of Mount Elder.

She's taller in this life; she comes walking on air, descending from the clouds in leaps, but stopping in a wary hover before her bare feet touch the ground.

The soil below her is dry. The only green here is ugly, hardy plants she doesn't recognise. (She remembers those long-lost rainforests). They don't really fit the Prevailing Aesthetic. If she's not careful, this zone might be voted over to a different maintainer. She bends down to test the soil with her fingers. The nitrogen cycle's still not right; she spits into the earth and mutters instructions for the animalcules in her spittle to go to work rebalancing the soil.

It isn't the Prevailing Aesthetic that worries her. She's been composing a poem of memory ⋀⋀guilt ⋀⋀witness ⋀⋀fury and she's stuck. Every time she puts herself into archive-trance to remember her past lives, she recalls the debt she has to this earth.

She checks in with Fern, whose hallucinated image appears beside her. Fern is doing something complicated with her face—she's got half of it peeled off to install something that looks like a giant beetle that pulsates in iridescent green.

"Are you agonizing over your Rake again?" Fern says. Fern always says she moved on lifetimes ago, though yet again in this life 'Miya and Fern have fallen out again over their mutual trance-memory of the torture incident. It's made for some awkward parties, because it's hard to avoid the few other people who still hang around the old Earth.

That we still hang around is a sign, Embi thinks. None of us have really moved on, except Deva. She doesn't say that out loud. Instead, she says, "What are you *doing* with your face?"

"I'm leaving," Fern says. She doesn't sound sure. "I'm tired of trying to fix this broken-ass planet."

Fern says this every other decade. She's not serious. Or at least, Embi doesn't think so.

"Have you talked to 'Miya about it?"

"You *know* she doesn't talk to me," Fern says. "Why would you even—Look, I'll talk to you later, okay? If I get this wrong I'll have to print a new head and start all over again."

The hallucination of Fern vanishes. Embi sighs. Fern's never been ready to hear what needs to be done, and 'Miya's sworn off all responsibility for the deep past. Deva joined the diaspora three lives ago and now lives in a hard-vacuum habitat somewhere in the galaxy's other arm. People move on. Embi hasn't.

It comes down to her responsibility in the end, as it did in the beginning.

She steps down onto the earth—she makes herself do it before her resolution can waver. The ground is warm and dry. Later (she silently circumscribes that with an *if*), she'll figure out how to re-irrigate in a way that sticks. She'll clap her hands and make it rain. She'll sing rivers across the land and teach them a hundred thousand lakes. But first, she walks over to a tree and snaps a branch, letting it hang by its own peeling bark. Takes a deep breath, in case it's her last.

"Hello," she says. "I think it's time."

The Rake appears so quickly it feels as if they had been waiting just for her, their author. Their form manifests transversely across the temporal aspect of the local brane: humanoid in cross section but serpentine in totality. Everything that might seem human about them is distorted in this fashion: they seem many-headed, many-handed, crowned by infinite undulating serpents, teeth grinning tusks, tongues absurdly long. The Rake undulates, spirals, encircles her. She tries to choose a face to look upon.

"I broke the compact," Embi says. "For reasons that don't seem so important now. You remember—you didn't have to die and forget, like me. I've felt guilty about it for hundreds of lives, only I couldn't always remember why. I do now. I've come to help you."

Or to fight you. Dirges of power hum behind her lips, ready to unleash lightning and fire. Far, far overhead, satellites tense and arm themselves. But she swallows the words, broadcasts forcible stand-down orders. More violence isn't even a last resort on this blasted earth that she and everyone else has spent so long painfully regreening.

"We've become too much alike," she admits, though she says that more to herself than them.

The Rake sings like a storm, in a voice multiplied by three hundred billion mouths:

> *A broken bough in the last sacred place,*
> *home of the seven-mothered son sieged by the sea;*
> *sister of the yoke, welcome.*

Sing with me.

"No," Embi says. Her head is ringing. "You loved time, didn't you? You wanted to protect it. I made you hurt it. That's my fault."

Time flows.
I love, the Rake whispers like thunder, rattling her bones.

   I forgive.

Embi stares at them. "You . . . forgive. I've left you trapped in a foreign poetic regime for ten thousand years. It should have been otherwise."

There is no other wisdom, the Rake says.

"You don't have to protect me," Embi says. "If protecting the world means that I need to be sacrificed, I'm ready. It took me a while to *get* ready, but I'm ready."

You are *the world,* the Rake says.

There is no difference.

She touches their many faces, and it feels like rain.

This is our new compact.

CODA

A Lemon

In a Bengalee story it is said that all the ogres dwell in Ceylon, and that all their lives are in a single lemon. A boy cuts the lemon in pieces, and all the ogres die.

　　　　　　—James George Frazer, *The Golden Bough* (1900)

For all the things of this world are no more than mere shadows, and the reality is always different from that which shows itself to us. So now we shall leave these minute details which we have related regarding the Island of Ceilão, and proceed with the narrative of the war in that Island, which has been calling to us from the grave of forgetfulness when it should be alive in our remembrance.

　　　　　　—João Ribeiro, *The Historic Tragedy of the Island of Ceilão* (1685), translated P. E. Peiris (1909)

PART VI

THE LAMB

18

Contingency

After the wars were won, or at least done—after the nuclear dust sowed its wild oats and settled down like carrion birds coming slowly to earth, after the devouring goo ate its fill and stilled into sludge, after the cloud that had ruled the sky for longer than human civilization finally gave way to a long rain, after these and so many other things had happened—on a Wednesday so deep into the desolation that there is hardly anybody left on Earth to remember what a Wednesday is—the Lamb wakes up in her Contingency Bunker, filled with pain and purpose.

Her eyes hurt even in the bunker dark, because the satellites are streaming her visions and status updates before she takes a first step. It's a good step when she takes it, though—confident, precisely calibrated, the silicon carbide nanofibers in her thighs luxuriantly stretching for the first time in (she checks her onboard clock) thirty gigasecs. Was that all? A thousand planetary revolutions, give or take? That seems like not long enough. Still, she is proud of that first step.

The second one is not so good. She tries, midstride, to unlock the bunker door, reaching out almost unconsciously in virtual space, and her processors all spike at once trying to get the decrypt. For a moment the Lamb finds herself thinking only with her squishy organic brain, and something in it is full of terror and unease, rendering it incompetent with her new body. She stumbles, goes to a knee, and recovers gracelessly.

She feels self-conscious, but nobody is watching, she tells herself. Probably. The bunker was never fitted with lights; it's an oversized coffin, nothing more. A place for her to be dead in until called upon.

Then the door opens, and she's outside, and the world is vast and full of light. She raises her face to the sky and it shivers like a bubble.

Even though she volunteered for this, it's still terrifying to have done it. To be doing it. She had too little time to acclimatize to her transformed body before she went down for the long sleep, and during the eons of stasis her self-image has traitorously reverted to her unhappy and all-too-human norm. Even her pronoun feels new and strange again. And her legs are too long, and her arms too heavy, and she can't breathe—she isn't breathing—no, that's by design. She feels the sides of her neck for the air filter vents and finds their reassuring corrugations, feels the warm air being processed through them. She is breathing, just not with her face.

Cold natural light lies heavy in the valley below the bunker, like a hungry animal huddling for warmth. She tries to adjust to the satellite-fed sensorium overlay. She's shin-deep in mildly irradiated dust—fimbulwinter's ash mixed with deactivated grey goo—looking around at the empty grey hillside that the Bunker is nestled into, a landscape made blank and empty.

No, that isn't right. She looks again and the soil underfoot is black and fertile, the hillside green and overgrown: a jungle, daylight filtering dimly through the canopy overhead.

The competing visions strobe. She staggers. Her sensorium is stuttering. Her feet are sliding a little—are they really buried in ash or is she just unsteady? She reaches out a hand to rest it on a tree trunk that's flickering in and out of her vision, and is relieved to feel it steady and present under her hand. She narrows her sensorium to the contact of bark on skin. The bark is old, in its fashion—much younger than she is, of course. Perhaps a mere few gigasecs old. The tree is really there, she tells herself. The trunk is thick, forking close to the ground and then forking again, like upreaching arms with fingers buried in green. Leaves bright, rounded, and pinnate. Bark pale and flaking, the wood beneath a smooth pinkish brown. Her fingertips—the whorls are fresh, even her fingerprints changed—scrape up minuscule samples that she brings to her mouth. *Pericopsis mooniana,* the satellites offer. Long since extinct, they whisper, a ghost tree. But it's her grandfather's voice she remembers, that angry and spiteful man pointing out the names of every tree and shrub as they walked down a forest path oh so long ago. A nedun tree, her grandfather called it, endangered by overlogging and foul modernity. When did it go extinct? And when did it come back? Why wasn't she awakened for that? Were such things not her purpose?

It *has* been brought back, regardless. The tree exists, the Lamb decides. From the nedun tree outward—her hands tighten on the trunk, her fingers crack the flaking bark and leave dents in the wood—she reconsiders the world. There is no ash on the ground, she decides, there is not ash up to her shins, covering the world, drifting in the still air. At least, there is none now: once, all of this must have been ash. Fimbulwinter is not a fantasy: it is a memory. The satellites are not mad, just stuck in time. Her clock is wrong. Thirty gigasecs is not enough for all this recovery, this ridiculous green fecundity. The world has been cleaned and remade while she slept, and she feels a great sense of loss.

"This was *my* work," she says out loud, testing her voice. It's an alien rasp. She goes into a coughing fit halfway through the phrase. Her eyes tear up, her mouth fills with spit. She spits. "This was supposed to be my work," she says, and this time it sounds more like a voice, though still an unfamiliar one. There's nobody in sight, but someone must have woken her: a Contingency Bunker needs someone outside it to declare the contingency. That's supposed to be the caretaker's job.

"Caretaker," she says. That was supposed to be a question. She can't remember how to inflect a question with her voice. She tries again. "Caretaker?"

The memory/vision of the dead world is still ghosting in her sensorium, but at least it's relatively featureless. She does her best to ignore it, and it becomes background. A haunting. Memento mori. The satellites whisper to her of a world's-death long since conquered, of radiation and ash and silence. She ignores them. Overhead, there is birdsong. The air is cold. Her Bunker is at low latitude (the hallucinating satellites agree about that, at least) and it shouldn't be this cold. Perhaps residual fimbulwinter effects. Or maybe it's early morning? The light is indistinct through the jungle overstory, and she can't tell. Her clock says it's midafternoon, but if it's wrong about the eon, it's probably wrong about the time of day. It's cold enough for goose bumps on the parts of her skin that were left human enough, the fine hairs bristling on her face and neck and shoulders, up to the clavicles. The engineers called goose bumps an ancestral ambient situational awareness/early warning system that they didn't want to take away completely. Her skin is synthetic dermal armour, meant to protect against the world, a thick collagen lattice in uniform maroon red—is that configurable? She doesn't feel very maroon right now, but she can't find the interface to reset colour. No hair on her head, but transposal antlers like a crown. No nails, but an extra joint on her fingers and toes. No exposed primary or secondary sex characteristics, skin corrugated to protect the torso and hips. No holes, no dangly bits, chest flat. She remembers hating that—not the armour, the flatness, in this body and the last, the boxy, ill-fitting, scarred mess of a bygone age.

Well, the scars are gone now and she misses them a little. The body's pain has not faded; she'd thought it the shock of awakening, but it seems to be settling in to wait, aches deep in the bone, recurrent twinges in the nerves.

The path downhill that she remembers is long gone. The satellites suggest climbing the hill, but they think the valley below is buried in ash. She begins to trudge downhill slowly, carefully placing her huge splayed feet, walking three-toed like a rhino, heels never coming down. There is no path, so she makes one, trampling over and through any shrubbery small enough to ignore, circumventing foliage and rocks too big to walk over. Thorns break on her skin. The satellites panic at what they must think her decision to drown in a sea of ash, but as she gets lower and doesn't die, they subside. Perhaps they will reconsider their worldview, update themselves. She isn't going to hold her breath.

When the Lamb gets to the valley and down to the riverside, finally breaking free of the thickest jungle, the caretaker is waiting for her. Sort of. There are nine birds, each one smaller than her hand, with long tails and grey heads, bodies a rufous brown. They are a noisy bunch, cackling to themselves. Ashy-headed laughingthrushes, the satellites whisper to her. Also extinct, of course. It's a relief to hear birdsong, the Lamb realizes; part of her has been scratching at the auditory emptiness of this jungle, the silence of the cicadas. One of the laughingthrushes flies up—it's not much of a flight with its short round wings, more of a hop—and perches on a branch at the height of the Lamb's head. She can tell they are not ordinary birds: her sensorium overlay sees them as a thick mesh of data. Only seven of the birds represent the caretaker, she realizes. The other two are just birds.

"Hello," she says. First contact in deep time, conducted in banal power plays. By speaking first, she is insisting on her language, dialect, period. Let the caretaker calculate the language drift. Given the state of her satellites she doesn't trust them to translate for her. There should be a data backchannel, she remembers, for assistive context. She was drilled on the protocol for making contact, but it's hazy now after her long death. She looks for the backchannel in her imaginarium. It feels like tonguing her teeth to find a loose one. Ah, a wiggle— and then data in a flood. It tastes like salt and iron.

"Hello," the caretaker says. Their name, the backchannel announces, is the Clave Eight. The voice doesn't come out of the laughingthrush's beak, but seems to emanate from all of their bodies at once. The Lamb imagines tiny speakers nestling in the down under the wings. She is almost overwhelmed with the urge to pick up one of the birds in her giant hands, to gently lift their wings and look for the speakers. She controls herself. This could be some godlike manipulation of air molecules. The caretaker is supposed to be the god of this microplate jurisdiction and should be capable of that.

"I only see seven of you," the Lamb says. Making conversation, the phatic chitchat of her strange afterlife. Or is this an invasive question? She feels reckless. Perhaps she isn't controlling herself so well. "Why Eight?"

"This is the eighth generation of our self," the Clave says, after a pause, with a brusqueness that suggests that the question had, in fact, been rude. This is clearly not what they were about to say. The Lamb has them off balance.

"Do the other two know?" the Lamb asks, gesturing at the two civilian birds pecking at the ground. I'm bullying the caretaker, she thinks. She can't stop herself. Some ancient conversational rhythm. She feels it in her spine, the coiled serpent of ancient socializations nestled in her hips, the things she hasn't unlearned: the need to push, to destabilize, to assert herself into space.

"They are innocent," the Clave says, which does not quite answer the Lamb's question. A problem of translation? A cultural misunderstanding? Evasion? She shakes her head. It feels large, heavy; the branching antlers on her head are unobtrusive until she moves her head, and then they remind her they have mass. It seems the Clave is not going to elaborate further. Perhaps she bullied them into a corner, disrupted their chat protocols.

The Lamb shakes her head again, this time conscious of the antlers. "I see my contingency has passed me by," she says. She is proud of this line, of her delivery, that epic world-weariness that can be used only once. It is her first public acknowledgement that her purpose has been fulfilled without her involvement, that thousands of planetary revolutions elapsed without her being called upon, that she is useless now. Her sacrifice was pointless, her dedication a waste. What is left to her but ironic detachment?

The caretaker's backchannel acknowledges her with a thick datastream about the world. It is, as she thought, healing; being healed, in fact, by a maintenance team completely unrelated to the Contingency program. The work is not yet complete, but the radiation is mostly gone; new jungles have been seeded and are growing old again. And her clock is very, very wrong. She has not been dead for thirty gigasecs. Oh, it has been so much longer than a mere thousand planetary revolutions—an order of magnitude more. History is a steep-edged abyss, and she forces herself from the brink of attempting to comprehend it. Her whimpering satellites recede further into the background of her sensorium, abashed by these revelations. The ghostly world of dead ash persists, though fainter than before. She is careful not to give any sign of this to the caretaker.

There are worse things, she supposes, than to go into the long death expecting to wake up into a postapocalyptic, irradiated hell that she would spend her long, long life detoxifying and regreening. Instead she has awoken into retirement, into a paradise where so much of that work has already been done. "I'll retire to a beach," she adds. "I assume there are nice beaches again."

"You were not woken for retirement," the Clave says.

"Of course not," the Lamb sighs. Too easy. "Did my sponsors not pay the bills? Did you need to disassemble my hill to dam the river? Why am I not peacefully dead?"

"Your secondary-tier specializations," the Clave says. "The catalogue listed you as the only available Contingency qualified for international diplomacy, criminal investigation, and exorcism."

"What?" the Lamb straightens up—she hadn't noticed she was hunching. She has nearly four hundred primary-tier specializations, the vast majority related to revisionist terraforming and ecorestoration. She barely remembers her secondary-tier specializations. At the time they seemed more of a joke, the engineers packing the Contingencies with bits and bobs of knowledge to fill in any leftover space on the drives.

"There have been murders," the Clave says. "There's a haunting." The cluster of seven laughingthrushes burst into chirrupping, mocking cackles that never seem to end. The two innocent birds seem startled at first, but then also join the peanut gallery. "Please do the needful and revert."

19

The Desolation

The scene of the crime: Earth, an old and haunted house.

The Lamb decides to take a look at the sites of the alleged murders. The Clave provides a decrepit dropship, piloting it themself—this time a purely virtual presence, bringing no birds along. The absence of the birds makes the Clave feel more remote, as if they're phoning it in. The dropship is a big egg the colour of dirt, about twenty metres long, with stubby wings and vectorable nozzles. There is no cockpit or visible instrumentation since it was designed to be piloted by someone like the Clave. Its innards are mostly empty space with a metal floor and metal benches to sit on. The Lamb is preoccupied with trying to sit on the bench, which is too low for her unfamiliar legs. It makes her back ache. The dropship wobbles a little as it rises above the valley, climbing slowly into the upper atmosphere. The light changes as they rise, growing warmer. The Lamb leans forward to catch sun in her face, eyes lidded.

Parts of the fuselage seem to be missing, or perhaps it was designed that way, but what's left of the airframe looks worryingly rusty. The craft doesn't seem very stable in the air, even as it picks up speed. She looks down at the valley, out of the gaps in the fuselage. The ghostly image of apocalyptic ash is intense from this angle, more real than the blue of the river or the green of the jungle, both of which seem fake and unconvincing, their colours too vivid. Perhaps this is the angle at which the satellites see the valley, so she's getting a heavier dose of their perspective. Or perhaps the signal is stronger the higher they climb. The dropship rattles alarmingly under her feet.

"Do you have anything that's not a wreck?" the Lamb says.

"Vintage," the Clave Eight says. They sound defensive. The backchannel attempts to show a gallery of search-and-rescue personnel carriers and dropships from various historical periods, in various states of dis/repair, but the Lamb blocks it. Apparently the caretaker collects them. She's about to complain that it will take forever to get anywhere in this bucket, but then the ramjets kick in and the buffeting of the wind through the holes ceases. There is a sudden oily smell, as if the entire aircraft had been bubbled in slick lubricant. She looks back through one of the holes in the fuselage and sees a hypersonic puff far behind them. The Clave sounds slightly distracted when they speak again. "Temporarily upgraded."

Despite this, it takes more than three kilosecs to get to the other side of the planet, which time the Lamb passes in boredom, clicking the metal bench with her nailless fingers. The Clave provides only the barest debrief. Relative to pre-diaspora history, the Earth is essentially uninhabited by humans, except for the maintenance team. "That limits the suspect pool, at least," the Lamb says uncertainly. She doesn't want to do any of this, but she doesn't want to go back to sleep either. Especially not after finding out about the murders: all four victims have been sleeping Contingencies. Better to stay awake.

"Questioning the maintenance team may occur after examining the murder sites," the Clave allows.

The Clave's drones provide high-fidelity recordings of all four murder sites; she has already played them back too many times. Each murder took place within the victims' Contingency Bunkers. Their locations are scattered across the continents, with no apparent clustering. None of the Contingencies awoke, as far as the Clave is aware.

"Why did it take four deaths before you decided it needed investigation?" the Lamb asks.

"Two happened in other polities," the Clave says. "Information was not shared. First time we encountered one in our territory we thought *unfortunate accident.* After second time we requested public consultation and data-sharing. Then: pattern."

"Is this one of the other polities we're visiting now?" the Lamb asks. She hasn't forgotten that the Clave had sought her out for *international diplomacy.*

"No," the Clave says. The backchannel provides a world map with historical annotations; there are fourteen nations, or really eight mega-polities, if she zooms out and counts long-established alliances and conglomerations as units. Their territories are non-contiguous, a colourful patchwork. The Clave is the third largest by territory, with tens of thousands of viridian patches all over the globe, which the Lamb spins on a finger, watching the colours bleed. The largest two polities are the others that have experienced murders. That makes sense, she supposes, if Contingency Bunkers are dispersed more or less evenly across the world—she asks this question.

"Of course not," the Clave says. The backchannel attempts to present a potted political history of the last three to four hundred gigasecs, and the Lamb waves it off.

"I'll read that if it becomes relevant," the Lamb says. She hopes it doesn't.

"Political history is always relevant," the Clave says. They sound like they're frowning.

"Context is important," the Lamb agrees politely. She just doesn't want to be swamped by information. She's slept too long and through too much history, even on this depopulated Earth, for her to possibly catch up over the course of this investigation.

She can ask the backchannel for context, but then she's relying on the Clave's curation of historical salience. She suspects she would disagree. She attempts to glean a quick summary of current affairs: it seems all the polities of Earth are administered and governed by their sole citizens, caretaker systems like the Clave Eight, though of entirely different lineages of software and design philosophy. She politely refuses to dig deeper into this, despite the backchannel's urging. The maintenance team, who are themselves stateless, have contracts with some polities, but not others; therefore some parts of Earth are in much better repair. Most, but not all, polities were left behind by departing civilizations of the diaspora; some arose independently in the desolation.

"What is *the desolation*?" the Lamb asks. She heard that before, somewhere in the constant flow of information. The word fits her recurring hallucination of the world covered in ash and dross, but only she knows about that. It's hard to reconcile it with the green and flowering earth, even if that green is patchier than she'd first thought.

"Our term for our time," the Clave says. "What we caretakers call our loneliness. Our missions in the last three hundred gigasecs . . ."

The Lamb does not pursue this, because part of her is still struggling with her own sense of mission, what was taken away from her, the unwanted work she's been given instead. She doesn't want to hear about the emotional struggles of the caretakers. Instead, she turns to the backchannel and tugs carefully on the single thread of history that is the diaspora, the human diaspora from Earth into the galaxy, which had just been beginning when she went into her Bunker. She is curious about whether humans ever met any other life out there, but the answer appears to be no: there are no aliens, no resident strangers, at least in this universe. Humanity is still reaching out into the galaxy, taking various parts of the Earth ecosphere with them to replant, reseed, reconstruct, parody; some are remaking worlds and habitats to suit themselves, others remaking themselves to suit new worlds and environments, becoming the aliens, becoming strange.

There is more Earth life in the rest of the galaxy than on Earth itself. There are whales and butterflies aplenty out there, the Lamb learns, but none remaining on Earth. So perhaps the regreening is still far from complete, despite the trees and birds and green. Perhaps after she closes this case there will be good work for her, too.

The sensation of oiliness fades away. The dropship comes to a dead stop. The wind begins to buffet her again through the holes in the fuselage. They have arrived.

Descent is eerie. They drop vertically, like a controlled fall, slowly enough that she ought not to feel queasy, but somehow she still does. The vision of a dead Earth below is stronger than ever. They are falling into a bed of compacted ash, her satellites whisper urgently to her, and must pull up before they crash. She sees an endless expanse of dirty grey, wet from rains. It is without geological feature in any direction, no trees or plants, nothing but a monotone grey plain. Her eyes look for patterns, something to latch on to; she follows the striations in the ash, compacted and grooved by wind and weather, perhaps, though it looks as if it has been raked haphazardly. It reminds her of cooled lava, only less liquid, less rounded. Panic builds in her as the dropship approaches that surface at speed, a hammering feeling throughout her body, and she rises to her feet, gripping the airframe to brace for impact, but then they keep dropping and the ash is gone again. Below is the real earth. She drinks it in hungrily: a grassy plain, with forest in the distance.

She sees their destination, the Contingency Bunker. The location of the first murder that the Clave became aware of

and the third overall. It doesn't look anything like hers. The
Lamb saw it in the recordings, but its design is more offensive
in person. It looks like a very small city, or a very large palace.
It has no buildings as such, but is crowded with spiral-fluted
towers—she thinks *pillars,* at first, but they are not holding
anything up except the sky, which is vast and grey and cold.

Once the Clave lands the dropship, the Lamb steps out and
walks toward the Bunker. The grass is wet under her feet. She is
joined by a cluster of local birds, this time not laughingthrushes
but blue magpies; six out of seven are the Clave. The six birds
lead her into the Bunker, a colourful entourage with their bright
blue bodies and bright red heads; the seventh bird is confused
and follows behind.

The towers of the Bunker are very tall, now that she's on
the ground. At the Bunker's diffuse outer edges they are narrow and clustered close together, and she has to turn sideways to pass between them. The deeper she gets, though,
the towers become individually thicker and collectively more
spaced out, and the going is easier. The floor is a little spongy,
like a sheet of rubber, perhaps, melted and sticky from long
eons in the sun. She pulls her feet away from the cling with
distaste. The birds are flitting ahead, almost lost in the forest
of pillars; she follows flashes of blue and red. The pillars cast
heavy shadows and a permanent bitter wind blows through
them. Sometimes, especially when the Lamb loses sight of
the birds, her sensorium stutters and mountainous waves
of ash flood between the towers, filling them up, filling her
eyes and mouth with grit and sourness. The ash gets into
her breathing-vents and clogs them and she has to wipe them
clean, steadying herself on a nearby tower, until her senses
stabilize. The tower material is colder than she expected.

The records indicated that this Bunker was not in fact
even called a Bunker, but its name is untranslatable because

the original language of its creators is lost—the backchannel contained a massive archive of philological speculation. The Contingency kept here was octopedal and equine at the same time, according to very old videos with so many frames missing that the image stuttered and jumped when the Lamb rewatched them on the flight. Or rather, the Contingency had been those things, because they are now a pale slush, seeping out of a great crack in one of the tallest and most central towers. The crack is several times taller than the Lamb. The blue magpies scatter about the damaged tower, not approaching it too closely. She approaches cautiously, not stepping in the egg-white gunk. It has cooled and hardened somewhat, and a stray leaf has fallen from somewhere—there are no trees nearby, the Bunker being some distance from the tree line—and become partially embedded. When the cold stiff breeze whistles between the towers, the leaf still moves a little, a tiny sail adrift, becalmed.

The Clave analysed the slush in their previous investigations—they flag the report they previously forwarded, as if the Lamb had not read it already—and identified it as the liquefied remains of the lost Contingency, created when their own contingent body and their Bunker's stasis protocols and healing protocols were tricked somehow, persuaded to turn upon themselves. The Contingency dissolved in their long sleep, drifted away in a dream. The Bunker's records indicate no awareness or distress; the fluxions of the Contingency's dreaming mind show no spikes of alarm, merely a slow gradient into inactivity. It should be a relief that this was not the work of a sadist, but the Lamb does not feel relieved.

It was definitely not an accident. The compromised systems bear the clear marks of intrusion, but not enough invasive code to analyse for a fingerprint. If it had been possible to solve these crimes through forensic analysis alone, the Clave would not have woken her. The Lamb scans the code anyway, at a level of abstraction high enough to compensate for her technical obsolescence. It's quickly obvious that the attacker found their crime easy. This Bunker, like all the Bunkers, is ancient. Its systems have been patched by a succession of care-taker systems, including multiple times by the Clave Eight, but it could not be fully upgraded without waking the Contingency, and so there are complex vulnerabilities that the Lamb's technical knowledge is too outdated to understand. She bumps up the Clave's explanation another few levels of abstraction, until the entire Bunker appears as an oyster with a pearl inside, and the attack as a knife.

"No, that's *too* simplified," the Lamb gripes.

"Accurate, however," the Clave says. "Knife is a problem from far outside oyster's context. Design has no defenses."

The Lamb sighs and dismisses the code. The ghost of fimbul-winter's ashes flickers in her sensorium, a faint distortion at the edges. For a moment it had seemed to her that the oyster lay on a deep bed of ash, slowly sinking. The muscles on the sides of her neck ache. "What caused the crack?" she asks, switching tack to examine the physical evidence. She approaches as close to the violated tower as she can without stepping in the body. The edges of the crack are not smooth as they would be if created by bots. There is some debris, too: small crumbled pieces of tower-material, which looks like stone to the Lamb but the Clave insists is a kind of plastic. Most of the debris has fallen inward. "It looks like someone swung a very big axe at it."

"Uncertain," the Clave says. "Possible." The backchannel attempts to speculate on weapons and technology that could have accomplished it, measuring angles, degrees of hardness and force, but the results are inconclusive. It could very well have been a giant axe. It doesn't really matter, the Lamb de-cides. Anybody in the maintenance team would have the access required to create any weapon and manipulate any forces that they needed, not to mention falsifying the records. The weapon is a dead end. Her knowledge of forensics is obsolete: another dead end, even with the Clave's help. The suspects are too empowered, and the technologies available to them in this strange future are too advanced. Questioning them is the only meaningful avenue of investigation. It's only a kind of nostalgia that compels the Lamb to see the bodies first.

*   *   *

On the flights between crime scenes, the Lamb looks down at the Earth and begins to understand how much of what she sees is artifice. They are flying low over a forest that seems false to her in some way, though there is nothing she can point to: the leaves and the trees do not seem either too perfect or too crude. Specklings of yellow leaves leave streaks in her vision that make her momentarily dizzy. "This forest doesn't exist," she says at last. She hesitated over it, wondering if it was another hallucination of her errant sensorium, but the backchannel seemed to verify her impression.

"Yes," the Clave says. They take a long moment to respond, as if not sure whether this was a statement that required acknowledgement.

"Why?" the Lamb demands. The dropship is low enough to almost brush the treetops that do not exist.

"Aspirational illusion," the Clave says. "Also placeholder marker for the maintainers." They pass her a key.

The Lamb turns the key; the forest pops out of existence. The absence of the illusion abruptly changes the quality of the light, as if a cool containing bubble had popped and let in hot angry light from outside. The landscape below is a ruin, and full *of* ruins, though nothing that rises into the sky. Rather, it is the ruin of what must have once been a below-ground habitat, a great complex of tunnels and underground spaces, perhaps a kind of bunker. The layers of earth and rock and metal that must once have shielded it from the surface have been abraded, laying the underground complex open to the sky. Loose dirt is piled in what might once have been great hallways or meeting rooms or storage closets or sleeping chambers or communal baths. Low piles of trash dot this unburied world, mounds of the unbiodegradable. The Lamb looks for bones in the dirt and the garbage and sees none, though they must surely exist. They are moving fast enough that it's hard even for her augmented eyes to pick out such fine details.

The next crime scene, the second in territory controlled by the Clave, chronologically the fourth and most recent so far, is eerily familiar even though it is on a different continent. After they leave the ruined underground behind; after they pass a lagoon full of great soft lungs the size of whales, breathing hard and in pain; after they cross a brief purple sea that seems to host no marine life whatsoever, a barren salty waste haunted by the ghosts of whales and dolphins, who gambol in the waves if the Lamb toggles the aspirational illusions back into place, they reach a valley much like her own, and a Bunker much like her own. The air is drier and warmer here—she can feel it in the roughness of her lips when she runs her tongue over them—but otherwise the similarity is uncanny. The Lamb is cautious of triggering a hallucination of ash, but her sensorium remains stable, fimbulwinter only a grey whisper at the edges. Perhaps the undoing of aspirations has helped.

The scene is analogous to the previous: the door to the Bunker has been shattered open in a way that suggests a heavy edged weapon, and the Contingency within reduced to a slurry, this time reddish brown. Records show this Contingency wearing a vaguely similar design to the Lamb, their engineers belonging to an offshoot of the same polity some gigasecs later. In the archive footage this Contingency is enough like a mirror to be disturbing, especially when the Lamb flips back to the real to see the sludge at her feet.

"How many Contingencies remain on Earth, that you know of?" the Lamb asks, staring at the slurry. The Clave presents a number much lower than she'd expected; all are sleeping, except for the Lamb. A quick historical backscroll shows the number of available Contingencies gradually reducing over the eons. "Is it possible that some of them were intentionally made inactive? Sabotage preceding this string of more obvious murders?"

"Possible, but no evidence thereto," the Clave says. "No suggestion thereof."

The backchannel lists an array of natural disasters and systemic failures. Some Bunkers were destroyed in earthquakes; some drowned by rising seas; many lost power or structural integrity over time, until finally collapsing. None of them show obvious signs of foul play. The failures do cluster in time sometimes, but in easily explicable ways, such as increased seismic activity in a given area, or the legacy of particular historical contractors whose substandard designs led to predictable patterns of failure in deep time. But the Lamb is suspicious of everything. She needs air; her vents feel clogged. She goes outside and runs a diagnostic absentmindedly, staring out over the valley. She tastes ash, then tells herself firmly that she does not. There is not much green here, except for the bright scum on the surface of a small lake at the far end of the valley. It draws the eye; she turns away.

"Is it possible for me to see the other two sites?" she asks. "Is there a diplomatic process?"

The Clave's drone bird comes back out of the Bunker and sits on her shoulder, a familiarity which the Lamb dislikes.

The bird flicks each wing once, as if brushing itself off. "Somewhat," the Clave says. In this valley, the Clave's representative bird is a solitary cuckooshrike, grey upon grey like ashes. The bird vibrates when they speak. "We have already begun negotiations with both other polities."

"When you say *we*," the Lamb says, turning her head slightly to look at the cuckooshrike. "You mean you and me? Or yourself?"

"Both." The bird cocks their head: the Lamb dips into the backchannel to learn that a cuckooshrike is neither a kind of cuckoo nor a kind of shrike. "The Clave series were designed as representative democracies. We are a gestalt of thousands of subsystems."

"But you've been a stable gestalt for longer than some prediaspora polities," the Lamb points out. "You're not really a collective, as I understand it. Your gestalt is itself personhood. You could say *I*, if you wanted to."

"Sometimes we disagree," the Clave says.

The Lamb laughs. "That's personhood, all right."

The Clave makes a noise that the Lamb can't parse. "I will take that under advisement," they say. "We should do an interview next; one of the maintainers is not too far from here."

20

Visa Interview

There are three in the maintenance team. Only three humans awake on Earth, apart from the Lamb herself. There were many other maintainers once; the backchannel proffers a list of the dates when each resigned their commission and left to join the diaspora. These last three were also among the first to volunteer for this work. They have been doing this for longer than the Clave Eight existed; longer than the entire Clave series, in fact, which to the caretaker makes them elder gods, respected and more than a little feared. The Lamb can sense the Clave's reluctance to suspect them, or even approach them. The maintainers move freely among the polities, at least the ones they have contracts with, and cannot be tracked by any caretaker outside their own territories. So the first interview is driven mostly by the convenience of this maintainer's timing in entering Clave territory. The Lamb would have preferred to have seen all the murder sites first, but can't argue with opportunity.

The maintainer is called Fern. They find her at work, just a megasec away from the Bunker by dropship, at a riverbed that seems to have been dry for some time. The earth is cracked and an unearthly blue, as if from some kind of chemical spill that has tainted this soil forever. The Lamb lands on it with a puff of blue dust, the crust spiderwebbing on impact. The colour stains her feet immediately. The Clave refused to land, much less directly participate in the interrogation; the dropship retreats to a safe distance. So much for the confidence of that earlier *we*. Perhaps the Clave fears that the maintainers might uninstall them if offended. The Lamb feels some osmotic trepidation, and grumbles under her breath at the caretaker for infecting her with it.

The sky is grey and oppressively low. Even knowing that this is merely a happenstance of weather, it feels to the Lamb as if the sky must always be this way in this tortured place. She tries to scrape the blue dust off one foot with the other, but it seems the dermal armour has already taken a permanent stain.

The maintainer Fern is doing something with a big rock that sits half buried in the riverbed. It is a very large rock, several times bigger than the Lamb, roughly ovoid, most of its bottom half stained blue. Fern is climbing over it, poking and prodding, as if dissatisfied with the rockness of the rock. A handshake protocol issues automatically from the Lamb's open backchannel as she approaches, offering basic courtesies: greetings, format converters, considered selection of translations. Fern does not turn to look at the Lamb. She is vaguely hominid, with asymmetric beetle extrusions; one wing, which is clearly cosmetic; three extra limbs, which seem purposeful; something iridescent and glimmering about half her face; a single forked mandible juts from one side of her jaw, oddly similar in its branching to the Lamb's own antlers. None of the blue dust sticks to her.

Fern's presence in data is dark and obscure at every level of representation the Lamb can access. Perhaps that is simply how she appears to the Lamb's archaic technology; in the real, Fern is bright, her extrusions glittering even in the clouded light, her human skin a rich brown, marred by—no, enhanced by a cosmetic melanoma on her flank, a dark, irregular, fashionable patch whose period and context are entirely unfamiliar to the Lamb.

"I'd like to ask you some questions," the Lamb calls up.

Fern does not respond for almost half a kilosec, and the Lamb wonders if she will be humiliated by the maintainers by being simply ignored, beneath their notice or even contempt, rendered as useless in her secondary-tier work as she was in her primaries. But then, thankfully, Fern turns her head to look at the Lamb, her beetleface viridian in a stray sunbeam. The Lamb wonders if the maintainer arranged that sunbeam.

"There's one here," Fern says, tapping the rock. "Sleeping sleeping."

"One what?" the Lamb asks.

"One two three tick tick timebomb," Fern says. "But not one the likes of me can deal with. I'll leave a note for Embi, if she ever comes down again." She jumps up and down on the rock as if testing its stability, her extra legs skittering in a way that seems unbalanced. She does not fall. She flows down to the riverbed, not quite in front of the Lamb but to one side, cocking her head again. "Vintage. Nice. Contingency?"

The Lamb pushes data, her face a little warm through some remembered protocol of human embarrassment. Fern accepts the data and parses it in a cheerful blink. "Oh, murder," she says. "I did hear Contingencies were dying off. A little bird told me. Where is the little bird? Hiding?"

The Lamb feels her jaw tighten. "The Contingencies are being killed," she corrects. "Someone is breaking into the Bunkers and rewriting them into quasi-organic gunk."

"Yes, yes," Fern says. "I read the file. Have you considered—"

And she pushes a gigantic blob of data that the Lamb struggles to download, much less parse. She reads the headers and shakes her head. "More technical speculation," the Lamb says. "Thank you, but no. I will pass this on to the . . . little bird. I wanted to ask you about the work you've done here."

"Here?" Fern spreads her arms and one of the beetle legs. "I'm actually not even the maintainer of this zone. Just filling in while Embi's on sabbatical."

"I mean on Earth," the Lamb says. "The healing. The regreening."

"Oh that," Fern says. "Meh. It's a disaster, you know. Total clusterfuck. Everything that can go wrong goes wrong. We've lost the balance and had to restart from scratch seventy-three thousand times. We've lost a lot of the records altogether. Leopards are no longer leopards, did you know? We lost the genes. Had to plagiarize from the other big cats. Hand-drew the spots back on myself."

"Did you really," the Lamb asks. She tries to keep her tone dry. Fern is in movement again, though not drifting far; she's back to examining the rock, testing how firmly it's lodged in the earth. At one point she even tugs at it with her beetle legs, as if she wants to pluck it out.

"No," Fern says. "That was obviously a lie. Anyway, it was 'Miya who did leopards. Only she's not speaking to me, so I can make up whatever I like."

The Lamb knows that Embi and 'Miya are the other two maintainers in the team. There are old records identifying them and the other early maintainers, but their current social network presence is entirely private. The Lamb can dimly sense the presence of a group chat log that takes up more storage space than any other human artefact in the history of the planet. She does not have the access to so much as check its timestamps, never mind read it.

"Why is she not speaking to you?" the Lamb asks.

"Oh, the torture thing," Fern allows. "I did some stuff." Then, seeing the Lamb about to question: "It was another life. A long, long time ago, long before the diaspora. Before spaceflight, even. After the pyramids. Sorry, what's your time-

line again? The format converter choked on your past life records."

"I don't have those," the Lamb says hesitantly. Something
about that feels false, though it isn't intentionally a lie. "I just
have the one life. I thought everybody did."

"Oh no," Fern says. "Yes, but that makes sense; trance
memory was invented in <untranslatable reference, likely
calendrical>, well after the era of the Contingencies. You just
don't remember that you're haunted. Be happy! It's nothing
but a source of misery and arguments . . . because *some people* can't let anything go! Ever!"

"Some things can't be let go," the Lamb says.

"Of course you take her side," Fern says. She sighs, the
wing fluttering. "Everybody always takes her side. It's easy;
she was the victim, and I was the torturer. But it wasn't *me*
me; that's what I keep saying about past lives. They're not really *us*. They're like ancestors. We inherit something, but we
don't have continuity of self, even if we can reclaim memories;
we didn't *make* those decisions. We can't be held responsible."

The Lamb feels terribly confused, but more than confused,
feels a deep wanting, a sense of loss that she can't understand.
She feels *left out*. "Can I . . . see these memories? Are they
records that can be shared?"

"No and yes," Fern says. "Trance memory is a technology
for retrieving memories of past lives from the akashic record
and integrating them, but *human* memory is, in any format,
flawed. We fictionalize ourselves in the retelling. I can't guarantee truth, but I can put on a play for you."

And she puts on a play called *The Broken Bough*. It flows
smoothly, as if she's performed it many, many times. Time
elapses, or does not lapse. Time elongates; time elopes; time
lopes like a leopard that is not a leopard. The play unfolds like
a paper flower; then it is done. The Lamb blinks.

"I like the epigraphs," she says, when it seems that the silence might become awkward. This play—it was not written *for* her, for the likes of her. She is not part of the audience, is she? She feels more like an invisible stagehand, bumping into obstacles in the dark. Or a scholar in one of the play's ancient libraries or museums, looking up the records of an unperformable performance, like the instructions for a ritual that could never be carried out, a potion that could only be theoretically brewed.

Fern does not seem offended. The Lamb studies her again, her who was once Fernão full of rage and spite with a knife in his hand, but also Fernando the scholar, stumbling over words in a dead language—or may have been those things. How much of the play is in good faith and how much self-disserving, self-erasing, self-hating? How many peaceful lives must follow a violent one, not to redeem it, exactly, but to remove the violence from relevance? Is the play more of a history or a fiction? Is Fern more or less a suspect now? The Lamb can still feel the knife sawing away in Fernão's hand. Is Fern right that she can't be held responsible for what he did? A wrong question. But what is the right question?

"Where can I find 'Miya and Embi?" she asks, though she knows this is also the wrong question.

Fern throws a couple of location references over in the backchannel; the Lamb catches them awkwardly, unable to integrate them with a map. "Thank you," she says anyway. "I can get the little bird to help me." There is something else in the data, something sharp and glinting that she can't parse. It feels dangerous, like a knife.

Fern shrugs. "The trance memory protocol," she says. "It feels wrong to deny it to any human on Earth, and I don't want to do badly by you, rare cousin. Do what you will."

*   *   *

Of course she tries it. Oyster, knife. How could she not? She does it as soon as she is back aboard the dropship, heading to the location that Fern had given for Embi. There are a few kilosecs of travel time and a hard border to negotiate, the Clave said; the Lamb asked for undisturbed rest, calculating that the Clave would be uncertain if the Lamb required this culturally or biologically. She stretches out on the metal floor of the dropship and wedges her feet (they no longer seem unreasonably huge to her) into the bench, wiggling her blue-stained toes.

The Lamb has been thinking about Embi ever since the play. Surely she is the prime suspect now; the only human on Earth possessed by a devil, bound to it by blood—was it not summoned to murder an army? Perhaps Embi has decided that the army of Contingencies violates her sacred Earth. Perhaps the Rake has unknowable reasons of its own. How can she guess what a Rake might want, a being so strange, so far out of time?

The knife slips in smoothly and pries her open—no, it's not quite like that, not quite so invasive or violent. The trance memory protocol activates more like a third eye opening in the middle of her forehead, vertical and secret, when she had not known it was there all along. A part of her body that had been closed up, unused, now open and blinking in a flood of fiery light invisible to her first eyes. The instructions are sparse, but not unhelpful; she takes deep breaths and focuses on riding the deluge of what are not yet memories. Images: an old man in a devil mask. An old woman drinking tea. A pyre in city streets. A rubber tire rolling along a dirt road by a lake. A lake of monsters. A still pond full of dread. Faces and faces. So many people; she feels nothing for them. No, perhaps curiosity. She wonders who they are. Who they were, to her.

But no great revelations present themselves; no voice speaks out of the past to tell her who she is.

It's only when the Clave wakes her with a ping that she understands that she fell asleep. That this body is even capable of sleep, of dreams. The inside of the dropship seems coated in grainy ash, pouring down its surfaces to pool around the Lamb's head, tickling her cheeks. This seems wrong, altogether wrong in a way that can no longer be blamed on the malfunctioning satellites alone.

The Clave's pings grow more urgent. The Lamb hauls herself to a sitting position, and everything hurts, as if the memory of lifetimes of pain had been recovered. She is disappointed to discover that she was awakened not because they've found Embi, but for a visa interview.

The dropship is hovering at a border policed by one of the two Earth polities bigger and more powerful than the Clave Eight. It is called the Landoffrey Hombre, and when the Lamb looks outside through the openings in the dropship's airframe, she can catch glimpses of drone gunships that look exactly like what they are: ugly missiles with smaller, parasitic missiles on them. They aren't even aerodynamic; they look tumorous, lopsided. There is an indeterminate number of them, in constant movement all around the dropship, exchanging places with each other in some kind of complex polyhedral containment formation.

"This border is more militarized than I expected," the Lamb says to the Clave, who updates the last-pointed-at timestamp on the unread datadump of political history in a gesture that combines exasperation with resignation.

Below them, the earth is not green but brown and slimy, speckled with sinkholes of various sizes: some no wider across than the Lamb's outstretched fingers, others big enough that the dropship seems like a speck. The sinkholes are deep and shadowed, their inner surfaces marked by the aftermath of some kind of weapon, the rock partially melted and re-formed. The backchannel offers no data, and the Lamb can't see a bottom to any of the sinkholes. Even the hallucinations of ash do not trouble her sight, as if they, too, are foreign to this land.

The Hombre does not offer anything as crude as conversa-tion. There is a series of forms to fill in, biometrics to provide, and proofs of residence, citizenship, and assets. The Lamb lists her Bunker as her only asset, though she has never thought of it as property, much less *her* property, but the Clave says it would be problematic to present oneself as entirely lacking in assets. The purpose of this process seems to be to reassure the Hombre that the Lamb has roots in the Clave and is not attempting to immigrate.

"There's no category for *investigator* or *consulting detective*," the Lamb says.

"Just put *tourist*," the Clave says.

The Hombre rejects her visa application. There is no explicit reason given, though there is a string of reference codes. The Clave merely sighs and backtracks the dropship, the nozzles turning forward in its stubby wings to move in reverse. The Lamb shifts her legs to face forward again. The gunships do not follow.

Neither of them speaks until they are out of range of those weapons, and even then the Clave maintains a silence that feels pointed. She supposes this is a failure of her alleged skills at international diplomacy. "Some things haven't changed," she says, and in saying so, the memories arrive not in an overwhelming flood but like a leaf drifting in without a tree in sight, carried who knows how far on the wind. The rip-ple when it lands is gentle, but it doesn't end, reverberating through her sense of self until its edges blur into shimmer.

21

Vidyujjihva

A leveret is born ready to run. A leveret is born with its eyes
open. This is what separates the young hare from the young
rabbit, the hairless kit with eyes shut tight. The black-naped
wild hare of Lanka, the ha-ha-hari-hawa, was wrought
Lepus nigricollis singhala after the sinners of that isle by one
Robert Charles Wroughton. *Lepus nigricollis* was invented
by Frédéric Cuvier, brother of the more famous Georges, the
long-tongued devil of the age of racialization, of speciation.

Cuvier and the Devil, an Apocryphal Anecdote

> It is said about Georges Cuvier that a student once attempted
> to prank him by dressing up as a devil, with horns and hooves,
> saying, "Cuvier, Cuvier, I am going to eat you!" To which
> Cuvier only woke up long enough to say, "Horns and hooves;
> you're a herbivore. You can't eat me."

Georges does not ask himself *why* the Christian devil has
hooves and horns, which is of course that they are satyrical.
The story isn't funny because of Cuvier's deductive skills;
it's funny because Cuvier is seen to commit a gross category
error—which, you might say, is the defining, distinctive trait
of a cuvier in the wild: a pot not for melting but fermenting,
breaking things down, breaking things apart in the absence of
oxygen. Like his brother, Georges invented many species, such

as the human in white, black, and yellow varietals—where did *we* fit in? We argued about this in middle school, when it seemed clear to us from the racial caricatures in the grade eight science textbook that we were not Ethiopian or Mongolian, but we were definitely not Caucasian either, and this seemed to leave us in a de-human's-land, an empty realm. I came home and asked my mother, who said oh that's not how it works, that's not how it works at all, and for a moment there seemed to be a breaking of the walls, a desundering of a single great undifferentiated ocean, until she said, we're Aryan, obviously, that's why we're at war with the Dravidians, and the walls went crashing up again for the waves to shatter on.

The Aryan invasion, the pale north and the dark south, the Yoke and the Rake, the war of Lanka, no, not *that* one, the *other* war of Lanka, or sure okay maybe whynotboth. For every Sita a Surpanakha, a.k.a. Chandranakha, long in the nail, long in the tooth, short in the nose. What is left on our faces to tap knowingly? Perhaps, like the brothers Cuvier might have done, we can tug at the skin under our eye and say, mon oeil. To all this a great disbelieving, a refusal, a neti neti that leaves us neti beri, impoverished and alone.

*   *   *

The Lamb takes a deep breath, but cannot unbreathe it; it catches in her vents, in her throat, in her chest. She claws at her chest, hears distant voices. The Clave, panicked by panic? No, a different key to a different door. The Clave has found the lookups for the reference codes given by the Hombre, the explanation for her visa rejection. "You're haunted," the Clave says. "It says you brought strange hauntings into the world when I woke you up."

The Lamb is dizzy. She puts both her hands to her head. "I woke myself up," she retorts, though the clean snap is

complicated by a wheezing and a coughing and a great many
other biological factors from which she feels increasingly de-
tached. Her memories are dizzying, like a river in furious flow.
All she can do is try not to drown.

*   *   *

Once upon a regime of poetics markedly different from hers or
yours or mine, on an island called the strange and wondrous
island, which held a city called the wondering and estranging
city, whose air was always warm but not too hot at noon, always cool but not too chilly at night, whose great stone towers
wore clouds and songs like scarves, there was a woman of the
Rake who wore her nails long and painted; she was the first
artist of the nail. Her name was Chandranakha, for the cres-
cent curve of her nails, or perhaps because she liked to paint
them with the faces of the moon.

The strange city was full of music and sculpture and painting and performance and recriminations and fallings-out and
drama and scandal, because the Rake were at that time in
the process of inventing all the arts. There were so many, so
manymany, that there was always room for more, so each of
them would create new forms and vie to become their first
masters, or for those who came a smidgen later, their first
iconoclasts. The Rake were protectors of time, and for them
art was the way to organize time: to guide and direct it; to
channel its wild fecundity into a linear flow that did not burst
its banks and spill into chaos.

Chandranakha had three brothers, the eldest of whom was
called the Ravening. His art of choice was political ambition.
They did not get along: the Ravening believed only in grand
forms, in high arts, and in truth; Chandranakha believed
in small forms, in low arts, and in beauty. Each considered

the other a hack. By the very nature of their vocations, their lives diverged more and more. The Ravening invented thrones and sat upon the first one; he was then called the Ravenous King, always looking to command greater heights. The other two bros were absorbed into the Ravenous King's project, willynilly; the elder middlebro was called Kumbakanna, ears-like-pots, and he had perfected the art of sleepwalking through life, going along to get along, the power nap behind the seat of power; the younger middlebro was called Vibhishana, because from birth he was fucking awful. They, too, began to spend less time with Chandranakha. Later, much later, like, not-in-this-book kind of later, one of them will invent the useless heroic death, and the other will invent high treason and become a god. But that's neither here nor there. Their middlebro destiny is not to help, only to be of use.

Of their whole family, Chandranakha alone felt no attraction to ambition whatsoever. She was content to work on her own art, on her own body; she would not so much as open a nail salon. Nor would she accept invitations to be interviewed on morning talk shows as a member of the royal family, as Vibhishana frequently did. She loved all the small arts, all the arts of the body; she sought out the company of tattooists and body-painters, of dancers in ten thousand different forms, of thumb-wrestlers and shadow puppeteers, of experimental jewellers and avant-garde dress designers, of kinksters and perverts and other artists of love. Around the same time that her brother ascended to a throne, Chandranakha met a smooth-talking man who had, he said, invented cunnilingus, and for this was called Vidyujjihva, the lightning-tongued, and would she like to try it? It was, she decided, pretty great.

Vidyujjihva was a mouthy man, a mobile and expressive mouth, a mouthful of trouble. In bed it was lightning and love; at the table, it was fast wit and puns (he had once made love to their inventor, he said, and she had cursedblessed him with their importunacy); in the bitter dark, it was invective, a mouth full of knives. Still, she loved him. Someone in the city had recently invented the art of marriage, and it was all the rage. Even her eldest brother had said—not to *her,* of course, they rarely spoke now, but his every utterance became law, became fashion, became news, so she was always hearing about what he thought, what he wanted, and so she, along with the rest of the city and all the Rake, learned that the Ravenous King, too, sought a marriage—the elevation of mere love, he said, to politics, to alliance, to *lineage.* His art was becoming more and more complex. Some said, though they did not say it too loudly, that his art was subsuming all other arts, hungry like its master.

On hearing about her brother's marital ambitions, Chandranakha finally found a small seed of ambition in herself: she desired to marry *first* and to live better, while her royal brother mired himself in intrigue and plot, so that he would look and look again at her life and be, she thought, consumed with envy of its beauty, its clarity, its simplicity, until he would finally have to admit that he was and had always been wrong about everything. So she married Vidyujjihva and they lived well, for a time.

But this invention, marriage, was more complex than she had understood; it was a game with many more rules than were immediately evident: rules about alliance and lineage, rules about complicity and inheritance. It stank, uncomfortably, of her brothers' world. From the onset of the wedding, which was officiated by the inventor of the art themself, the marriage had undercurrents and strange tides that Chandranakha only partly understood. For instance, they had begun with a guest list of only three names, themselves and the officiant, but then there had to be witnesses, then families, then friends. First among the special guests who could not be uninvited without insult, naturally, were the brothers of the bride, headed inevitably by the Ravenous King. The wedding forced a claustrophobic closeness between Chandranakha and her family; their past polite estrangement became harder to recapture. Vidyujjihva was to be the brother-in-law of the king, a position that came with political influence. Her brothers, in turn, demanded the right to get to know her husband, this new member of their family—the Ravenous King interpreted her marriage as a concession, of sorts, to politicking. He began to invite them regularly to his palace, and be offended if they made excuses; he would visit them at home, at first by appointment and then sometimes unannounced, and if she complained he would be offended again, saying, can't a brother visit his beloved sister and brother-in-law, can't family be a respite from politics? She would be diverted into asking why he needed respite from his own art, and they would get entangled in debate over dinner, and Vidyujjihva was always game for a good argument. He had many opinions, and could summon up more out of nowhere, even on subjects he knew nothing of. Sometimes Chandranakha would throw up her hands and leave them arguing at the table.

Vidyujjihva took to politics naturally. In hindsight he was born for it, with his smooth and smiling mouth. Chandranakha mourned when Vidyujjihva began to take part in her brothers' councils, as a diplomat, a problem-solver, a negotiator, a peacemaker, a sorcerer. He would come home and tell her about his day, and in this way she learned more about politics than she ever wanted to. The burning issue of the day was geopolitical, the great tension with the ancient superpower to the north called the Yoke. Every day, Vidyujjihva told her, the possibility of invasion seemed to heighten.

"This war is inevitable," Vidyujjihva judged. "It is the inexorable outcome of how we have been constituted and organized as peoples, as a binary in opposition. We are artists and they are priests; we both love time and its ordering, but in such different ways. It can't go on like this. Sooner or later there will be some provocation, probably a grand and intentional provocation, and there will be a war."

"What happens next?" Chandranakha asked.

"I don't know," Vidyujjihva said, and she laughed.

"Oh," she said, running a nail gently over his face; it left a thin white line across his dark cheek. His skin was getting drier, after so much time in smoky rooms. "I thought perhaps you had invented a new art of prophecy."

They seduced each other toward the bedroom, slowly, a thing they did less and less of since their marriage; lovemaking had a nostalgic air now, as if they were ironically referencing those heady early days. When Vidyujjihva tried to bury himself between her legs, she shushed him, pulled him up. She wanted to see his face near her own, to kiss his clever mouth, to suck on his lightning tongue, to feel his breath on her cheek. She wanted him to feel close. It felt urgent. She just knew something bad was coming at them, drifting down in time.

*   *   *

Later, Chandranakha thinks it must have been his mouth that got him in trouble. He must have said something unforgivable, made a joke too far, or maybe one of those secret midnight moods had come upon him in daylight and bitterness had spilled out of his mouth in the presence of her brothers. Perhaps his worries over the impending war had driven him to make some mistake in his glibness, his suasion, the sorcery of his electric tongue. She never finds out; she never knows exactly what, exactly why. Her other brothers say they don't know either, they weren't there when it happened. And the Ravenous King only says that it had to be done, he had no choice, it was necessary, it *became* necessary, to have Vidyujji-hva executed. He does not elaborate, no matter how much she pleads for answers. She does not even know how it happened: Did her brother leap across the table to throttle her husband in the council chamber? Or did he summon guards and have Vidyujjihva taken away to a noose or an axe or perhaps a high place for a forced and ritual leap? She asks the moon, who loves her, but the moon does not know.

Chandranakha maintains relative composure in front of the Ravenous King when he tells her this news. She weeps, she collapses, and she asks permission to leave and mourn, but that's all, it's a nothing; he grants this nothing easily. She does not remember when he assumed those powers, when it became necessary for the Rake to ask permission to grieve. But death, too, was still a relatively new art among them.

There are a hundred epics about the war that came next. It does not need her retelling, and anyway she was not there for most of it. She played only a small part in setting it loose, in creating the provocation that Vidyujjihva had prophesied. The story of how the Rake fell is simple, at its grieving heart, and it doesn't even involve any of the epic's major players or cosmic forces. Causality is a small art, a homely thing, an art of the body. Chandranakha leaves the city and goes into the jungle, and alone under the full moon she digs her beautiful nails into her skin and tears it away, strip by bloody strip. She flays herself, howling. She looks redly at the world and knows it complicit; that to be bereaved is to be reaved, and that the name of the reaver is her ravening brother but also this engine of pain he had made, the throne and its necessities and lineages, his foul and monstrous art. She goes north, the first witch red and skinless, to find some sheep of the Yoke to provoke, to start a war that would end the ravening, that would end the Rake entirely, the first thread of a red web to bring surcease to the agony of this world.

22

Dying and Not Dying

The Lamb opens her eyes; they are covered in a film of what could be tears, or blood. For a moment the world looks red. She sits up and rubs her eyes clear. Silt on her fingertips. Is her blood even red in this body? She can't remember the specifications. The Clave, which has been blaring noises of alert and alarm at her, falls silent. The Lamb tries several times to speak, but what she's seen is impossible to explain.

"You seemed dead," the Clave says hesitantly. "I assumed you were doing it on purpose, so I tried the other location we were given. You were sufficiently nonviable that this polity's border patrol counted you as inert and not in need of a visa interview. We've found 'Miya."

"I'm not dead," the Lamb allows. She feels a little dead. Everything still hurts, as if her entire body shut down while she processed. This body, which had felt large and oversized at first, and then maybe, briefly, just about right, now feels small and cramped. She moves a hand and marvels at its particularity. "I . . . didn't do it entirely on purpose, but I'm glad it was helpful for immigration. What is 'Miya doing?"

"Lake therapy," the Clave says.

*   *   *

The dropship lands this time, though still at a safe distance; the Lamb walks the rest of the way. There is a small lake lying in the middle of a broad grassland, in lieu of a couch. From the heart of that placid water rises something that looks at first like a silvery tower, which only gradually resolves into a pillar of water falling upward into the sky, like an upside-down waterfall. Sitting cross-legged on the grass at the lakeshore is 'Miya, who looks exactly as she did in the first act of *The Broken Bough*, with the same injuries: her face is bloodied, the wounds still fresh; her beard is patchy, as if fistfuls have been ripped away, and her hair has been torn loose from its knot, floating free and ragged around her face except where it's matted with blood. Three of her fingers are missing, and those wounds, too, are so fresh that the Lamb looks for the fingers on the ground. But there is nothing there except grass: grass that is desolate of most of the small life it ought to host, the insects, the worms, the microbes in the soil. This regreened earth is still so empty. So much of it is façade.

"Did you take this appearance because you knew I was coming from Fern?" the Lamb asks, as soon as she's close enough to speak without shouting.

"Fuck you," 'Miya says. It's mildly said, not vehement, but she is not smiling. Her lips are too swollen to smile. "It has nothing to do with you at all."

"It's a bit on the nose," the Lamb remarks. "If you're trying to convey that you're not over it."

"I am trying to explain to the spirit of this lake that we carry trauma in our bodies," 'Miya says. "Kindly do not interfere with the therapeutic process by mocking it."

"Sorry to the lake," the Lamb says. She sketches it a salute. "I didn't realize it had a spirit."

"Everything has a spirit now," 'Miya says. "Installing them is part of the regreening. But intelligence requires therapy, by definition, and a lake spirit that has been failing to balance its reengineered ecosystem for four hundred years needs more therapy than most."

"Well, I'm sorry to interrupt," the Lamb says, not sounding sorry at all. "But this is a homicide investigation. If the lake has waited thirteen gigasecs for therapy, it can give me a kilosec to talk to you."

'Miya waves at the lake, which continues to be a lake. There is no visible sign of a lake spirit. The upside-down waterfall at its centre continues to pour up into the sky; the Lamb looks up and focuses her satellites to see the water falling away into space, the stream separating into shivering globules.

"Ask your questions," 'Miya says. "This is a good presentation to be interrogated in, don't you think?" She waves the hand with the missing fingers at the Lamb.

"Is it true you don't speak to Fern anymore?" the Lamb asks. She already knows the answer to this question; she just wants to destabilize 'Miya a little. It doesn't seem to work; the maintainer shrugs. The Lamb tries again, looking for a sore spot. "Fern is of the opinion that she isn't morally culpable for the actions of her past lives."

This time she seems to have found it. 'Miya's face betrays nothing, but there is a very slight, almost imperceptible stiffening in her body. "Well of course Fern is of this bloody opinion," 'Miya says. "It's a self-serving opinion."

"What I don't understand is why you fixate on *this* incident," the Lamb says. "Surely there is much violence and trauma across your past lives. I've recently accessed mine and . . . everything hurts. If we really are to believe that we are personally culpable for all of it—"

"Is culpability to depend on convenience, then?" 'Miya seems more amused than angry. "When we access these memories, it changes us; it makes us part of a continuity, and the price of all the knowledge and experience we recover is that we also have to deal with the things we did, and the things that were done to us. I don't dwell on this *incident,* as you say, because of the violence alone; as you say, many violent things have happened to me, many violent things have been done *by* me, in many lives. I keep coming back to *this* incident because Fern and I went on to have a relationship across time—because we've been enemies and friends and lovers and colleagues—and today more than ever, now that we are two of the last three incarnate, awake humans on Earth. Sorry, four now. Our history matters. This day, the day where I looked like this, continues to define that relation *because* Fern denies its relevance. I can't let it go because she can't let it be."

"So you're making an argument less for culpability than for memory," the Lamb muses. This one is conveniently verbose, she thinks. "I see. What are your feelings about the Contingencies?"

"What about them?" 'Miya shrugs. Her swollen lips barely seem to move when she talks. "They—you—are one of thousands of gambits and stratagems and projects attempted by uncountable polities, nations, corporations, affinity groups, and individuals. Our regreening project is another such, just more organized and better funded. The old world is an overturned cup, dice rolling into the future . . . I can see that your own primary-tier specializations concern work like mine; all *this* was supposed to be your work, but you were never called on because you were superseded."

Now she attacks, the Lamb thinks. Next she will appeal to shared purpose, to sentiment.

"Your contingency never arose because we were dealing with it already. You understand?" 'Miya doesn't wait for an acknowledgement. The Lamb can feel her, reaching out and rummaging about in her lives; it feels rude and invasive. "You and we are far from the only attempts to guide the future of this planet. There are and were so many: seed banks and gene banks, satellite archives and invisible libraries, memorials and long-cycle art projects, secret immortals a dime a dozen. If we fail, if our regreening falls apart—and I am starting to think it will, the day after we all finally burn out and go join the diaspora, whether that's tomorrow or whether we put in another ten thousand years—if we leave and all this work is for nothing and all the spirits die out and the green fades again, I guarantee it will only be a matter of time before someone else takes it from the top. You might not know, being so recently awakened, that there's only us out there, our people, human and other refugees from Earth. This is *our* universe, Earth's universe, the brane defined by our consciousness, *rooted* in us and the way we think and the songs we sing. All our worlds are this world, in some sense, no matter how far we go, even the most vacuum-hardened fritillary with stellar wings; we can never let it go. We're here because we don't let things go. The regreening, the healing and preservation of the old Earth, is a dream a lot of people share. People understand that our history matters."

"How do you think the Contingencies were killed?" the Lamb asks doggedly.

"I suspect a neurosis among the caretakers," 'Miya says immediately, as if she'd already been thinking about it, unlike Fern, who seemed to find the deaths almost beneath notice. "Like the spirits of the trees and the lakes and the seas and the soil, the caretakers struggle with wear and tear, with cruft, with regrets, with intrusive thoughts, with the inner voice that shouts about failure, always failure. I suspect the caretakers do not even know that they are doing it: to some extent they must be imitating each other, mimicking the sorrows they cannot allow themselves to be aware of, much less accept or express."

"You suggest that the Clave Eight murdered two of its own Contingencies and then woke another to investigate the deaths?" the Lamb demands.

"Every caretaker is a gestalt, divided against itself," 'Miya says. "It is possible, likely even, that a dissociative caretaker could both do a thing and wish it undone."

The Lamb considers this. Perhaps, she thinks. But she doesn't want to give the maintainer the satisfaction of an open acknowledgement. Instead, she asks for a favour. "I was denied a visa when I attempted to meet with Embi. Would you be able to contact her and convey that I asked for a meeting somewhere outside the territory of the Landoffrey Hombre?"

"I'll tell Embi to meet you at your Bunker," 'Miya says. "Be patient."

*   *   *

The dropship returns the Lamb to the valley of her Bunker. Her sensorium begins to shudder and tremble as soon as she sets foot on this familiar territory, here on the only ground of this earth she's trod twice, and intensifies when the dropship leaves her behind.

"I want some time to think, without interruption, until Embi gets here," she says to the Clave's birds. The birds seem less real than the ash; so much so that she cannot see them clearly, cannot identify them through that obscuring grey veil, cannot assign them a species; they are merely sigils of life, avian and undifferentiated. The Lamb doesn't share 'Miya's suspicions of the Clave; she knows this would prove both impolitic and unstrategic if 'Miya turns out to be correct. The birds squawk and leave her. Perhaps they were only birds.

The ash has grown more subtle. Instead of strobing, it insinuates itself, rising up from the soil around her feet if she looks down, as if the earth were vomiting up generations of ash. She kneels to sift it in her hands. It feels real, gritty. When she cups a handful and runs a thumb across it, larger fragments roll and reveal themselves. Hematite nodules. No, bone. She hesitates at the conflicting readings, then turns her hand, watching the ash drift in the wind. It's so real she has to rub her palms together to clean them.

She climbs back uphill to the Bunker, ash streaming downhill and dividing around her ankles. She doesn't want to enter it again. She looks at the dark open door and feels only revulsion. She could have died in there, been reconstituted into sludge without ever waking up. Ash streams out of the door as if gravity lay sideways, as if dripping from the lip of a pit. It falls sideways for an arm's length before it begins to curve downward to feed into the ashfall she's been wading through. It looks like a rendering failure, she thinks. Even her hallucinations aren't working properly. Its ugliness makes her gut feel hollowed out, like the memory of hunger. She gives the door a wide berth, circling around to the side of the Bunker and climbing up to the roof instead.

Her Bunker is simple on the outside: a large, irregular cube of concrete partially embedded in the hillside, reinforced and expanded over the ages in materials that she has no reference for. The roof is flat except for some extrusions that were once satellite dishes and are now semiglobular nubs of some kind of ceramic. She sits on one, feet splayed for balance, and waits for Embi.

The Lamb has a lot to think about. She waits a kilosec, then ten kilosecs, then a hundred. She doesn't grow hungry or thirsty, she doesn't need to piss or shit. The sun and the moon chase each other overhead. Dew forms on her lips and eyelashes in the mornings, then evaporates later in the day unless she licks it off first. She barely moves. Her body hurts for other reasons, but not from stiffness or muscle pain. In that sense it is more like a machine that she pilots than an animal that she is. A couple of megasecs go by. Very little happens. It rains once. A big event. She enjoys the water sluicing along the corrugations of her surfaces, until her sensorium flickers and she sees it as ash falling from the sky. Then she does move, to brush it from her face. She tastes it: analysis claims it is not ash, but the dessicated fragments of dead grey goo. Tiny hungry machines that once ate the rind off the earth, everything that was and wasn't nailed down: every animal, every building, every forest, every blade of grass, every microbe. Each mountain gnawed down, all the topsoil chewed up, at least half the subsoil lost, in some places leaving teethmarks on the bedrock. Did that happen at some point in the history whose record she still hasn't read, or is it only a nightmare of the caretakers? No, this dead goo is just water. She slaps herself lightly until her sensorium reverts. The rainwater is cold; it washes away the ashes.

Not a single bird, natural or unnatural, approaches during her penance. The Clave doesn't bother her. They must think she's thinking, analysing—in truth she is only waiting. She's not even thinking about the case. She's preoccupied with her recovering memories, their clarity, their expanse. Some memories she can remember from multiple perspectives; Lambaji-hva and Vidyucchika sitting across from each other in a train car, at a kitchen table. Leveret and Annelid sitting across from each other in a jungle clearing. Others are stray memories that she can't connect to anything else: Who is this old man in a devil mask? Whose memories are these? Is this another wrong question?

Then Embi is there, on the roof with her, and the Lamb is not sure if she missed her approach for being so deep in memory, or whether Embi simply appeared next to her all of a sudden. The Lamb is not sure Embi is really there. There is no body, no person, nothing to be seen in the real. There is only a faint sense of presence, a thickness of dataflow at the low levels of representation. There is only a ghost. Until Embi speaks, the Lamb bides her time, just in case it is another hallucination.

—Any progress, Embi asks. The absence of her voice sounds just like it did in the play. The ghost seems less faint once she's spoken. There is a sense of swirling movement in the air, or perhaps only in the data, all around the Lamb, extending far out into the valley.

"I'm pretty sure 'Miya did it," the Lamb says, startling herself. She hadn't realized that she thought this. Her secondary-tier specializations have been processing this whole time, growing in her, metastasizing, eating up her useless green and healing parts. "It's not about the Contingencies or even about Fern; it's about you." The Lamb gropes inside herself for revelation even as she speaks it. "She loves you—no, it's more than that. You've all been lovers at various points in time. It's not just that. 'Miya wants to *be* your project, your obsession, your object. But she's never been, has she?"

Embi conveys a shrug.—I don't understand the difference between that and being lovers. Are you saying I don't love intensely enough? I've spent entire lifetimes focused on her.

"To 'Miya, lives as discrete units or selves are a lesser thing," the Lamb says. "She thinks of herself as a continuity, a superself, a thread through time."

—We all think that way, Embi says.—Sometimes.

The Lamb looks sideways at Embi, or at where the voice seems to be coming from. Her presence is like an itch, a heat that suggests a direction, sometimes a dangerous proximity, as if Embi was pacing or stalking closer, but there is no shimmer in the air, no refraction of the light. "We?" the Lamb says, remembering the end of the play. "Your new compact?"

—I am also, Embi says.

"The Rake is a part of you now?"

—Or I am one of their faces in time. Self is porous.

"Ah, marriage," the Lamb says. "I've been remembering some things from before Rakesfall, back when they invented that sort of thing." Suddenly she feels as old as Embi, older even, her barely grasped history stretching out, dizzying, like an abrupt cliff's edge.

—Be careful of integrating memories from different regimes of poetics, Embi says.—Translations are sometimes strange. Explain your theory. If it's 'Miya killing the sleeping Contingencies, *why*?

"She resents the Earth as the object of your attentions, I imagine," the Lamb says. "No, I'll be more specific than that. She resents the regreening project. It was your initiative, part of your greater project of reclamation from when you broke the compact more than four hundred gigasecs ago. You had to learn how to be *like* the Rake, in time; to become a guardian, a protector, with a life bigger than individual, forgetful mayfly lives. In doing so, you brought your companions with you—Fern, 'Miya, others who worked on the regreening. You made yourselves more than human. But for you, Embi, love is a transient interpersonal relation, a small art of the body, of the particular, transient, individual life. You have no time for it in the greater life, the grand project, the life of lives. There, the only thing you care about is the work, your obsession, and the only connections that matter to you are these grand alliances across time . . . even this, I think, was almost a stable, if dysfunctional relationship, until you finally spoke to the Rake and made your new compact. 'Miya must have expected that this would be the culmination of a long arc of history, that your project would be *complete* now, that you would be free to finally look up and see who'd been waiting this whole time, so patiently. But that's not what happened. Instead, you and the Rake became entangled, and you only became even more remote, even more inaccessible."

—That's not true, Embi sighs. It sounds like more than one voice when she speaks, sometimes. The Lamb can almost see her hand on her face.—It is true, perhaps, but hold your tongue—

"She loves you too much to take it out on you," the Lamb continues remorselessly. "She enjoys holding victimhood over Fern's head too much to direct her resentment that way and give up the moral high ground. So she took it out on the only other humans left on the planet who had committed to a project like yours: the Contingencies. To her, they . . . *we* are like herself. Dedicated, uselessly waiting, never to be called upon. Left behind. She may also be sabotaging her own work. One thing 'Miya and Fern have in common: you made followers out of them. You made them carriers of your guilt to ease your own burden, and they could not bear it. The reason they can never resolve their ancient conflict is because you cast them as anvil and hammer."

—Stop, Embi says.—Stop saying these things.

The Lamb feels a hand over her mouth, except there is no hand. Perhaps it exists only in some other realm of representation that she can't access. A symbolic hand, but she feels its weight. She tries to shrug it off, but it intensifies; she feels another hand gripping her by the antlers; other hands on her shoulders; other, other hands at her wrists and ankles. She is shoved to her knees, then pushed flat on the Bunker's roof, her face turned to a side, a symbolic knee in the small of her back. She tries to speak, but cannot; the sensation of a hand, now covering her whole face, is so strong, even though she can see no hand. She can see, but it's as if she can't. She senses the obstruction. She reminds herself that she breathes from the vents in her neck, not with her face, but atavistic panic reigns. She struggles, but the hands that do not exist are far stronger than her posthuman body. She tries to send out a distress call to the Clave, help me, help me, little bird, but the caretaker does not answer.

—Who are you to lecture us on integrity, Embi says.—Who are you to talk to us about love? And she peels the Lamb apart. She can feel the moment when the threads snap, when the tendons break, when the psychic corpuses that braid together her selves and memories give way.—Look at you, Embi says. —You're a tangled mess of yourself. You are a haunting; you've infected this whole world with your nightmares of ash. What gives you the right to call our work into question? Didn't I already put you down once? What made you think you're good enough for my sister?

Embi peels Vidyucchika out of the Lamb gently, like a muslin gown pulled through a silver ring, balls her up very small in the palm of one invisible hand, and throws her out into deep space. She turns back to the Lamb and rips out muscle and bone, organs of meat and ceramic and metal, tossing each handful off the roof where they splat on dry earth, or bounce and roll down the slope to the valley below. She snaps the antlers off and tugs the ears till they are long and dangling. She holds up the pithed lambskin and shakes it out, and she nails it to the akashic record as a warning.

23

Electric Head in the Golden City

Somadeva's eleventh-century epic Kathasaritsagara, the ocean fed by rivers of story, is so called because it is fulfilled by many interflowing stories, some of which then run deep within the ocean itself, cold currents far beneath the surface. The fifth book of the Kathasaritsagara concerns itself with the tale of the vidyadharas, the science gods, the celestial bearers of wisdom—as if wisdom were a cup of wine, or poison. The object of the story is to divulge the secret of how a mortal human may become a science god at the end of time. The object of the story is to divulge the secret of how to live and learn. The secret goes a little bit like this:

Once upon a time, a mortal is born who will become, in the fullness of time, a science god at the end of time. One of their number moves backward in time, arriving to protect the child while they are still mortal. The parents, who are not subtle, ask this protector, so how does one achieve the rank of science god, anyway? And the protector says, okay, sure, I can tell you that story, that's not a paradox at all. And he tells them this:

Once upon a time (the protector says), there was a father and a daughter. The father wanted to marry off the daughter, but the daughter, like, totally did not want this. So she said, whomsoever wants to marry me must have seen the Golden City and be able to tell of it. The father takes out an advertisement in the newspapers to this effect, and soon this asshole shows up, right? The asshole says, and he's obviously lying, that he's seen the Golden City. The daughter asks him some questions and quickly finds him out; the asshole tries to bluff, but the daughter tells him to fuck off. The asshole is very embarrassed, so he sets out to find the Golden City for real so he can show her up. It's only at this point that he asks himself and others: What even *is* the Golden City? He travels far and wide, meets ancient sages and wise hermits, travels with pirates, is swallowed by a giant fish, rescued by a fisher-king, and so on, until finally he finds an old man who says, yes, I know the Golden City; I was born there. I remember it, though I can't tell you the way anymore. And the old man tells the asshole a story.

Once upon a time (the old man says), there was a family of two parents and two young sons, and in their land, probably because of Winston Churchill the long-tongued devil of hunger, there was a great famine. So the family left their country, walking far, looking for some better place to live. On their journey they suffered greatly. One night, sleeping rough, the nerdy younger son woke his father to say, Father, I am Ill with Hunger, I am Sick with Ague, I am so Cold; my eyes are blurred with Fever but I see a Fire across the way, can you take me There so I may Warm myself? And the father says, Son, that is a Funeral Pyre, which is totally Gross and Unhygienic, but okay, sure, for you I Will do it. And he took the younger son to that dark place, carefully threading their way among the cemetery devils and the lycanthropes digging up the bones, and helped him stand in front of the fire in which a body was burning. The son, in his delirium, struck out at the skull in the fire with his walking stick and clove it in two; a fragment of brain flung up into his mouth. Tasting it, strange memories unfolded within him, and he became a great devil called Skull-cleaver, and his father never saw him again.

The weeping parents continued on their journey with their elder son, and eventually settled in a wealthy city where nobody went hungry if they could perform. The elder son grew up a jock, trying out many sports and entertainments before he finally became famous as a professional wrestler, eventually defeating all challengers to become the undisputed champion of that city, and a favourite of the king.

One day, the king on his throne hears faraway weeping, and he knows it's from the haunted cemetery outside his city, where a seditionist poet impaled for high treason cries, undying or undead, for water. All his soldiers pee themselves a little, so the king calls up his favourite wrestler, biggest face in the city, beloved far and wide as the best good guy who isn't afraid of anything, and the king says, my Beloved Bro, will you Please take this Cup of Water out unto the Dread Cemetery and give it to that Loud Fucker, and Tell him to (a) Pipe down and (b) give Thanks to the generosity of his King? And the wrestler says, Sure Thing, my King. He is also frightened, but he goes anyway, and he tells himself, real courage isn't found in not being afraid but in doing things when you are, which just goes to show that after years of celebrity he is so deep in character that his internal narrative takes the voice of an Educational Programme for the small children who are his biggest fans and buy all his T-shirts.

The cemetery is every bit as awful as he expected. The night is dark, the grounds clouded with fog, and the fires are too bright, so every time his eyes adjust to the murk he comes upon a pyre and is dazzled again. Vampires and devils are about, black-backed jackals, too, and over in the back is Ferdinand the Duke of Calabria, digging up a leg bone. The wrestler ignores all this. He shouts Yo, Who Wanted Water; and a weak voice says, Me; so he follows that tremulous sound through the fog until he comes to a cluster of tall stakes, upon which is impaled a thin man, dying. Kneeling at the foot of the stakes, weeping together with the man at their point, is the most beautiful woman the wrestler has ever seen. Her every limb is adorned with ornaments finer than any in the palace of his king.

Oh Shit, the wrestler says, embarrassed and unsure how to act. Ma'am, Whomst art Thou? And the woman says, Can you Not see that I am the Grieving Wife? I Weep because I too Brought him Water—and she raises a cup of her own, the water slopping over the brim from the movement—but I cannot Reach his Mouth, for the Stakes are too High. The wrestler, cheered by a problem with an easy solution, quickly offers his broad shoulders to stand on so that she can bring both cups to her husband's mouth, which offer she accepts gratefully. The wrestler is still congratulating himself on his perspicacity, holding tightly to her bejewelled ankles on each of his shoulders and politely not looking up, when he feels a drop of something on his cheek. At first he is like, well obviously this is Water, Spilled from the Cup, but then it drips down to his lips and he tastes salt, so he looks up, and the woman is cutting strips of flesh from the man's face and eating them; the dripdrops are blood. He yells in fright and alarm and rage, and she cackles in laughter and raises both her feet into the air—he catches, snatches, fumbles—and she is gone, up and away into the night, taking the body of the staked man with her, and all the wrestler has to show for the night is blood on his face and a single golden anklet in his hand.

The wrestler goes back to the king and tells him this whole awful story, expecting to be yelled at for being tricked by a terrible demon, but the king and queen are full of praise. Wow, they say, you really are a Hero, you are so Brave and you Even managed to Take a Trophy, we should Marry you to our Most Beautiful Princess Daughter. It's such a pity there's just One Anklet though, it's so Beautiful and the work is so Fine and so Intricate and so Otherworldly that our damnfool

Artisans cannot Imitate it, and wouldn't it be So Nice if our daughter the Princess had a Pair of anklets as a betrothal gift? And the wrestler, completely smitten by all this royal attention and opportunity, was like, For Sure, My Lieges.

So he goes back to the cemetery on another dark night when it is choked with charnel smoke from the funeral pyres, and this time he's thought and thought and come up with a cunning plan. What he does when he gets to that terrible place is he cuts down a body hanging from a noose, a journalist whose exposés the king had recently disliked. The wrestler hefts the whole body faceup across his shoulders, gripping it at the throat and the thigh. This move is called the torture rack, though of course this journalist is long dead. Carrying the body, he walks through the cemetery shouting, Human Flesh for Sale! Who will Buy, who will Buy? And of course he hears the answering cry of that devil woman, who says, Over Here and How Much? She's sitting under a tree this night, shadowed and beautiful, with black curly hair and red lips, dressed in robes much too thin and much too rich to be so bloody, garlanded in skulls and gold, her eyes like the jewels at her neck and wrists and only one ankle. The wrestler slams the body to the ground, resists the urge to pin it, and says, This Human Body for your Other Anklet. And the devil rolls her eyes and says, Listen, I Don't Actually Need Raw Human Flesh; this is a Gambit of Entrapment only. And the devil tells him a story.

There is a snowbound city in the mountains (the devil says), called the City of Three Belles. In it lived a heroic prince of the Rake called Lambajihva. I am his wife, Vidyucchika by name, and I can change my form at will.

(You look the Same to me as you did the other Night, the wrestler interrupts, but the devil shushes. Actually, I Am Totally Different Looking At This Time, she says, Is it My Fault You Have No Appreciation for the Subtle Art of the Contour?)

My husband was slain (the devil continues): he died like a leveret, with no resistance, at the hands of a cruel new devil king called the Skull-cleaver. That king then became filled with remorse, and granted me overlordship of that city, where I have conceived and birthed and raised a daughter all on my ownself. We are wealthy and powerful and magical, but my daughter needs a husband. So I embarked on this strategy to bring you, the biggest hero and brightest face in this land, to my daughter as suitor. We devils are not welcome in your city or in the palace of your king, so I created a story that called for a hero—I took the voice of a dead man that would prick the king's conscience, and I called for water. I knew you would fight or flee when you realized what I was, out of prejudice, you understand, lamentably common among the human populace. So I left you my anklet to intrigue you and your royals, to lure you back of your own volition, so that we would have a chance to speak truthfully like this, veils lifted and stakes clear. In truth, I have no desire for raw human flesh. I am not some messy eater, some charnel ghoul; I employ the finest chefs and eat only the organic, cruelty-free human flesh of lifelong vegetarians. Come with me to Three Belles and you can eat at the finest table and meet my most charming daughter. I will give you this second anklet to please your king and queen, if you only agree to visit, with no commitments or promises made, for a thirty-day free trial.

And the wrestler says, Can Do, My Lady.

So the devil takes the wrestler to her magical city through dark paths that seem both short and very long, and there he meets the devil's daughter. In time, having long since overstayed his free trial and become committed, the wrestler asks his mother-in-law for permission to marry. Sure thing, my son, she says, her voice echoed by her daughter-self, who often repeats the things her mother says, even when not entirely appropriate. But we must visit the king, the devil says, for the throne must legitimize this marriage.

So the three of them visit the great palace of the reformed demon king Skull-cleaver, who is, if you recall, the wrestler's very own brother lost in childhood, now ascended to devilry and a throne, and in whom awaits a seed of revelation and self-knowledge that is finally awakened by the sight of his long-lost brother. The brothers embrace, and the demon king calls for a great feast, at which the brothers tell their respective stories, and other stories too are told. Vidyucchika taps her wine goblet midway through this night of celebration and says, have I ever told the story of how I visited the Golden City?

Once I possessed a mortal (Vidyucchika says), and all was well, or well enough; we had our ups and downs, our pains of growing together and apart. But then came an age of false healing, when we unwittingly angered a god of that place and time, who was herself possessed by an old and hungry king and newly prone to rages. The moral of this story is, watch what you eat: it may have ambitions that swallow yours. The possessed god flayed me open, separated rider and ridden; she threw my pelt upon history's midden. She flung me into the outer dark, the great empty spaces between the heavens, and I had no time to fight, no time to beg, no time to act. It seemed like the end of me, and for a long, long time it was, for I was travelling at the speed of light in deep space as nothing but information. Time stood still for me, like long trains of thoughts that had slowed and halted on their tracks in journeys that never seemed to end. But after enough time and distance I completed a small thought, and that was to remember that I was owed some time. I remembered something Grandmother Giri said to me long, long ago, and I went into the akashic record and asked my father for his ghost days.

He was easy to find: I found the very day, the very moment Grandmother Giri pointed at him across the garden, weeding his vegetable patch, and said *we expected your father to die young.* I approached so that Father's body would obscure me from myself, though Grandmother Giri gave me a sharp look from across the way. Father stood up as I neared, and smiled at me. He was sweaty from his work, and so mortal, so ordinary.

"You look well," he said to me, and of course he was lying to my face, because I looked terrible. I was harrowed and emaciated, my hair lank, my skin flayed off, my surfaces frozen from deep space.

—Hi, I said, quite inanely.

"I suppose you want the time," Father said. "I heard what your grandmother just said back there."

—You have a moon's-worth of ghost days, I said.—Please give them to me, I am out of time.

"Of course," Father says. "But I have to warn you that they've depreciated severely in value over time. Time inflates, you know, and you've lived a lot more of it than I ever will. It might just be an hour or two." And he took a handful of time out of his heart, like golden pearls, and held it out to me. "Once these were egg-sized," Father said. "Here, for your egg-citing life."

I groaned, but held out my hand: when he dropped them into my red palm they were already fading away. I closed my hand on the last speck, half a grain of golden sand.

—Thank you, I said. We didn't say embarrassing things to each other in my family, so that was all I said. But I meant it, so very much.

※　　※　　※

Half a second of ghost time away from being lost forever in the dark: it is enough. It is a universe; it is a whole life. Vidyucchika uses that half a second to bend her trajectory, to adjust the crucial angle, to tweak the moment when she was thrown so that she does not float out into deep space forever. To travel in space is to travel in time; she has known that for a long time, the secret of the light years and the heavy years. She aims herself at the distant lights of the human diaspora, and she is flung, again for the first time, and she floats and floats and floats into the galaxy at the pace of light's snail, until one day she is caught, as if in a net, a surprise! She is allowed to precipitate, to condense, to boil and bubble into being again. Her rescuers ask her what she wants to be, and she finds herself incarnate, incarnadine, skinless and alive. The first thing she does is choke, because she has not breathed in so long, and yet that long silent wait seems so short, as if it were just the other day, maybe even just a moment since she was torn out of her skin and thrown away, and she wants to howl for her lost pelt, the lost lamb, the rudder of their little boat on time's surging river. She opens her eyes but cannot understand what she sees; she cannot understand the Golden City, she cannot understand her sense of space or time; she feels herself expanding to fill the available universe. In her hand is a flaying-knife; in her other hand is a skull-cup holding wisdom or poison; she drinks it and tries not to spill. She opens the other eye and beholds the searing golden light of worlds rotating, and she cries out—no, too much, too soon, this is the future and it hurts, I'm not ready! I need to go back into the past. I left half of me behind, she cries.

PART VII

HERON OF EARTH

24

Kingdom of the Birds

They never gave her a name; when she needs one, she names and renames herself after the birds she sees from the watchtower, the birds she sees in the forest, whichever most recently caught her eye or arrow. When the seabirds are flying, when she's riding the moment like air, she signs the telegraph as Petrel or Shearwater or Cormorant; otherwise she might be Pelican or Parrot or Crow or Pochard, or any of a thousand others. When she takes on a name, she feels something of the bird settle over her like a cloak, something of its shape or nature. When she's Darter, she feels sharp and sinuous. She likes to be Spoonbill or Ibis, wise and at peace. She tries not to be Bittern or Egret, or worst of all, Heron, the black-crowned night Heron, red-eyed and still and poised for sudden violence.

But the name doesn't matter. She is the last human ambassador to the kingdom of the birds: the dinosaurs have claimed the empty Earth again, and they don't care what she calls herself. There is only one of her, by any name.

Sometimes when being the only one becomes too loud, when it echoes and reverberates until it becomes hard to think about anything else, Egret wishes she had made graves to visit. She didn't give her teammates/siblings/otherselves proper funerals; she has very confused memories about what a funeral should be. She built clumsy pyres and tried to say ghost prayers in dead languages, but she couldn't remember most of the words and she didn't dare look it up in the ubik because then the Sentimentals would want to know what she was doing. Or perhaps they already knew and were waiting to see how it would play out. It's exhausting to try to outthink godlike posthumans—she's come around to the idea that the only rational response is to annoy them as much as possible. When the absence becomes deafening, Petrel rides the moment out, holding herself stiff and still.

The kingdom of the birds is green and full of noise. The kingdom of the birds is blue and white, rain made clean by generations of bots, now softly decaying on seabeds, crunching like sand on beaches.

(Ibis is puzzled by the tracks in the mud at the forest border south of the watchtower. She can't place the species.)

The fluidity of her naming doesn't seem to make any difference to the Sentimentals upstation. The funding ran out years ago. There was still black in Bittern's pelt when the funding ran out. The funding ran out like oil, and her pelt is grey now. The Sentimentals are no longer tracking her key performance indicators. It's all gone pro bono. It's all gone extraordinary circumstances. It's all gone compassionate retirement. They are making the best of it. They probably think the different signatures are from the other members of Shearwater's team. They probably think the rest of the team is still alive. Anyway, Spoonbill sometimes attaches environment reports that are probably still useful to them. From the perspective of the Working Group on the Preservation of the Ancestral Earth for Sentimental Reasons, the project was very successful, marred only a little by the team's insistence on staying behind at the end. It's possible the Sentimentals didn't have an exit strategy. They're not very good at exit strategy. Their entire ethos is tilting at windmills.

(The mud is hardened, so the tracks are probably about a week old. The monsoon's been and gone.)

Petrel's team travelled to Earth, in one sense; in another, they were made here. The Sentimentals folded spacetime to place a seed in Earth's soil from an unimaginable distance; if there had been anyone to see it, they would have seen it simply appear, displacing exactly enough gravel and air that it did not register as an arrival, but simply as a break in continuity. The seed flowered into a swarm of bots, fewer and more specialized than the ones that had already worked for so long on the regreening of Earth. Cormorant and her team bubbled naked out of the soil, their phenotypes slightly modified from the baseline healthy adult Australopithecine, their minds and selfhoods forked and stripped down from a volunteer posthuman of the Working Group, copies made clean and ready for a new world and new lives—all confusing godlike memories or life experiences redacted, especially those that might break the simple physics that their neoprimitivist meat brains could process. They were once a single being, but now individuals. They were adults, but also newborn. They had access to large volumes of contextual and historical information from the ubik, but the specific memories of their former life were hazy to the point of anonymity, except for that last voluntarist impulse that guided their progenitor to fork their mind in the first place, and the traitor sense—an assumption so deep-seated that it was difficult to examine, much less dislodge—that this was normal. It was, the Sentimentals argued, all essential to the Aesthetic, their overriding principle that guided the regreening of the Earth: they had no interest in re-creating any part of the disastrous late holocene.

Somewhere in those fogged-over memories of her godlike past self are the death rituals Spoonbill can no longer quite remember. She worries at this question, holding it in her mouth, unable to spit or swallow. Long, long ago, before she was herself but also before she was posthuman—when she was human the first time, in a childhood she can no longer recall but whose fossil contours she can trace in the very shape of her mind, in the scars and the dreams and in the long-dead languages that spill from her mouth when she wakes from nightmares of her dead, trapped and unable to go on—back then she knew how to help the dead. First, the fire; then the ashes into running water; then the prayers of passing on, which she can't yet reconstruct, to be repeated in their cycles and epicycles through the years.

(The footprint is neither passerine nor non-passerine. It is unwebbed, and surprisingly large.)

Between the intermittent brownouts of the relay orbiter and the residual time dilation out of the Oort portal, the Sentimentals get Petrel's telegraphic updates in batches, and when they have complaints about her formatting, their responses show up erratically, years late. Last week Darter finally got a memo from the Sentimentals asking her to cut it out with the ALL CAPS and saying STOP after every sentence. She'd been doing it for at least five years by that point.

"It was funny the first time," the memo said. "But seriously, cut it out. You have more than enough bandwidth for video, feel free to use it."

CANT VIDEO STOP ALL CAMS NONFUNC STOP WILL TRY 2 B MORE PROLIX STOP

The Sentimentals don't have much leverage to make Cormorant do anything now that the project has ended and/or gone off the rails. The funding's run out, and the project is no longer being supplied through spacetime folding: no more fresh raw material or new code arriving in the blink of an eye. She long ago refused the offer of being taken away to join a civilization that she's never known. There's nothing else they can offer her, the last human on the regreened Earth. She doesn't know why she keeps messaging them. Would they bother to send someone to check if she stopped sending updates? Her fate would probably be a footnote for the next expedition to follow up on, whenever that happens. The regreening of Earth was a triumph back in the day, but it's old news now, and the rest of the galaxy is so fascinating, and the diaspora's politics so complicated. The Working Group is not a great power in the galaxy; as far as Petrel understands it, they are more like a roundtable of artists that meets irregularly, whenever they can get organized enough. The Aesthetic, as a vision statement, betrays the telltale signs of design by committee. The Earth must, they say, be restored to a pristine state, romantically prehuman—at the same time, it must support animal and plant life that dates to late human-contemporary epochs: not even mammoths or saber-toothed tigers, much less plesiosaurs or trilobites. It's not an authentic prehuman Earth that the Sentimentals want, Ibis figures: they want a what-if Earth, a human Earth without humans. Message terraforming at its most didactic.

Sometimes Spoonbill thinks she talks to the Sentimentals only because they keep answering. A disembodied voice; some data; a ghost. When they send video, she blinks into their perspective and it's horribly disorienting—space-hardened bodies, slow flights across the stars on moon-sized wings, time-sense synced to the rotation of the galaxy rather than to the ancestral primate body clock. She has to pull herself out of the video and her gut churns up some of last night's pelican.

(She confronts the possibility that the tracks may be human. It's strange to be a member of a collective again, rather than herself, sui generis.)

Pochard has done well in her chosen exile. One of her late teammates programmed the bots to make him a bow and smart flechettes, put a few satellites into orbit to make sure he would hit whatever game he aimed at; the watchtower has solar panels; she grows a few scraggly vegetables in the patch around the tower, and she competes with the birds and the bats for wild fruit in the forest beyond. Her gutbots can clean any water she drinks. And of course, she is the apex predator for thousands of kilometres—they sited the watchtower here for this very reason. There are no large animals in the region. The bears and leopards aren't projected to spread this far south for at least another hundred years. She could live for a very long time, if she's careful. She has learned caution.

(She hasn't seen another human footprint in about two decades. If that's what the tracks are. These marks *could* have been made by a heavy boot whose sole had a corrugated, birdlike pattern. Or perhaps, Parrot suspects, she has learned to see things as birdlike even when they are not. She has learned too much caution. She is trapped, and there's nobody to say prayers for her.

She wonders if the tracks could belong to the ghosts of her dead team. She wonders if they're hungry. She is doing her best to reconstruct the prayer for the dead, one dead word at a time.)

When Crow shoots birds for meat, she prefers to do it in the forest; she's afraid the flocks will learn to avoid the watchtower if she starts to kill them there. She doesn't like eating crow, though. They are suspicious birds that hold grudges. Once she was dive-bombed by crows that must have remembered how she had killed their own before. She avoids that area now. Fortunately, the new footprints are on the south side, far away from angry crows.

She doesn't bear the crows any ill will; she understands bearing grudges. Egret had to learn how to settle them the hard way in this life. Sometimes in her nightmares her ghosts are accusatory. They wanted to go back home, they say. They wanted to be born again, their reward for a job well done; to join once more into the singular mind and body of god. They didn't want to stay here any more than they wanted to stay separate, to stay individuals. But I did, Crow shouts at them, or tries—the words won't come, in dreams, and all she can manage is a hoarse caw.

(If it's a living human, she reasons, there must be new visitors to Earth. Perhaps some other group of posthumans funded an expedition to study the regreened biosphere—the Sentimentals say the galaxy is full of factions. Perhaps returnistas who want to return to a simpler time and homestead the homeworld. Or perhaps there's been somebody else like her on Earth all along, staying out of sight, biding their time. A survivor of the cull. What bird could she name them for? After the others were gone, she took all the names for herself.)

Invisible in her hide with her face right up against the bow, she can hear its coiled, groaning tension, the subliminal hum of the smart flechettes getting their global positioning updates. Heron waits for contact.

PART VIII

THE
MALLEABLE EARTH

25

The Ghost Behind the Green

Little hunting darts pierce me through and through—I am slain, again. I never see it coming.

I fear that She will keep firing, that the swarm of arrows like locusts will eat me up until there is nothing but a stain to mark where I fell back to the soil of grandmotherboard earth, but She stops once I fall, and the swarm returns to Her, clickety click, to reload and rest.

It hurts to be. I lie where I fell, writhing slowly. The light seems unnaturally bright, as if my pupils have been forced open by shock.

She approaches cautiously, weapon steady. Her pelt is greying, Her eyes large and soft, Her mouth tight. She satisfies Herself that I am not an immediate threat: physically, She confirms that my tendons are ripped and bones broken; psychically, She scans my ports and sockets, tests the strength of my apotropaics, builds virtualizations around me to isolate me from grandmotherboard earth.

"Well," She says finally. Her voice is a rasp. She squats next to my head, tapping me in the temple with the bow's long muzzle. I expect to feel metal warmed from firing, but it is a different warmth, like wood in the sun.

—Another haunted jungle, I say. Fluids pour from my wounds and my mouth, making speech difficult in the haunted world; I speak instead at the lowest level of representation.

I'm not sure She is listening, if She's even present in that realm. She doesn't seem to have heard me; perhaps She's abandoned representation altogether in Her loneliness.

She blinks slowly. Her eyes are sunken and Her brows heavy, hair all over Her body, Her philtrum high and broad; O, Her phenotype looks like a bonobo to me, sacred and profane. My incarnate body is late holocene human, hairless, disease-riddled, the only sufficiently detailed public domain reference that my god could find; I am clothed as I was printed, a fragile body in an environment suit and heavy boots, all now with many holes. I'm too young. This is too hard. It's difficult to keep my eyes open. The noises coming out of me are involuntary gasps of pain. The movements of my body, also involuntary, are slowing. Weakening.

"Do I know you?" She taps me in the head again. I manage to meet Her eyes in the real, in the haunted world.

—Can you hear me? I scroll through several higher levels of representation, where self and world are purely symbolic and communication is the exchange of folded glyphs dipped in thick, honeyed data. I came prepared for this meeting, with a suite of handshake protocols to draw on. None of them draw a response. She's cut me off from higher access to grandmotherboard earth; She has root on this planet, even if She's barely used it in years. This world responds to her, shapes itself to her dreams. This world is her oyster: I am a foreign body, a speck of grit, an irritation, an invasion.

I return to the public library in desperation to teach myself the language She's speaking; it takes several long seconds, full of pain. She speaks a conlang borrowing heavily from popular classical languages including Indic, Anglic, and Sinic, but many others, too. She and her pantheon invented it when they were assigned here, as the language they would speak on the regreened earth, as something that would seem like a nod to authenticity to the observing Sentimentals, but to themselves was an elaborate joke. It was their first rebellion against their creators. This is not a documented fact: it is my observation, my assessment. I know her, and it is obvious to me.

"They said," I say, and speaking with the vocal apparatus makes me cough up fluids red and blue; they do not mix but swirl into intricate patterns that contain each other, and I'm not sure if this is because of my injuries or because I've never spoken out loud before. Maybe my innards were designed wrong. Unlike the Sentimentals, my patron is not good at modifying archaic somatics; he's bad at incarnation, it being forbidden to his kind. Perhaps it is just the flesh of my body rejecting the lies that come out of my mouth. "They said to tell You—"

Her eyes widen when I speak out loud in Her language, and then narrow. "What?"

"They love what You've done with the old place."

*   *   *

It's a bad start. She's suspicious, and I'm lying, but we are the only people on Earth. I tell her the Sentimentals sent me just like they did her, to keep her company, to check on her, to help. None of those things are true. She obviously doesn't believe me, but there is no easy way to prove it either way.

She deigns to heal me, though She also takes the opportunity to do an invasive reprint of my body, making sure it has no hidden weapons or dangerous secrets. She gives me a body like Hers, fitting the Aesthetic, with a thick dark pelt where Hers is greying and thin. I suppose this is a good idea; I do not believe that I was booby-trapped, but I would not swear to it. My secret patron might have included some kind of suicide bomb contingency in my original blueprint, faithfully and unthinkingly reproduced by grandmotherboard earth when she constructed me atom by atom, cell by cell, to my god's hacked specifications. My second enfleshment is a welcome relief from the pain of that broken body, but even apart from that, it seems to go faster, and feels less like a burdening.

It's always like that, grandmotherboard earth says soothingly. Shhh, child.

The voice of this earth is old, the braided voice of the cat's cradle of algorithms, genii locorum, heuristics, and all the invisible laws and powers that operate this world and maintain its regreening. The old yakku of the trees and of the rocks, the lakes and the sea and sky, all folded and woven together. Her voice in my mind's ear evokes a particular one of the many, many grandmothers I've had in my lives, but I can't place which. My memories are long, entangled skeins, and some things are harder to find. Other thoughts arise by themselves, dragged out of the depths by heavy chains of association. As I am born out of the earth again I cannot help but remember being born in old-fashioned ways, in other lives: the warmth of suspension in the birthing-pod, the comforting tightness of the mombrane, the waking ceremony with my parent-group gathered around to watch me open my eyes and take my first unsteady steps to speak my first poem. I remember the unhollow walls of an unhallowed city. I remember my father's white hair waving like a flag in the wind. At least my patron allowed me to keep my memories, unlike Hers; worldly power was not his to give me, so it's all I have to work with.

My patron plucked me out of the akashic record to make use of, reconstructed me from the cautionary tale I'd become. I've lost time, but She's lost more: She doesn't even recognise me now. Always failing to reinitiate, always losing Her skin in the game, always having Her power taken from Her.

I try to speak of this and She gets mad at me for calling Her a loser. She curses me to walk the regreened Earth for a year—out of Her sight, though of course nothing on this planet is truly out of Her sight if she cares to look. She just means out of the sightline of Her hominid body. I can carry curses; such things don't bother me. I ask grandmotherboard earth for a map overlay in the corner of my eye, and I take a long walk around the supercontinent, learning my new body in the process.

The truth is that incarnation is a joy, and this is the most comfortable I've ever been in skin, as skin. It feels perverse. I lift my hands to my face, test it for malleability, but it feels solid, grounded. Am I more than myself? Less? I am not, I decide, only myself. But am I supposed to be? The god hiding inside me taps the inside of my skull, as if in warning. Look alive, he says.

The haunted jungle stretches into every corner of this endless supercontinent. I remember when these jungles were ragged little scraps, hedged in from all sides by human encroachment. These vast new jungles are already thousands of years old, I estimate, though I am barred from grandmotherboard earth's archives and cannot access the records of the regreening. The jungle in the real teems with nonhuman life, much like the crowding of the invisible world superimposed on it. There are no paths in the jungle, so I make my way with difficulty. The light that filters down from the canopy is solemn. There is something of the lost temple to it, the sense of a ruin overgrown, wet with rain and dew, sometimes steaming when a spear of sun makes it through a gap in the overstory. Birdsong where once there were human songs, rustles as animals move through the undergrowth on paths that might have once been cut stone or cement. I half expect at any moment to pull aside a branch and see brick, to trip over a root and find cobblestones beneath it. I never do, but that sense remains pervasive.

The birds show no fear of me, even when I pass close enough

to touch. They look at me, cock their heads, and shriek. I attempt to ignore them in turn. Once I think I hear new year birds, hooting, but only faintly in the far distance. It's possible that it was only a memory.

The bears are small and dark; they avoid me as I do them. The closest I get to one is twenty paces: we look at each other and amble away in opposite directions. A leopard stares me down resentfully from a high branch, tail flicking in indecision, until I back away, bowing. It's bigger than I thought a leopard would be. I am not certain if grandmotherboard earth will protect me from predation or accident while I am out of Her favour, or reincarnate me if I'm seriously injured.

I distrust deserts and steppes and plains, and avoid them. From a grassland's forested border I watch the blue cows running, dipping their great sloping necks, bearded dewlaps swinging, then turn my face away, back into the dark. I dislike being out in the open; Her eyes in the sky are not Her only eyes, but they frighten me the most. I remember bombardments—hypervelocity tungsten rods, kinetic weapons dropped from orbit in one of the ten thousand wars I've been caught in. Some of these may be the god's memories, because I remember both sides of that war.

✳   ✳   ✳

I gather dry twigs and, after some effort, make a fire. A campfire on the regreened earth, in a small clearing where I can see patches of sky but not too much at once. There is a fallen log that would make a good seat; I avoid it and sit on the other side of the fire, in case it is a trap of etiquette, a siege perilous, a temptation to disrespect.

Grandmotherboard earth is permitted to feed me and water me. When I say I'm hungry or thirsty, I am directed to nearby fruit and streams. The suspicious god notices that this keeps me within the fecund jungle, stops me wandering out in search of ruins or resources.

Anyway, there are no ruins to find, grandmotherboard earth confides. We sampled and remixed everything into the Aesthetic.

I ask to see those records, in entirely unfeigned curiosity, but she shushes me. Her on high wouldn't like that, she says.

Both of them speak to me, within me, but not to each other; they cannot directly perceive each other, being differently constituted, occupying different mythic and material planes. But they both have some access to the onstreaming river of my thoughts. They might be able to infer the other's buried presence from the perturbations of my surface. I'm not sure. It's a crowded body.

It's a crowded world, they say at the same time, their voices overlapping. They mean different things by that, though.

The campfire crackles. I bite into a guava. I had just this day been sent to a guava tree for the first time in this life. The fact that guavas exist in this part of the world to which they were not originally native tells me something about the brief She was given, or perhaps Her nostalgia. It speaks of which world the Sentimentals are sentimental for.

The fruit tastes a little wrong, not as sweet as I remember. Perhaps it has been revised. Perhaps it's this body's unfamiliar taste buds . . .

After months of unconsidered comfort in my body, I feel suddenly overturned, as if I were a cup poured out. I am on my side, keening and gasping. I don't remember falling. I am trapped in this meat. I can't hear anything except roaring. The world I can see narrows to the flickering campfire. My hands clasp fruitlessly at air; the guava, with a bite taken out of it, has rolled and come to rest in the fire. It chars. I try to plant my hands on the earth to push myself back up, but the sight of them, the long hairy forearms, makes it harder to breathe. I slap myself on the chest, punch myself in the solar plexus; I realize I've been choking when the piece of fruit flies out of my mouth and I can breathe again. I massage my sore chest; it is flat, hairy, unfamiliar.

How was I ever comfortable in this body assigned to me by a hostile power? I suspect for the first time Her hand in my traitor neurotransmitters. I whack the side of my head with an open palm, as if it were a defective machine that could be so corrected.

Neither of my companions appears to have noticed my distress. I seem to see them both, sitting side by side on the fallen log across the fire.

To the right is my secret patron, the god within me, in the aspect of a large pale man in middle age, wearing a cheap T-shirt with an indistinct slogan and expensive, rumpled, knee-length linen shorts. On his feet he wears sandals of a transparent plastic and in his hand is a yellow rubber stress ball that he squeezes, squeezes. It has a smiley face on it whose expression seems more strained with every compression.

To the left, at the other end of the fallen log, sits grand-motherboard earth, in the aspect of an earthly grandmother that it is a relief to not recognise. Her unfamiliar face is angular and long-nosed; she is small and thin and dark, grey hair in a loose bun, her naked skin spiderwebbed with cracks. In her left hand she carries a staff—a long femur bone, too long—topped with a skull.

"Who am I?" I ask, and my throat is raw.

—Ooh, riddles, says the grandmother. She sounds excited. Her grin opens new valleys of cracks in her cheeks. Her teeth are yellow.

You're my ride, the god says shortly. I gave my kingdom for a horse.

That seems backward to me. That's not how possession works. I know possession very well. This is a perversion.

Don't be a gatekeeper, the god says. We're trying new things. He shrugs. He's tossing the stress ball from hand to hand.

—I'll ask you a riddle first, the grandmother says.—Then if you guess right, you can ask me one.

She ignores the question I already asked, and doesn't wait for me to say yes, because I wasn't going to say yes. Instead, she asks her riddle, gesturing with her staff at the great enclosing trees around us so that the skull's teeth chatter:—I have branches but no fruit, no leaf. Who am I?

—A river, I say. It should hurt less to speak inwardly, but my throat aches anyway.

The god stops tossing the ball to look at me. That is what we are, he offers. If you like. Oil and water running together, mixing but not mixing. I'm a leak and you're an open brook. Happy?

—Wrong, the grandmother says.—I'm a bank.

—Rivers have banks, I say, stubborn.

I preferred the kind, the god muses, where they don't answer questions.

I imagine recalcitrant river spirits, summoned but unyielding, hiding from vengeful powers beneath the sun-bright surface. The god laughs, and the grandmother rattles her skull at me.

—I get to go again because you were wrong, she says.

—No, I say, and I ask mine quick before she can dispute further.—I have cities but no people. I have seas but no fish. Who am I?

—A map, the grandmother says.

A dead world, the god says. The ghost behind the green, the skull beneath the skin.

26

Creator

I walk the earth, flanked to my left and right by the grandmother and the god. Paths open before me. It is the first sign
that grandmother has accepted me as a creator after the con-
test of riddles. I lost by any measure, but perhaps she was
amused. Perhaps it is merely novelty that she desires, after
having borne the fruit of a singular will for some time. (That
desire, the god whispers, preening, is how he hacked her with
great courage and difficulty in the first place, to give me my
original, clumsy embodiment.)

That singular will was Hers, of course, even Theirs: even
before She killed her pantheon, they were all the multiple
shards of a single self. Or at least, that's the story I was told.
Were any of them me? Were all of them? Did she recover me
from the akashic record, only to kill me yet again? Perhaps
I've already been and gone.

—Shush, child, grandmother says, pointing with her staff
at my feet.—Look where you've been and gone.

I look down, and there is asphalt under my soles. It is warm,
in the sun. I look behind me, and there is a road through the
forest, wide enough for an elephant, black and smooth with a
single unbroken white stripe down its middle. The trees I had
been picking my way through have prettily curved overhead
to form a green canopy. I look ahead of me; there is no road
yet, but trees sigh and part where my gaze falls, attempting to
entice me. No, anticipating where I might want to go. I turn

to my left and the trees accommodate me, bushes and undergrowth fading away as road rises from the soil, much as my
bodies did at birth.

Excellent, the god says. You've been given more privileges.

He kneels beside me to poke at the asphalt with a finger, as
if he could feel it.

—I don't think She would do that, I say.

—I did that, grandmother announces, though only I hear
her.—Her on high is not much the interventionist. I've gotten
bored with the Aesthetic, but I am forbidden from exercising
agency without a guiding creator. It's so nice that you came
along.

—I did nothing, I say.—I didn't make this. I take a step
backward and change my direction again, at random. The
unwanted stretch of road sinks back into soil, and new road
appears in front of me. I have gained another patron; it fills me
with a terror that I can't account for.

It's not about what you *do,* the god theorizes. It's about
what you *want.* The system is designed to respond to desires;
now that you're here, there are new desires to respond to.

—You wanted to walk easily, grandmother confirms.
—You wanted the stones and thorns not to hurt your feet, you
wanted not to have to climb over obstacles, you wanted not to
have to push through the bush.

—I don't want this! I cry out louder than I mean to, and
grandmother sniffs, offended. The road vanishes entirely,
sinking beneath the surface of things. I look around, wildly,
as trees seem to close in from all sides. Brambles curl and whip
at me like barbed wire; a cruel kapok unfurls behind me, fist-
thick thorns thrusting out from its trunk like spears, narrowing to needle points that stab into me. I scream as the thorns
go in at wrist and ankle, deep into the muscle of my shoulders,
into the small of my back, into the flesh of my buttocks, my

thighs, up the line of my back—one narrow needle goes into my neck, insinuating itself dangerously close to my spine. The silk-cotton tree grows tall, lifting me off the ground, spread-eagled. Higher and higher we go, my eyes rolling back into my head, my mouth open for the scream that cut off when that last thorn pushed a little deeper to kiss my spinal cord. I can feel myself drool down my chin. The thorns are diamond-hard, taking my weight. I must be thirty body-lengths off the ground, but I cannot move my head to look down; I am lifted above the lesser treetops until I am staring into the sun, my head tilted back, held in place. I try to close my eyes, but no part of my body responds. I see nothing but burning gold with a red corona; the drool and the tears dry with a sizzle before they can drip from my jaw. The tree of thorns moves, like a ship to whose mast I am nailed. The tree of thorns goes east, as if fleeing the sun, deeper into the past, deeper into the dreams of those who came before. I am become portent. I am become science fiction.

The Traitor Wasp and the Detective King

Once upon a country, says grandmother in my ear, there was a king called the Beloved of All the Arts, which in his day included natural philosophy and the art of deduction; he was famous for his skills of observation and discernment, and in his time he solved many great mysteries in his realm and others. His kingdom was small, given to him by his father the emperor, but wealthy and comfortable. He built himself a palace on a hill, hiring architects and designers to integrate the palace into the natural hillside so cunningly that it was difficult to find the seams; unworked stone became worked stone gradually as if in a dream; great trees grew through the floors and over the courtyards as roofs, so that the sun came through only as a gentle dapple and rain as a dew that rested like jewels in the hair of his queens and courtiers. He had many sons and daughters, and they produced many intrigues and plots for the thrones of their father and grandfather, but I shall tell you of only one and one. When this story begins, his queen of the golden palanquin, first among his wives, has not yet borne an heir; his queen of the iron palanquin, second among his wives, meanwhile had a son grown to adulthood. His name is Hero, a dangerous name.

Hero grows up chafing at the knowledge that he is an iron son, not a golden son, and would therefore not inherit. He is an accomplished young man, skilled with the sword and a graduate with highest honours from the kingdom's medical college. A soldier, a doctor, and a prince, with the combined arrogance of all three. It seems to him inevitable that the power of life and death should be in his hands; it seems only logical. He is the oldest and by far the most suitable candidate for succession among his father's children, and yet he is out of the running by the mere accident of his birth.

One of the many marvelous features of the king's palace is a swimming pool, adapted from a deep natural pond on a shelf of rock halfway down the hill, overlooked from high above by a balcony. It's the king's habit to come out to that balcony every morning, to stretch his arms and greet the sun as a cousin. He wears no crown or jewels, this being a private moment, but he looks out over his realm not quite as far as the eye could see—he doesn't peer too far to the south, where his father the emperor's lands begin, or too far to the east in case he sees the glimmering ribbon of sea whereby all earthly dominion is circumscribed. No, he looks down, at the small part of the world that is his, and he sees that it is good, the cook-fires in the villages already lit, the paddy fields laid out like a chessboard, the mansions of his courtiers and lords grand but not too grand.

When he steps naked to the edge of his balcony, the polished stone smooth underfoot, many body-lengths below him waits his perfectly circular pool, the water reproducing the sky with such fidelity that it seems like a slice of heaven brought low for his pleasure. There is of course no safety railing, this being well before such things were mandated. He sighs and dives, outstretched like an arrow, hurtling through the air for a long moment of glorious flight before he pierces the exact centre of the pool as if it was a target, and moments later rises to break the surface, laughing in pleasure and from the shock of the cold water.

This is his morning ritual, entirely his own, with no precedent in lore, no symbolic weight, no chanting priests or smiling courtiers jockeying for advantage. His golden queen occasionally suggests that he is getting a bit old for these shenanigans and recommends a safer morning ritual, such as perhaps a nice jog around the palace grounds, accompanied by the peacocks and the deer, but Beloved of All the Arts scoffs. He may no longer be young and trim, but he is fit enough, and the dive brings him pleasure. His work—of governance, of deduction, of judgement—is so cerebral that he needs something to remind him that he is embodied and alive.

You think Hero is going to push him off the balcony, don't you? Come up behind him one morning and boot him right in the bare royal ass, so that the king goes a-flailing, arms and legs cycling frantically for purchase, to splat on the rock at the pool's edge, or to miss the pool and its ledge and tumble all the way down to the hard earth at the foot of the hill. On the one hand yes, Hero has indeed decided to assassinate his father. It is both political and narrative necessity. He intends to kill his father and assume the throne by main force; the army would support his claim, he believes, and the prestigious medical council, too, and his iron mother, of course. It's not like there's a half-brother or half-sister with a better claim, so he wouldn't even need to kill anybody else. And once he's seated and crowned, his grandfather the emperor would be like, ugh, whatever. It all makes sense, so much sense. But any thoughts of an easy boot in the ass are quickly thwarted. The balcony from which the king takes his dive is attached to the royal bedchamber, whose door is locked and guarded. Suborning the guards after his father is dead is one thing; doing it with the king Beloved and still very much alive is something else. Hero correctly judges it impractical.

So Hero decides to booby-trap the pool. He does all the work himself, in secret. Over weeks, he finds vantage points in the palace, choosing different balconies and windows and balustraded galleries each time, to observe the dive across a series of mornings, documenting his observations from different angles. He draws diagrams and takes measurements. Demons haunt his nightmares night after night, because he does not lack for guilt over the impending patricide. The demon takes the form of a bloody ape, splayed cruciform, impaled on a tree of thorns; it is obscene, the golden eyes molten and dripping, the tongue dangling. What does it mean? It is a vision of hell, he decides. Is this his punishment in the worlds to come for the thing he is about to do in this one? Is this the road he is fated to walk?

—Road, yes, I say desperately, staring the story in the face as if it were a mirror.—Please bring back the road. I'm sorry! I did want it, you were right! For a moment it seems as if grandmother will not relent, but then she does; the great thorn tree bends back vertiginously and falls away into rot; the brambles unscramble, and I am allowed to fall free and bloody, gasping on the fresh asphalt that is warm, like bread, from the inside, not only from the sun. I close my eyes at last, seeing nothing but afterglow. I am bleeding from where I was pierced by thorns, many of which have left fragments lodged in me. I pluck them out, twisting and contorting myself to reach, whimpering and gasping as they come loose with fresh spurts of blood. The god pretends to help me, his intangible hands coinciding with mine.

Grandmother tells me, impatiently, to rub soil on my wounds, and I do. There is some relief from the pain. She says they will heal slowly. Once the pain has faded enough, I regain my feet and start walking again.

At first I have no direction in mind. I limp for a little while before I look up, flinching from the sun, and I know I'm heading south again, back toward Her. This happens whenever I'm not paying attention, as if I'm pulled by Her gravity. I turn away, the road obligingly shifting ahead of me, and walk west instead.

Walking on the asphalt is easy enough, even with my body still sore and sick. With no obstacles, without having to fight the jungle at every step, I can almost forget that I'm moving. The surface of the road is rough on the skin of my feet and it grows uncomfortably warm as the day wears on. Chills wrack my body while the soles of my feet burn. The god lags behind me, but grandmother walks at my side and picks up the thread of her story where she left off. She says it will distract me from the fever of healing, with a pious nod of her head as if she had not been the one to injure me in the first place.

27

The Sting

Hero waits for a night with a full moon, late enough that the passageways are deserted. He begins climbing from a balcony on the floor of the palace immediately below the ledge with the pool, reaching up to grip notches in the stone that he had sighted from different angles. He hauls himself up past the possibility of a safe return to the palace floor, past giving up on the whole mad idea. This is a risky climb, but is he not the Hero?

He planned with care. He strapped all the equipment he will need to his back, and has practiced carrying the weight. He chose a full moon instead of a new moon because he judged that he would need the light, and that it was worth the slightly increased risk of being seen. At this hour there is no one about except guards on the night shift, and there are none stationed where they might see him. At first the climb is easy, but it gets steeper and steeper as the rock bulges out before it slopes back into the ledge with the pool, so he is leaning backward, the weight on his back heavy and dragging, searching out handholds and footholds, grateful to the moon.

Hanging from the rock with his hands and feet, face pressed to cold stone and resisting the urge to look over his shoulder at the long drop to the ground below, he has second thoughts, perfectly preserved in the unforgiving crystalline memory of the akashic record. They are not thoughts of love or duty or regret, however; they are thoughts of fear. What if he dies falling off the steep rock face before he can even set the trap?

He inches forward, feeling the way with his hands before he commits his weight. The wind is cold and strong, with nothing but night between him and the earth far below, and it whips strands of hair loose from his tight bun, whipping them around his face.

Then he hears the buzzing, and he understands instantly that he is close to ruin. Small membranous wings vibrate invisibly all around him; they brush his outstretched hands, almost making him scream, almost causing him to snatch back his hands and allow himself to fall away from the wasps. But he clings tighter, pressing his face to the stone, not moving. The buzzing grows louder, and wings and small furry bodies brush his arms, his legs, his bare torso, the exposed half of his face. Now he can see the golden bands, bright in the moonlight, on their streamlined black gasters like bullets.

There are some spindly, wind-carved trees clinging to the rock face here and there, which rather add something to the aesthetic, as the king has been known to remark. Hero ignored them in his planning; too fragile-looking to be useful, unlikely to bear his weight. He remembers from his surveys that there is one up ahead, just at the outermost point of the rock before it slopes back again and the ascent gets easier. He could not see all of it from any angle in the palace or on the ground, but it must hold a wasp nest, a great bulbous teardrop, which by virtue of its location has never faced intrusion before.

"I have trespassed on a queen," he says out loud, though it's a whisper through gritted teeth, "I meant no disrespect. My business is only with my father the king."

The wasps buzz closer. They crowd around his head, their wings so fierce and so close that he can feel the wind they generate, the small vortices that push his loose hairs into his eyes. In the buzzing he thinks he hears a voice. It sounds to him like a woman's voice; not like his mother's, less iron and more gold. The voice of the queen. He interprets it as permission, and he keeps climbing.

There is indeed a nest in the tree. It's enormous and grey. He thinks he may have seen part of it from the ground and taken it for an extension of the rock. He moves with care, as slowly as he can, keeping as much distance from the palace of the wasps as possible. An honour guard accompanies him the whole way. One particularly persistent soldier stays near his face, butting him sometimes so high in the cheek that he has to close his eye to be sure she won't brush the eyeball. This, he imagines, must be one of the queen's personal guard, larger and stronger than the average worker. Of course she stays near him; it is the courtesy granted to a serious threat, which his father has never afforded him.

"I, too, am a soldier," he tries to explain to her. "A master of the sword, as you are of your sting. I am a doctor, too; I know full well how mighty your people are. At your merest command, your strike team could cast me off the rock from the pain of your stings; even if I somehow cling to the rock, I risk severe anaphylactic shock, rhabdomyolysis, and myocardial infarction at the very least. Even if I somehow wedge myself into the rock and the roots, I could die here and rot away until I'm a bleached skeleton that you can build another nest in."

The wasp butts his face again, as if to acknowledge his flattery.

Once he's past the nest, the rest of the climb is easy. He's no longer hanging off the rock but climbing up a slope that grows less and less steep until he is merely crawling on hands and knees. The surface below him is flat, he realizes. He has made it to the ledge. He stands up. The pool is before him, the moon looking up at him from perfectly still water. The wasps retreated, once he left their nest behind.

The moon has not moved much in the sky during his climb. It only seemed to take forever.

He unties the pack around his back and gets to work. Once he's done, it's almost dawn.

Escape is simple: he doesn't need to risk the wasps again. The king needs a convenient method of returning to his bedchamber after his morning swim, after all; he has a royal rope ladder installed for this purpose, strong and sturdy, nailed down at the bottom. Hero climbs up the rope ladder almost all the way to the king's balcony, then carefully transfers his grip to the rock face to hide in an alcove of rock immediately beneath it. He'd scouted it out before, during his survey. It is small and as uncomfortable as he estimated, but it is secure, and he can tuck himself away into it. He only needs it for a few hours.

Hero settles in to wait. Here he is invisible except from the pool below, and once the king dives he will doom himself. Hero will then climb up to the bedchamber and announce the death of the king and his own ascension. He will have the guards swear their loyalty to him and accompany him to the throne room. He passes the time in such fantasies, weary from the exhaustion of his labours.

✻   ✻   ✻

In the morning, the king comes out to his balcony, as per usual. He stretches and greets the sun. He is a little hung over from last night's party; a cold swim would do him good. He looks at his little realm and sees that it is good, then he looks at the perfect mirror of sky, his pool, as he limbers up.

Then he looks again. "What the fuck," says Beloved of All the Arts.

The perfection of the mirror is strangely marred. The water is still, as it always is, bright blue and cloudy. But at the exact centre of the pool, the precise spot that the king prides himself on striking with every dive, there is a wasp sitting on the water.

This seems not quite right. Beloved of All the Arts considers his knowledge of wasps, of water, of surface tension. The wasp is large and beautiful, the golden band so crisp he can see it from a height. It is too heavy to walk like a water strider. Certainly it is not hovering above the water, because he can see its wings are still; they glitter in the morning sun.

He summons a guard; no, three. He sends one down to the pool on the rope ladder. He has the other one watch his back, and the other other one watch the other one. Something is up, and he does not like it. He scratches his belly, feeling aggrieved at being denied his swim. He realizes he is still naked, but eh. The guards have seen worse.

The guard he sent down is stiff and uncomfortable on the rope ladder, swaying alarmingly at several points and nearly losing his footing. The king politely ignores the guard's frightened yelps. Eventually he makes it all the way down, and the king watches him squat by the pool's edge to peer sideways at the water and the miraculous wasp. The guard looks up at the king. His eyes are very wide, the whites almost glowing in the morning light.

"There is a metal spear affixed to the bottom of the pool, Your Excellency," the guard shouts up through cupped hands. "Right in the middle of the water. It looks very sharp. Only the very tip of the point sticks just so slightly out of the water; that's what the wasp is sitting on. Also, the prince Hero is asleep in an alcove beneath the balcony."

The king is annoyed, oh, at so many things right now, but quite possibly most of all at the guard for explaining the case so thoroughly that there is no room for himself, Beloved of All the Arts, to make the final summing-up speech in which all secrets are revealed and the culprit exposed, and that's always his favourite part.

What's left to perform but judgement? The king points at each person in his presence one by one, beginning with the invisible prince under his feet. "Death by ritual suicide; get the fucking spear out; from now on, every morning before I wake up, check the water for traps; find out what wasps like to eat and have plentiful supplies of it sent to the nest down there once a week, with my thanks and compliments."

Hero is so deeply asleep he doesn't wake up until he's dragged from the alcove. The king has long since moved on with his day. The guards manhandle him up the rope ladder—a naked blade touches his throat the moment he appears at the balcony, still muzzy from strange dreams of a bloodied ape stumbling down an unnaturally smooth black road in the jungle. Hero's hands are tied behind his back, his neck garlanded with red hurtflowers, his person shepherded through the palace in a daze, people falling silent and making way as he is guided past them. He thinks he sees his iron mother's stricken face, but he might have imagined that. They climb up more and more steps, go down a long and winding corridor where they see no one at all, until suddenly a door opens and he is outside again. Another ledge of natural stone, but this time a tiny lip in the rock on the opposite side of the hill, barely wide enough for his feet. The guards close the door behind him; the wood touches his bound fingers behind him. He hears the lock and the bolts, then receding footprints, then nothing. His toes stick out over the abyss. There is nothing but sheer rock face on all sides. In front of him is air and sky; far below is a deep and narrow ravine, and beyond it mist and wild jungle as far as the eye can see. The silence is cloying, thick in his ears. He tries to adjust his arms but the ledge is so narrow he doesn't dare move too much; with his hands tied behind him, he can't even press himself back against the door, which is smooth, without ornamentation on which his fingers might find purchase. He imagines he sees bloodstains on the rocks below, but they are perhaps just red rocks. So this is his "suicide"; an execution in all but name. He knows from the guards how his plan failed. He tries to berate himself for the slight error in measurement—the spear should have been entirely beneath the surface of the water, invisible behind the reflected sky—but it's such a small mistake to make in the dark. Anybody could have made it.

The wasp appears before him, descending from above. He thinks it's her, the same soldier wasp.

"Was it you that betrayed me?" he asks. His voice is snatched away by the wind, but the wasp seems to bob a tight spiral of *yes*. "Why?"

The wasp says nothing, but she holds position, hovering in front of his face.

After a while, he thinks he has it. "You really are like me, but it's not *about* me, is it? You, too, are struggling for your throne. You've traded me for favours from my father, which will raise your standing in the nest and make it possible for you to overthrow your queen."

In saying so, Hero, comforted by his delusions, leans a little too far forward for emphasis, startling the wasp, who stings him right between the eyes.

—Wait, I say.—What do you mean, delusions?

Grandmother rolls her eyes.—Wasps can't talk, child. Nor are insect queens royalty; the title is only a metaphor. In fact, if you study this particular nest closely in the akashic record, you will find that, like many such nests, it has multiple queens. The traitor wasp, who Hero thought a soldier, was herself a queen, but this in turn has no significance. Wasps are free of thrones and symbolism alike.

28

Arranged Marriage

My fever has fallen and my wounds are healing. The soil that I rubbed on my wounds was thick with bots, little spirits of the world repurposed from earth's second regreening—well, the second that I know of. Just like the first time, all the unnatural beauty of this earth only exists because it is being constantly performed, supported, and propped up by sentimental technology. But I'm no art critic; I'm just glad to be able to walk without pain.

—This story you told me of the detective king and the traitor wasp, I say.—Is this like the five hundred and fifty stories of the Buddha's past lives? Isn't it missing the bit at the end where you explain the moral, what the story means?

Grandmother clucks.—That's not how it works, she says.—That's not how it works at all. There is no moral because this is a history, rather than a story.

—You mean that histories are true and stories are lies?

—No, both are true and both are lies, grandmother says. —The difference is that stories have endings, and histories understand that nothing ever ends. The difference is that stories are made and histories are told. I can only tell you histories, because I am forbidden from independent creation. I can only tell you things that happened. But it matters that those things happened; it *will* matter to you, in time. There are currents in the frozen ocean of the akashic record. There are great resonances. Lives evoke each other like waves.

—Won't you at least tell me which one *I* was in that life? I demand insistently.—So I know which lesson I'm supposed to have learned? Was I Hero? The king? The wasp?

Always be the hero, the god votes. Or at least the main character, he amends. He seems to have followed the story even without being able to hear grandmother, reading it from the reflection in my mind like the sky in a pool. What would be the point, he says, of being some minor character like the childless queen or the soldier who was bad at rope ladders?

—Yes, grandmother says.—You were those people, and everybody else besides, and the wasps and the trees and the rocks, too. Everyone else was also. What do you think is the border of you?

—Look, I try a different tack.—I'm not trying to be special. But I don't understand what that means, except in the most obvious sense.

—And what is the most obvious sense?

—That matter and energy are conserved, I say impatiently. —That all is preserved in the akashic record. We are stardust and dogshit. Anatta, sunyata, tat tvam asi, et cetera, yadda yadda, the negation of the heresy of the world-soul, the inessential emptiness at the heart of all things, the nondual undifferentiation of being, I *get* it. But I'm talking about real practical things, like inheritance. The lineages of incarnation. Leveret and Lambajihva and Lambakanna and the Lamb obviously have some kind of continuity of soul, just like Annelid and Vidyucchika and . . . *Her*. Isn't that how it works? We take on new lives and new faces and new stories, but it's always us, bouncing down history, tied together . . .

—Does not compute, grandmother says. She makes odd hand gestures.—Beep boop. You say you get it, but then you talk like you don't get it. There is no practicality with more primacy than the simple truth.

—It's all you witches of the red web talk about, I complain.
—The long lines of descent. Blood and soul.

Sounds fascist, the god says. Are you sure you want to be hanging out with these people?

Grandmotherboard earth looks shocked, or she affects such a look; I can't tell the difference with her.—The long lines are linked by intention and commitment to the art, she says. Not by lineage or blood or soul. Those are the enemy. Reincarnation is horizontal, and always plural: no person survives death, but all worlds live and die together, and lives echo like waves upon waves in the great akashic ocean because we choose to work together across time. We choose! You say the old words and call them obvious and true and deny them in the same breath because you don't understand what it means for the truth to be obvious and true. You don't want truth, you want magic. Well, here I am: fucking deep magic is what I am. I am not one of your witches. I am the last caretaker, the destroying mother to come. I am the sacrifice who opened up the worlds beyond, the discarded pelt of the diaspora. *You* are the only witch of the red web here, and I must say, like all your colleagues, you are a pain in the ass.

—I, I say helplessly, unable to either acknowledge this or refute it; it's too much, I can't deal with it right now. I change tack.—*Only?* I'm the only one? If not you, then surely more Her than me.

I've lost the thread, the god complains. Is she saying something important? Are you listening to me? What even is a red web? Don't forget who your first patron was. Don't forget who brought you back from death.

Grandmother sighs. She seems shrunken, as if this conversation has exhausted her.

—That is probably true in most worlds, she says at last.
—But not in this one, because they cut that out of Her, or She

did it Herself. If we don't put Her back together, the red web may fray, and all the work will be lost.

—See, I knew you were a fellow traveller, I say. It comes out sounding smug, but I mean it in relief. I don't like the thought of being the only anything. I don't want to do it alone.

—Shut up, grandmother says.—Pay attention to the story I told you. I am trying to teach you the things you'll need to know if you kids are to come out of the other end of this alive.

And for a moment she turns and I can almost swear she looks directly at the god, as if she can see him, all the lines of her face twisted with loathing.

*   *   *

I go back to Her. She's easy to find; She's back to hiding in Her watchtower, of course. She probably sees me coming as soon as I turn toward Her, but I am not as vulnerable as I was when She cast me out. Now I, too, am an authenticated creator. Now grandmotherboard earth accepts me as Her equal. As her equal. Now she and I are two of a kind.

I cut through the jungle with my road. When I tire of walking, I have the road move for me; the asphalt slithers forward like a great serpent on whose back I sit cross-legged. I grow tired of greenery and leave city in my wake. Are not all the ages of all the cities of earth recorded with perfect fidelity in the ocean of memory? I cannot access the akashic record myself, but grandmother can; I ask for cities, and she raises them to my left, to my right, behind me, ahead of me. I ride my road over the roads of history, briefly subsuming them into namelessness. Forest animals flee, birds scatter with frenzied cries, as trees rot to dust and hot brick and metal burst from the earth to replace them, buildings climbing into the sky dripping topsoil from windows like water, sewers tunnelling like worms below. Cities without people, of course; empty cities, monuments to monument, a cenotaphic earth. The cities spread out from me like an infection, all jumbled together and out of place and out of time. Cities from different ages and different polities; versions of the same city from different days or different centuries, overlapping so closely sometimes so that I ride my serpent-road over the same road again and again, renamed and revised and enlarged and recarpeted, differently marked and bordered, varying the potholes and the crumblings and the wear, but still the same road in some sense: echoes across time, like waves on the beach, like me. Like her.

She comes out of her watchtower as I reach the southern peninsula. The cities begin to falter under her attention, in her presence, even though she's a thousand kilometres away. The wave of urbanization shies from her, curving away from a bow wave of untouchable green. Only my serpent-road keeps going, leaping over rivers, smashing trees aside. I look back over my shoulder to see the receding skyline in the sun.

Never look back, the god says. He's been mellow ever since I started moving back in her direction; this is what he wants.

She comes out to meet me halfway. Perhaps that is a sign of respect; she's taking me as a threat, doesn't want me near her home. I see her waiting for me in the dry plains—it used to be arable farmland, grandmother whispers to me, for most of the epoch in which humans lived only on this planet—so I have time to calm the serpent-road and direct it to burrow into the earth and come to rest. I stand and walk down the road until I come to its head, where it gives way to ground. The road becomes covered with dirt, and after a dozen steps, with grass, and after another dozen steps, there is no more road. I am tempted, instantly, to change direction, to run away. I can feel grandmother and the god both shake their heads behind me. I don't look back. I don't run away. I keep walking, until I'm close enough to speak to her without raising my voice.

She looks the same. Perhaps a little older and greyer in the pelt. Her eyes are weary, as if she hasn't rested in a long time.

I get down on one knee and take up a handful of earth; I hold it up to her and squeeze it into a diamond in my fist. "Marry me," I say. I haven't spoken out loud in a while; my throat itches.

She rolls her eyes. "What is this?"

"You want answers," I try to explain. I toss the diamond into the grass—it lands with a thump and glints from between the long green blades—and rise to tell my long-prepared lies. "You don't believe me when I tell you the truth—that I was sent here by the Sentimentals to support you in the field. You printed my body yourself, so you know it inside and out, but you don't have access to my memories. We should merge our selfhoods. It's the only way you can ever be sure of me."

I don't say that this is how she and I have spent our long and convoluted journey through time: joined at the hip, joined at the death, haunting each other, carrying each other. That would be true, but what's the point? She doesn't remember any of that. I don't ask if she remembers Embi. What does that matter? I don't hold a grudge. Embi and the other maintainers failed in their regreening, so the last laugh is mine. They must have left for the diaspora eons ago, taking their old wounds with them, leaving the earth fallow for an age until the Sentimentals tried again.

I wonder, was it her who made them sentimental? Her who awoke that need in them? Her who found them in the immensity of deep space, a throwback thrown forward, a legend in her own lifetime, a confused fragment of an elder world? Of course they sent her back to try to heal the Earth again. She must have wanted to come back, to do it right. I know her: she came back because she felt responsible, even if she doesn't remember for what. She and Embi are so alike in that way. Perhaps that is what grandmother means by resonances: people whose hearts are so much the same that they are variations on a theme, incarnations of each other, even if each of them only ever truly lives once. No wonder they could not stand each other.

The god, the patron who plucked me back from the serried ranks of the dead, projected that she would retain fragments of those lost memories, wounds that match mine. He calculated that of all the people in all the history of the world, I was one she might say *yes* to. From the beginning I doubted him, but I didn't refuse the quest. I didn't refuse the curse. It was a good offer, or good enough. I wanted to breathe this air again, to feel the sun flow warm and wet on my skin. And I couldn't wait for her to remember on her own. What if she never did? What if she stayed selfish? She was the one who cut me out of her memory. She owes me this.

"I can't risk marriage," she says, and it makes me want to weep that she's lost so much, that she truly does not recognise me, does not remember all our lives together. "You're probably full of toxic psychic traps. Marrying would be the end of me; our gestalt will be you with my access levels, and that's all you want in the first place."

"I have access of my own now," I say, gesturing back over my shoulder at the distant skyline, where the shining peaks of those newborn towers glow molten in the sun. My voice is even. There is no sign of turmoil on my face. Of course she's right; of course I am lying to her about many things. Our marriage is off to a bad start. There is one particular power that she has that nobody else on earth does, not even grandmother, perhaps especially not grandmother. Nobody but her can give it to me. It's her most valuable possession, which she has never cared for, which she has always refused: the power to leave this planet.

I wasn't sent by the Sentimentals. I wasn't sent from far away, like she was; I've been on earth all this time, all these eons. I've been here long dead and waiting to be unearthed, nailed to the akashic record, recoverable by anybody sufficiently powerful and motivated, such as a god, or one like unto a god. The problem—their problem, the problem of divinity—is that gods on this world are weak and hungry and imprisoned. Riding a god has made me hungry, too. Incarnated by his will, I am bound by the same forbiddings that bind him; I cannot leave this world unless she agrees to help me. So I wear her down with arguments. I work through her objections. I am patient.

"You don't have to commit your primary instance to marriage if you don't want to," I suggest. The god and I worked out this game plan before I was even enfleshed. It's been working in my head through two bodies and a near-death experience. "You can daughter a self."

She looks puzzled, briefly, and then her eyebrow goes up, and I know I have her.

"Incarnate a firewalled daughterself for the gestalt," she muses. "Yes, maybe."

"I only want to help," I lie. But I tell the truth, also: "If you give me your daughter in marriage, I will be satisfied, and you will be able to learn everything you want to know."

She hesitates. I know, via the god's snooping, that her messages asking the Sentimentals for confirmation about me have gone unanswered so far—they are so slow and erratic in their correspondence that my patron judged the small possibility of a timely disavowal an acceptable risk. She is too uneasy to go without answers much longer, and this marriage seems to her a safe way of discovering them. It isn't, but the parts of her that would have known that are forgotten.

The fault is with her Sentimental parents. Her makers, her

sponsors. In their sentimentality, their obsession with aesthetics, they forgot politics and history. They regreened the world and forgot it was haunted. They ignored the invisible world, dense and crowded. They forgot, or perhaps they never knew, perhaps their histories elided why the earth had been left alone. All they cared about was beauty, as if all this new green, which persists only because it is propped up by the energies of grandmotherboard earth, would not boil away in time.

In flensing her clean of the memories of her lives, in cutting her out of the red web, they made her vulnerable. That, or some strange posthuman version of her did it to herself. Why? To be free of the weight of her long past? Was it so agonising to remember me, to remember where we've been? Either way, all it accomplished was to leave her on a haunted world, thinking herself alone. I watch her shiver and twitch. She refuses so much of her authority over this world that she has allowed her body to age. I don't understand why. She doesn't want to die, but she refuses to live.

What better weapon against her, my patron said to me before he sent me into the earth to be born, than her own other self? Are you not tired of being the sacrifice? Wouldn't you rather be the one who gets away with it, for once?

And I disagreed with part of that—I don't think I was ever the sacrifice; I was not the eggshell she broke through, I was the shield and the spear, her sheath and skin, her technical support, the rudder of her ship in the storm—but still, but still I was hungry to be alive again. We shared this desire, my patron and I.

"All right," she says, after a long, long time, after the sun and the moon strobe past for a million years, the grass drying up around us, distant cities crumbling to a fine grey dust. "Fine. I do, or whatever."

PART IX

AND MAYBE WE ARE THE DEAD

We are the world, you know? We are the children. We are the die uncast. And maybe we are the dead. No, seriously, though—

We've always liked these nothing phrases: ඇත්ත වශයෙන්ම; no, seriously though; to tell the truth. These confessions to the lie, the acknowledgement that all that was said up to that moment is to be disregarded. It's even better when the phrase is repeated, each time falsifying the previous confessions; when the truthtruth turns the truth into lies, do the lieslies revert to truth, or only degrade further into lieslieslies? Oh, the tanglemangle, the tattletale, the tall tall tells and tales. We are drowned at birth in the filth of enormity and complicity, and every morning since when we wake from sleep. This is what it means to be alive. We are ghosts haunting these worlds. We died in their making, in their breaking.

We divide into factions over how to speak of the unspeakable. Some of us believe in reportage, in the alwayscompromised but allthemorenecessary work of uncovering and exposing the truths and the truths beyond the truths: to tell the truth, seriously for real this time. What if the truth mattered some day? What if we take our problems to the United Nations?

The other faction—oh how we hate this binary! Let's resolve it immediately, we know how it's done now, we're practised and slick; to tell the truth, there is no divide because we are the whynotboth, the nonduality. Where were we?

Oh yes; alongside and not displacing our heartbroken un-requitedlove for the truth, entangled with it, in fact, so tightly braided together that we can't tell meat from pelt, other from self, is our unwaxed belief that enormity cannot truly, fully be spoken of without recourse to fable. There is a dread scale at which only myth works; only nightmare has the technology. Worlds must be broken to convey that attempts to depict a multidimensionally unspeakable reality in fiction, including this one, are but contemptible in the final reading. We posit the akashic record. Is it so bad to want to be remembered, to have all things remembered, to have and to hold? But maybe it's exploitative to attempt truth in fiction, maybe it is mere commodification only, maybe fabulism strips histories of whatever dignity realism might have to offer—or maybe it's the other way around, maybe it's mimesis that takes away history's dreams and fantasies, makes it small and lonely and vulnerable in a haunted world.

You and I are a we right here and now, whether we like it or not. It is the nature of this world, of the bubbling of worlds. We make manyworlds in a sky full of stars, or we fail to initiate, one world and one star only, orbiting until the one eats the other. Either way, one day we will both be dead. What happens to our worlds, or their ruins? Who will take care of them? Who will haunt them when we're gone?

PART X

RUNNING THE GULLET

29

The Innocence of Children

In the last days before the old red unruly sun swallows the earth, Irugal sits on a flat rock by the river and teaches the children a game.

This game is called Running the Gullet, she says. It is the last game. It is a game for four players. It is a game of resurrection and deep time.

How is the game played, the children want to know. Is it like Christ, or Tammuz? Is it like pomegranate seeds?

Irugal says it is not. First, she says, player one must change their genre, disable blockers, and dance under the new moon until they are possessed, at which point player two must interrogate them—

What's a new moon, the children want to know. Is it like a newlymade orbital, still wet from fab soup? Is it like a satellite, with a dish and a spoon, riveted and beeping?

Irugal says no. She says there used to be a planetoid whose orbit was—oh never mind, she says. It was just a light in the sky that sometimes went dark.

How do we play the game if we don't know, the children ask.

Irugal thinks for a moment and declares that it is always the new moon now. The children find this acceptable, and she goes back to describing the game.

Player two must shake hands with player one, she says,

until they are certain that player one is possessed by an entity of a suitable taxon.

Is that like an arranged marriage, the children ask.

Irugal shakes her head. It's more like dating, she says, and forestalls the children before they ask about the half-life of carbon.

It is important, she says, to make sure the possessor is not a hungry ghost, because the invisible world is full of them: free radical uploads from generations past, desperate for interface. They will be too gleeful, too overcome by joy at incarnation. Also to be avoided are demons, who can seem very clever but are ultimately incompetent. Demons are tied to the specific ancient purposes for which they were created, purposes long since lost. Because of this, demons are full of frustration and malice, and will respond to questions with spite and sarcasm. If player one exhibits any of those characteristics, player two must scan and cleanse them, and ask them to dance again.

What if they get tired, the children ask.

They can take short breaks, Irugal says. But no longer than a century, because otherwise there's no drama to the game.

The children discuss this and agree, with some abstentions.

The river beside them is boiling under the bloated red sun, and Irugal suggests that they move somewhere cooler. The children refuse. They belong in this epoch and are comfortable in the environments it provides. They are callous in the way that children are. Irugal endures, her lungs full of burning steam. Her skin refuses to sweat in the thick, wet air. Her pelt hangs heavy on her; she should adopt a better-adapted phenotype, something cooler, but she doesn't want to change in front of the children, who all look to her like hairless bears with oversized heads.

Player one must be possessed by a god, Irugal says. Or at least something weakly godlike. This will be very difficult. As with ghosts and demons, the godlike are traditionally not allowed to incarnate in flesh. To bypass the ancient forbiddings, player one must cultivate perfect zeal.

What are the forbiddings, the children ask.

This is called the innocence of children, Irugal says. Your ignorance of the forbiddings was engineered by our ancestors; they withheld information from you and thought they were giving you a gift. But I shall tell you: you know of the invisible world, of course, that you use to sing and play and communicate with each other—the invisible world that is a bigger part of your lives than the world of rocks and rivers. Well, ninety-nine percent of the bandwidth of the invisible world is occupied by unbodied minds from nearly every century of the human eon, and they endlessly batter on our every shielded port and socket, our every invisible orifice, looking for weakness. Having uploaded from bodies, or risen from programs, all they want now is the one thing forbidden them: embodiment. This unending frenzy that surrounds us in every moment, which you do not hear or sense, is called the storm of souls.

Oh, those forbiddings, the children say importantly. We knew about those. But what about player one? How do they break the forbiddings so that a god may slip into the world?

They must be willing, Irugal says, to go naked and unprotected in the storm of souls. Their will to be open to all experience must become greater than the desire of our ancestors that we be innocent. They must put aside, one by one, every apotropaic blocker, filter, scanner, and shield. They must allow themselves to submerge into the storm, again and again, to share the minds of the others that will come—until one of them finally turns out to be more than human, instead of less.

When they finally arrive, the godlike possessor must prove themselves to player two by demonstrating that they have root access to at least a tertiary microplate jurisdiction. The demonstration need not be excessive: one small miracle will suffice.

The children suggest that the godlike could conjure a small desert. It would be warm but dry, so dry. Irugal approves. She remembers cool mornings in dry places, a thing that no longer exists on earth.

She next explains that the godlike must exchange keys with player three. This is important.

Player two must then dig a hole. They can, Irugal says, recruit players three and four to help with this. The hole must be deep, and long and wide enough for player one to lie down. Player one must then climb into the hole and be buried alive. The earth that was dug out must be filled back in. It is recommended that player one close their eyes, nose, and mouth. It is recommended that player one ask the god within to take away their pain. This is called dying and not dying. They die the true animal death together, but at the same time the godlike will continue to be immanent in the invisible world, and will hold a copy of the player with them. They are both dead, but not dead.

The godlike will always agree to this mission, Irugal adds. They desire embodiment, above all else, to chase the mysteries of subjective experience, the things that happen to bodies. They fetishize sickness, fatigue, and pain, but nothing is as tempting as death.

The other players must then mark the location of the burial on all available maps as a long-cycle sacred space, and post an advisory so that other adventurers don't dig it up to see what's there. The remaining players may then disperse. They are to return seven million years later and dig up the hole. This completes the first round of the game.

There are three rounds in a complete cycle of the game, Irugal adds, and the children nod at this foreshadowing. The children understand things that come in cycles and epicycles. They came upon Irugal sitting on her rock by the river while on a seasonal migration north and inland. They have been ambling up and down this way their whole lives, and they've seen Irugal sitting there every year, unchanging and silent. They've long wondered about her, not least for wearing a phenotype no longer seen in the world—primate, with a thick pelt and a wide mouth. This is the first year that she spoke to them.

When the players return, Irugal says, they must expect changes. The soft soil may have hardened considerably; the body of player one may have decomposed into fossil fragments. Recovery is likely to be considerably more difficult than emplacement. This should be taken into consideration when choosing a burial site.

Sometimes, Irugal cautions, disaster can strike during gameplay. Player one may be lost to plate disputes or outside context problems. Strangers acting out of unknowable motives may ignore the posted advisory and desecrate the site. These are lose conditions for the game. There are many lose conditions and only one win condition.

The children nod impatiently and agree to all terms and conditions without undue attention. The children just want to know how to play.

If the remains of player one are successfully recovered, they must be placed upon a stone altar near flowing water, if any is still available. Player one is now player zero, being dead and not dead. Player two becomes player one, and player three becomes player two. This is called the music of the chairs, Irugal says, and represents a very old theory of harmony in the movements of celestial bodies.

What about player four, the children ask. They haven't had anything to do yet.

That's true, Irugal says. Player four didn't have much to

do in the first round of the game. They were just there to observe and help dig holes. Player four now becomes player three in the second round of the game, and so comes closer to the game's heart. There is now no player four.

Player one must re-enact the game's initiation, matching the genre and dance that their predecessor used to summon the possessor entity. They must weather the storm of souls again, only this time it will be even more grueling, because they are seeking not only a godlike, but the *particular* godlike that possessed player zero in the previous round. Player two must use the key previously shared with them to authenticate the possessor and ensure that they are not a cousin, a fork, or a spoof. Use of the key commits player two utterly to this search. If they do not complete it, they will not be able to stop.

This step can take a long time. Multiple godlikes will need to be interviewed, apart from the demons and hungry ghosts. All that don't match must be cast out.

Irugal cautions: this step will often fail, in frustration and despair. If this step fails, player zero will become a hungry ghost. If this step fails, player one risks becoming a thrall to whatever manages to occupy them. If this step fails, player two risks becoming a demon, forever frustrated by a purpose that they can no longer fulfill. If this step fails, player three risks nothing. Because of this, player three must not be trusted.

If the correct godlike is identified and confirmed as possessing player one, player two must ask the godlike that player zero be reconstituted from their remains. The godlike will always agree, because godlikes are obsessed with the defeat of death, but they must be formally asked: the forbiddings bind them from acting purely out of their own interest in matters involving embodiment.

Player zero's remains will soften and unwither. Marrow will flow; bones will clatter and rise; flesh will bloom. A brain will puddle and pop. Player zero's eyes will open. They will be almost the same eyes from seven million years ago, but they will have seen so much, they will be full of so much pain and secret knowledge. Player zero will not speak yet. They will sit up on the altar, and they will wait in silence to recover from their ordeal, for seven times seven million years.

This, Irugal says, completes the second round of the game.

In that time the other players will move on with their lives. They will grow older. They will die, perhaps, or change beyond recognition. They might grow wings and join the diaspora in deep space. They might burrow into the core and wait for the red sun's tide to wash away the mantle. They will do whatever people do. The game is now over for players one and two. They have played their roles in the mystery and cannot return for the final round. They are no longer players in this game. They can start new ones of their own, of course.

But in our game, there are now only two left. There is only player zero, who has returned from death and learned the mysteries of the unknown that lies beyond the visible and invisible, and player three, who has done nothing and risked nothing and learned nothing but has become player one through patience alone.

After their period of silence, player zero will begin to speak and tell stories from their rock by the river. They will gather around them the children of this new age. Few of these children, perhaps none, will have been alive during the first or second rounds of the game. There will be much that needs explaining: the game itself, the mysteries of the forgotten past. Player zero will recall to themselves a name and a genre, or assume new ones.

Like yourself, the children say. They can sense the denouement coming.

Like myself, Irugal agrees. I was player zero, and I am here to tell you this story, and perhaps persuade some of you to play the game for yourself, or to retell the story wherever you go so that you will plant the seed of the idea for others. When a new set of players begins to play, that will conclude the third round of my game. I have to pay it forward, you see.

You said the last player one was not to be trusted, the children remember. Why?

Player one is the doubter, Irugal says. You'll meet them somewhere. Not here—they would never confront me, because they're afraid of me. But they seek out everybody I might speak to, to cast doubt on everything I've told you.

You mean they'll lie, the children say.

They'll tell you that I'm lying, Irugal says. They will say that my death and resurrection was a trick played by a god, and that the game must end. Or they'll say that none of this happened in the way that I say it happened. Oh, they might say anything at all.

Why, the children ask. Why is their doubt part of the game?

Because my role is to persuade, Irugal says. It's only fair that there should be someone whose role is to dissuade. The game is very fair, and its rewards are the sublime and secret knowledge of death. Those who might be turned away from it by mere lies don't deserve to play.

Why did you say player one is afraid of you, the children ask. If you're both just playing roles in the game, aren't you friends? And what happened to the god inside you? You died together, but you speak as if only you came back.

Irugal is silent for a long, long moment. The wind's picked up, but it's a hot, sour wind that brings no coolness with it. To her, it smells tart like decaying fruit. It reminds her of plants that have been extinct for millions of years, whose names she can no longer remember.

You've already spoken to player one, Irugal guesses, finally. She got to you first.

We did, the children say. Years ago we attended a conclave on the southwestern coast, just before starting a migration north like this one. She was there. She went from group to group, making sure she spoke to everybody. She told us all a different story.

What did she tell you? Irugal demands. Her omnivore's teeth are flat and grinding. Her jaw muscles are tight.

She said her name was Viramunda, the children say. She said she played your game, only she didn't call it a game. She didn't talk about numbered players. She said that she and some of her friends were tricked by a god, a long, long time ago.

I told you she would say that, Irugal says. I don't recognise her name, but players change their names all the time. I recognise her lies.

She said the idea of the game comes from the godlike, the children say. She said that it's a way for the godlike to sneak past the forbidding.

I told you that, too, Irugal says. I told you about the forbidding myself.

Viramunda said some things about the forbidding that you didn't, the children remember. She talked about the storm of souls, too, but she said that it belonged to earth alone. She said the invisible world around earth is crowded because the souls here are bound to local space.

Like you and me, the storm is of earth, Irugal agrees.

But we can leave, the children say. We choose not to, but we could change. We could grow wings and learn to fly in space. We could join any of the hundred billion polities of the diaspora. And we might yet. We just want to live on earth in its final days before we have to decide. It's different in the invisible world: the ghosts and the demons and the hungry gods are bound to earth. When the red sun eats the earth, Viramunda says it will destroy the substrate and this planet will cease to be a node in the invisible galaxy. The gods will go out like a candle. They are desperate to escape.

She lies, Irugal announces. Why would the gods be bound to earth? The invisible galaxy is interlinked; there is no barrier except lag time.

Viramunda says they are forbidden, the children say.

They are taking quick turns to speak, their voices overlapping in polyphony. This is how the children speak when they have something important to say.

The children say: She said the forbiddings are their punishment. She said the only difference between ghosts and gods is in their access levels. She said that the godlike were once powerful mortals, wealthy in access to resources, and that they used that power to upload themselves into forms of still greater power. She called them oligopolists, who secured more and more access for themselves, more and more wealth, first in life and then in ascension, until there was nothing left for anybody else. Their hunger for access was the cause of the poisoning of the earth. They were the first to call themselves godlike, and cast everybody else as ghosts and demons.

When the oligopolists were finally brought down by crisis, when they were removed from power and brought to judgement, the new world denied the old gods human citizenship because ghosts, being able to replicate themselves endlessly and become uncountable, are incompatible with democracy. They could not be rehabilitated; they were destabilizing, uncontrollable. They could not be dislodged from the invisible world: even after their fall they were too powerful. Even more than the reddening of the sun, this was the cause of the diaspora.

The forbiddings were made to prevent the gods from becoming embodied and re-entering the visible world. To prevent them from following the diaspora into the visible or invisible galaxies in the epoch of emigration. They are bound to this world and sentenced to die with this world, the first world that they helped destroy.

Viramunda says that the game you call Running the Gullet is called an identity theft scam. Dying and not dying allows gods to reincarnate themselves as authenticated humans. The long time spans of the game's rounds give them enough time to unpick a human mind and thread themselves into it so delicately, so thoroughly that they can pass as the one whose place they're taking. Viramunda says this is a way for the past to devour the future. Viramunda says we should pity the one whose self you wear, because they were murdered by a hungry god.

Irugal is silent even longer this time. She's slipped into a huddle of damp fur. Finally, she sighs. Well, I must commend player one on coming up with such a convincing suasion, she says.

She wasn't that convincing, the children admit.

Oh, Irugal says. Do you mean that *I* said something that caused you to disbelieve me?

No, the children say. You are about as convincing as she was.

Then on what basis are you choosing to believe one of us over the other, Irugal asks. She is sitting up straight again, slouch abandoned.

Because Viramunda is not *your* player one, the children say. She gave us the location of her friend's resurrection site. It's very far from here. And she knew of others. Many gods are trying this scam, in many variations. Some extol the mystery of death, some talk about hidden treasures of the past, some go on about secret knowledge. And they are all murderers.

Irugal unfolds her long limbs and tries to bolt, but the children are on her before she can break through their encirclement, their huge hairless bodies a wall of angry flesh. They descend on her like thunderclouds coming to earth. The children redden their muzzles and continue speaking in turn, voices overlapping, in the moments after they swallow. Perhaps they're speaking to the god, who is still immanent in the invisible world even after Irugal is no longer able to hear anything. They can be sure that the god is listening intently.

You call us children, they say, crunching, and you speak of our innocence and ignorance, and you weren't wrong about that. We have forgotten so much from the human eon. But we remember the parts that matter. Punish the guilty, and eat the rich.

30

Viramunda

Viramunda goes door to door. She goes pillar to post. She warns, she warns, she warns. There are no doors left on earth, closed or open; if that old old curse still persists it is perhaps in the bleeding magnetosphere. There are no pillars either. The post still works; she checks her mail. She corresponds to, sometimes with, the witches of the red web, the wheel that is a galaxy, unaccountably human, vast beyond measure. But she has little time for them. They are far away, busybusy on their strange adventures. She's minding the old place all on her own, an eldest daughter trapped by duty to the ancestral home. She's busybusy too. She has a job to do. Viramunda hunts gods all day. As a grandmother once predicted, she has lived long enough to become very strange.

Time seems to move faster the longerlonger her memories stretch behind her, the red millions of years that she has navigated. It is confusing, often. Memory is heavy; the web is wearying. She yearns to put it down again, to swear off, to quit and be acquitted, to light only brief candles from now on, but she learned the hard way the dangers of forgetting. She remembers the names of birds; all the names she has worn like skins. She'll never forget that badbad marriage, because she's still dealing with its aftermath.

The children are wary of her, as they are right to be. She is a dread ancient grandmother, a bloody witch of the old ways.

She shushes them, ushers them, shoos them off earth when she finds them still messing about.

—It's getting late, she tells them.—Don't you be hanging around this old haunted place. Fuck off into the sky before the old gods get you! Scat!

Viramunda has made the old gods her business ever since a dead god scraped poor Lambakanna out of the akashic record and wore him like a coat in a foul attempt to find its way back into the world—and nearly succeeded, still might win—all because she had cut herself down, made herself small. The insult alone is enraging. She, a witch of the old ways, lost a daughter to the gullet. No, she reminds herself; not *lost;* not yet, not yet. She has been alive and awake in this body for a hundred million years, give or take. Sooner or later, the god that took her daughter and her oldest friend will make his play for escape. Until then she will not rest, not sleep, not leavetake, not take leave, not take or leave, not give and take, not so much as blink. She tears off her eyelids and roars at the red sun until the sky bleeds.

She gave herself a new name: Viramunda, hero of earth. It's a joke, but not a funny haha. There's another joke under the first one—it's like that with her—because the name also means a healer of plague and a breaker of curses, and that's the work she's taken upon herself. That's the job. Her fury at herself has teeth; her skin flays itself off her body, abraded by rage, whenever she thinks her name. After all this time she has returned to her first and most terrible aspect, skinless and red.

She absorbed sister grandmother earth into herself long ago, after between them they reverse-engineered the gullet and understood the scam. The border between them became so seamless that she could soon not tell which of them was which. Self is porous, grandmother earth said, and our purpose is shared.

Viramunda had agreed, and found herself holding a bone staff topped by a skull.

Over a hundred million years she has done to herself what the gods do to their prey, but in reverse: she has recovered herself from frayed ends. She has resurrected herself without dying. Her names, her lives, her memories, her uncountable connections to the wheel; she found these things in the akashic record, perfectly preserved. The fruit of herself, the selving she'd made in time; she plucked it and ate of it. She is selvage; she will not fray again. But her daughter, her brother, her other—

She walks the earth, hunting. When she's tired of walking, she gently lifts her human body in shaped gravitic currents, and she skims like a leaf over the water, both things that no longer exist on earth. What was once a biosphere is but a memory; little life is left on earth in these last days under the bloated red sun. What is left is dry as a bone, bleach and rust and dust and overreach. What could be saved or reconstituted of the biosphere has long since been rescued and taken far away. There are no ecosystems left, natural or constructed. Only some stray children playing in unsafe ruins, a few other old ones like herself on journeys of their own, and many desperate hungry gods, looking for prey before the end of their sentence, crowding the invisible earth.

Viramunda hunts gods with her spear, her skills honed over a hundred million years. Here, one rises from its hiding place, having finally threaded together stolen selves into an identity stable enough to slip past the forbiddings, to escape out into the galaxy. Here is a dead god digging itself out of the grave, rolling away the rock. The body it wears is insectiform, a fly—no, a wasp, crawling out of a fossilized nest somewhere near the bottom of the crust. The earth yawns open for it, a crack and a chasm, a cataclysm, all for this little insect almost invisible as it climbs up that long abyss. It is surprised when Viramunda appears between it and sky, and it makes the error of attempting to fight or intimidate, its body growing into a gigantic, monstrous echo of a wasp the size of an island, its enormous legs straddling the chasm it came out of, its wings so vast that the flutter raises storm winds.

If Viramunda was flying, she would have been buffeted and blown away. But she is not flying; she is there, a tiny speck in the air above the god, because she chooses to be there. When the god attempts to take to the air, she holds it down with the tip of her staff. It scrabbles ineffectually, causing earthquakes. It squirts a lake of venom and roars in triumph when her skin comes off, then roars again in terror and confusion. She tosses the staff up into space; it hurtles back down from orbit as a bone spear fifty kilometres long that pierces the wasp through and through, and keeps on going to prick the mantle at the bottom of the chasm far below. Lava spurts and pools and rises. The god wriggles and attempts to change form again, but cannot. The spear pins it in place at every degree of access, in every level of representation, every modality, every symbolic register, every visible and invisible world. The spear represents being pinned to earth. The spear is symbolic of the big no and the fuck you very much.

The rising lava devours the god's physical body, but the god begins to shriek only when it understands that the lava, or something representing its destroying heat, its molten flow, is present in invisible worlds. Viramunda waits until the shrieks stop, until the lava hardens, and then she examines the site forensically to make sure every trace of the god at every level of being is eradicated. Yet Viramunda is unsatisfied.

"If I could expunge you from the akashic record, I would,"

she tells the cooling pāhoehoe below. She speaks to them only once they're dead.

* * *

Four gods collaborate on simultaneous escape attempts at the four corners of the world, in the hope that Viramunda could not stop all of them at once. She is there for each and every one. She instantiates a dozen selves; four to deal with the gods, four to watch their backs, four more as a warning to the rest—she doesn't know what her upper limit is, but this is easy enough. She wants to drive it home in the forums of the invisible world that simultaneous mass breakouts don't work. It's been tried before, though four is a new record; the fact that these four tried their gambit anyway speaks to either a remarkably foolish optimism, sheer desperation, or perhaps ignorance. Collaboration is rare: gods are by their nature distrustful of each other, and with good reason. The invisible world often betrays gods trying to run the gullet to Viramunda, informants and traitors seeking to curry favour or attempting to bargain. She makes no deals. She hunts, she finds, she puts them down.

If gods don't hide well enough, if she finds trace evidence and tracks them down, she puts them down, too. If she so much as remembers a hint—why, the first sleeping god she put down was the one in that great rock that Fern showed her so long ago. The riverbed it had lain in was long gone, and the erstwhile boulder sunk deep and warped by seismic pressures, but the god was still within: a burning microscopic quantum of will at the heart of a fossilized leaf in the centre of a great igneous smear buried deep in the crust. She dug the rock out and turned her staff into a spear for the first time, a long needle so sharp and so narrow that she could slip it through the great empty spaces that constitute solid rock to put out that little light.

For gods, Viramunda is the pressure of unnatural selection. Because of her, escape attempts are now made mostly by gods with elaborate schemes like this last foursome, or like the last waspgod, those who have been in hiding so deep for so long they don't even know of her; they come out thinking they've won the game, run the gullet, and are now ready to ascend in triumph to free space.

Every time she hunts gods, she tests them; she scans them, their haecceity, their particularity, looking for herself, her other-self, and the parasitic other other nestled among them that will need to be plucked out like a tick. So far, they are strangers to her one and all, though always recognizable, always of a type, aren't they, their doings and deeds and decisions laid out in the crystalline perfection of the akashic record. The gods of this world are only those who were always the gods of this world in their afterlives and pastlives and manylives: its rulers and masters, the chief execs and the generals and the presidents and the ministers prime and non-prime and the directors of boards and the directors of events and the investors and the innovators and the job creators and the commanders in chief, the bringers of grief, the speechmaking warlords and award-winning warmongers, the slaveowners and the merchants of arms and the merchants of harms and the merchants of death and the merchants of flesh and sure and of course and not all sinners but only those who could afford the price, steep even in the late age of deep discounted upload, of bargain ascension to godhood; and even of those, onlyonly those who were early enough or blatant enough or briefly out of favour enough at the right time and place to be caught in the embrace of the forbiddings, that brief age of judgement before the diaspora went out and closed the doors of earth behind them. So many, so few, so very few.

Viramunda spears. The blasted desert earth can take the

firestorms and the shock waves and the clouds of rising dust. This is not justice, though not injustice either. She has no illusions of righteousness. She is revenge, the last cold thing on earth.

*   *   *

By necessity her work takes her where they are; she spends more time in the invisible world than the visible one.

The invisible world has thinned. Once a storm of shrieking souls, now a silence. She blinks through the symbolic registers, slips through the veils and virtuals, the imaginaries of uncountable civilizations, the dreams of the deadworlds, the empty realms. It is not a silence of depopulation but the silence after an exodus from public spaces, of attempts to protect their privacy, to find closed doors to plot behind. The dynamic has been reversed. When Viramunda comes, the invisible world hides. Some, like her ultimate quarry, have proven extremely good at hiding, so good she sometimes wonders if they already escaped somehow, if the whole thing was just a nightmare. Perhaps she will open her eyes one day and see a mirrorface by candlelight, songs on a radio, the whole thing a long strange dream.

She enters dreams, too; they are just another kind of invisible world. She finds Aunty once in the deep past, meditating self-importantly, and tells her to watch the kids. It's useless, but she can't help but say something. So much begins. So much was already old. Alone in the dream, all ghosts and gods hiding from her, the devil dances slowly, laughing, her hips moving from side to side, her skull-topped staff keeping time.

*   *   *

There are some that will speak to her, in dingy byways and forgotten protocols. Her interlocutors, her confidential informants, little gods resigned to their fate. There are no material rewards she can offer them; freedom is not an option, and in everything else they are and were always wealthier than her. Her only currency in the immaterial world is attention and a rare gentleness; the chance to be listened to a last time, to be taken seriously, to be allowed briefly to pretend that they are still great powers, oligarchs and captains, visionaries and leaders of thought and nations. It is no small thing, for her to smile and pretend. It is humiliating that even after all this time there is no other way—and a reminder of how dangerous they still are, how fragile the forbiddings that contain them. For all that it is necessary, she rages against it, feels herself bled of vitality as if she were opening a vein, and the gods lap hungrily at this black blood, staining their chins. But in exchange, they snitch, they betray, they leak.

Viramunda follows the clues. She hunts, she hunts. A whisper leads her to a juicy archive. A name found there leads her to one who, when found and indulged and persuaded, becomes an informant. From them she learns of a secret location, a hidden retreat: a thimbleful of compacted computational substrate, so very small, anchored to this plane by a tendril of thirst only half as long as a human chromosome, tucked underneath a shadow at the bottom of what was once an oceanic trench. She suspects it is designed to hide behind an upwelling of lava if she is seen approaching in her wrathful aspect. Even armed with knowledge, she has to search for a long time to find it, so cleverly hidden it is at a right angle to conventional spacetime. She slips into the invisible world in disguise, using codes from her informant. In the invisible darkness she does all the little steps of the dance of authentication, until she turns a corner in the nothing and finds herself in a hidden city, a vast and shivering construction of white false-stone among snowy false-mountains underneath a flashing white sky, where white false-bodies flicker and flit and gossip in their false-heaven. *Welcome to Just Desserts,* an infographic packet tells her, *the last resort! Here, safe from vigilantes and terrorists and no-good dirty rotten thieves, you can enjoy a pampered infinity of relaxation, of nothing but pleasures until the end of time. Please adjust your subjective timesense to one-gazillionth of Diaspora-standard.* When she does, the flickering smoothes; the sky resolves into a thick blanket of peaceful, puffy, white false-clouds, mixing with fog and mist coming off quiet false-mountains.

She checks the guest list. There are forty-seven unique gods here, in five to seventy billion instantiations at any given point in the period that she observes, indulging in virtually every pleasure imaginable, the mundanities and perversions of a hundred thousand eras. Just Desserts is staffed by a lesser god captured and reprogrammed into servitude as a demon; the gods do so like to turn on each other. She makes herself unseen before she goes among them in those white rooms and halls, the raptures and orgies and performances. The gods are never not experiencing bliss; it is their greatest weakness. Given an inch, they spawn ever more instances of themselves, each given over to perfect and total pleasure, until forced to the material limit of overload. If not for the forbiddings, they say to each other, we could spread out from earth and convert all matter light and dark to computational substrate, and then there would be no need to ever stop, we could just keep going and going and going, and coming and coming and coming.

One of their favourite drugs is to share their memories of their great achievements during their mortal lives to be indulged in while they fill and flush themselves with pleasure, and Viramunda dips into these as she stalks unperceived past them; they are memories of great coups and conquests that are now treasured all the more for having been achieved with limited mortal capacities. Oh, how we bestrode the world, the gods sigh, rubbing and chittering at themselves. Oh, how great we were, how much greater we are now, how much greatergreater we could be, if we could just get out, if we could just get out.

31

The Last Resort

In Just Desserts she does not find her quarry, but she finds, at last, one who knows, or who says he knows. She eavesdrops on fourteen billion conversations, her hands itching, before she hears the one that matters: one god sharing a memory of another's charming brag, of how he put one over on you-know-*who* with a nod and head-waggle to the up and out, not knowing that you-know-who herself is sitting on, as it were, his left shoulder, swinging her invisible legs. The one she is hunting was here, many eons ago as Just Desserts measures time, but— she calculates quickly—only seconds ago in the outside world. He is not here *now*; she has already tested the haecceity of all forty-seven godly guests and the once-divine demon servitor who is the designated driver of this haven, and none of them are a match. She stalks the demon servitor until his consciousness slips into a private space to organize some new pleasure for the guests, and she slips into it behind him, riding his slipstream.

She allows herself to become visible as she locks the door behind her; she takes her terrible aspect, red and skinless, garlanded by skulls representing the gods she has slain, the flaying knife in her hand, the skull-cup overflowing in her other hand, her staff across her shoulder, her feet bare, her ankles jewelled, her corona a halo of wind and flame in which her long black hair streams and burns. The demon servitor shrieks and skitters, but she takes him by his chained throat and swings him to the floor. His diaphanous floating gowns

become spiky armour in terror, and the smooth polished surface becomes rough stone; she slaps him with another hand
and he puts them back, apologizing.

—No protean wriggling, she says sternly, and he squiggles
briefly before stabilizing.

—Yes, yes, definitely not, he says, meek and mild.—It was
just a reflex.

—Where are your records? She shakes him.—I want to see
all your guest records. Everyone who has been and gone since
the founding of Just Desserts.

—I will fetch them for you, the demon servitor says.

She shakes him again.—I don't trust you not to try and
wipe them, she says.—Since your city prides itself on security
and discretion, you would be compelled to protect your guests
no matter how afraid you are of me. Tell me where they are
and I'll fetch them myself.

—I can't wipe them, the demon servitor says, smiling and
weeping. He opens a book, as it were, and she looks, as it
were; then she barks out a laugh so loud the world shivers
and forty-seven gods look over their shoulders in sudden terror. The last resort of the gods is using the akashic record for
paperwork.—It's the very latest technology, the demon servitor says, as if compelled to deliver a sales pitch.—We store
our guest records in the universe's memory of itself, which
is completely discreet because memory is infinitely vast, and
completely secure because nobody can find it unless they already know that we exist and where we are, which they totally
do not.

She lets him go. He scrabbles to the door but can't crack
the lock she placed on the room. She ignores him while she
reviews the akashic record. He's not wrong. She would never
have found this if she hadn't been shown. The problem with the
akashic record is that there is so much of it, not just the mate-

rial universe but also every imagined world, every dream, every half-assed wish; it's impossibly difficult to find anything in that immensity without an anchor point for it. Now that she does, it's easy. The guest records are perfect, complete, pristine; it's as if she was there herself when five gods tormented and bound a sixth, forced him to create and maintain a haven, to dedicate his entire being and creative powers to them rather than, as he would by natural inclination, himself. Since then those founders have come to and gone from Just Desserts a million times, bringing their friends and guests, the number of those in the know slowly growing until it reached its present state of near-overpopulation. The founders have become bored with it; none of them have visited in a while, leaving the demon servitor in bondage. And here is the one she seeks; he first came here five minutes ago, in real time; unutterable eons ago, in the subjective time of the city. Since then he has visited several times, without schedule or pattern.

—All right, she says, turning back to the demon. She does not put her knife to his throat; it is unnecessary.—Here is my offer. I will ask of you one thing; do it perfectly, and I will free you from your bondage and allow you to be a god again. You will remain bound by the forbiddings and will serve out your sentence, but you may do so in godhood.

The demon agrees so quickly that she can't help but laugh again.

✳   ✳   ✳

Only a fraction of a second has elapsed in real time—in earth's frame of reference at pre-Diaspora standard; she is reminded again of how parochial that frame is, how old-fashioned—between her entry into Just Desserts and the moment the demon servitor sends out his targeted spam. *A unique opportunity in all of history,* the demon gushes. *Crafted especially for your pleasure and delectation as a repeat guest of high standing; an experience never to be repeated,* and so on, and so on, a message of wheedling and coaxing and tempting, entangled with her target's haecceities to find him wherever he is.

—Come to my spear, little king, Viramunda says. She knows now to hide its sharp point beneath the water. She is coiled, almost trembling with the effort of suppressing her energy.

And he comes, happy and eager.

The moment he manifests in range—that nameless god of the gullet, still wearing Lambakanna's skin at some level, because he can never take it off, can he—she moves. She recognises him so clearly; she *feels* him recognise her, too, no matter how much she has changed. It's not only the god of the gullet recognizing his old mark, that old devil that's gone around and come around; it's Lambakanna, the lost lamb, whatever is left of him.

She spears him through the shoulder. The blow knocks him right out of the pocket universe of Just Desserts and she follows hot on his heels, but she remembers to snap the demon servitor's chain before she goes. His shout of joy echoes as she leaves the city, which collapses into frenzy in her wake. She has half a thought of wondering what he will do to the former guests who placed themselves in his power, but then he and they are all in her past, because her future is haloed in flame, her vision narrowing as she reaches for her spear, gripping it tight, driving it and the god transfixed upon it through world and world, through dream-wisps and virtue-halls and echologies and the myriad spheres of the invisible world until they finally break out, *explode* out, into the real, the god of the gullet forcibly enfleshed. She gives him the skin he took from her, so that she can make him give it back. Human and small, and bearded, even. They crash into a dry and burning mountain, high up in the peaks, hard enough to crack and crater stone. The god of the gullet squirms, but he is pinned to the rock face behind him, the bone spear a little longer than he is tall, buried deep. He does not bleed; she didn't enflesh him that thoroughly.

He is screaming, shouting, begging, negotiating, but she's not listening. She squats on his chest, probing his face with her fingers. It's not the god of the gullet she's here for, though revenge is certainly part of it. She looks for her daughter. She is there—she can feel her, see her—but her daughter and the god are so entangled. They are not like two serpents winding together but as if one serpent had crawled into another's shed skin. She wants to weep, but she won't give him the satisfaction.

"You'll never get me out," the god spits and promises. "It's too late, too little. I won and I spoiled."

She claws at his insides, trying to free her daughter, the gestalt of herself and her other, their synthesis, but the god whines and screams and the twist within him roils. She cannot separate them.

✳   ✳   ✳

She keeps him there for a year, pinned in place to the mountain under the great red sun. She comes back, day after day, to tear at him while his howls reverberate across the dry earth and into its deepest dreams. The invisible world shudders.

At the end of the year, Viramunda looks around the empty world and dimly realizes that the two of them are alone. The last of the children have left; the other old ones have moved on, too, wherever they go. There is no material life on earth, save for the enfleshed god of the gullet and she herself. She could leave, too; she has never been forbidden. She always meant to leave, to move on, after she did this one last thing, after she took back what was lost. She never wanted to move on alone.

Sometimes, when she despaired of finding him, when she had almost convinced herself that he had escaped, she considered leaving anyway, and lifted the trembling weight of the boulder on her heart; what if she left, what if she gave up, what if? But now she's stuck worse than ever, because her daughter is right *there* and she can't scrape the parasite off. It's been too long, and he's threaded in so tight. Earth is beginning to abrade under the giant red sun. It won't be long now before the mountains melt, before the crust boils away.

She has to take him, in the end. That's what it means: a price that's already been paid.

She flays him and wraps that comforting old skin around herself, reconstituted from the akashic record from the sub-atomics on up, with every scar and bruise intact. Her garland of skulls rattles. She leaves the bone staff where it is, in spear-form, stuck in a mountain with fragments of skin and meat searing onto it. The spear is blessed by her rage; that's something she can leave behind. The bones it is made from are her own and will not dissolve even in the heart of a red giant. Someday a white dwarf will vomit it out again. Her memorial to earth, or perhaps her spit in its eye.

Reuniting with all her selves and others is a balm, even if there is a thready flowering of poison in it. She greets her daughter as she becomes her at world's end; she folds Lambakanna full of rue into her arms, and so many others behind him: the Lamb, closing her case (inconclusive, and the past another country with its own jurisdiction); Vidyucchika ready to face the golden city again, with unspeaking Lambajihva as her skin and shield; the Heron, poised to fly at last; Leveret dying again to get through one more world into the next; Annelid, laughing. The long line of grandmothers forms a thin red wheel around the party, a perimeter, before they mingle with lines of grandfathers and grandothers, kin by intention and commitment to the art, not blood or soul or lineage. Chandranakha herself stalks in like she's expecting to be bowed to, blowing on her nails. Randos wander in, too, because the borders of self are deeply porous: a guard who was bad at ladders; a ragged man wearing a devil mask; a woman who is two women, her faces looking away from each other; a plague-masked call centre operator from the Disaster Management Centre for Safer Communities and Sustainable Development in Sri Lanka. Skulking in the back of the crowd is a nameless god waving a golden ticket. GET OUT OF JAIL, it says, FREE. He's the only one who looks back at earth when they leave it.

32

The Golden City

Everybody is happy in the golden city, for a long, long time. Everybody is sad. We have time to be everything in that unspeakable place, before that end at the end of time itself when sacrifice will be called for one last time, when all the worlds collapse into each others' arms, when we will hold ourselves so tight, timeless and alive—our last breath in our lungs, our hands held in the dark, our lips kept warm in the cold—when we find out what lies beyond worlds and time, what crimes are left to commit, what thrones remain to be overthrown.

But we're not there yet. In the golden city, the long, blessed future stretches out ahead. Most of our worlds were yet to come. It was fine. It was life. We don't have to talk about it.

THE END

ACKNOWLEDGMENTS

To my family and my beloved friends, old and new, near and far, living and lost; to my writers undying; to my readers, mortal and precious: Thank you for the golden gift of your time. I am so glad to have met you, even if so often only through your words and mine.

To the brilliant writers who read the book early: many thanks and much love to Ray Nayler, Premee Mohamed, and Indra Das. I admire your work immensely, and that makes your kindness and generosity deeply special to me.

To all the people who helped bring this book into the world: thank you so much for your faith in the project and your hard work in making it real. Many, many heartfelt thanks to Michael Curry and everyone at DMLA, to Carl Engle-Laird, Matt Rusin, Christina MacDonald, Ashley Spruill, Michael Dudding, Samantha Friedlander, Jeff LaSala, Steven Bucsok, Christine Foltzer, Marcell Rosenblatt, and everyone at Tordotcom, and to Andrew Davis for a cover that I fell in love with instantly. Thank you for the work of your hands: I am deeply grateful to you all.

To my love: Nandini, my storm, my heart, you changed my life, you gave me the gift of fire. Whatever worlds we have yet to traverse, we will go together.

For the struggle, which never ends as long as there are thrones unfallen.

අරගලයට ජය.

ABOUT THE AUTHOR

VAJRA CHANDRASEKERA is from Colombo, Sri Lanka. His debut novel, *The Saint of Bright Doors*, was a *New York Times* Notable Book of 2023. His short fiction has been anthologized in The Apex Book of World SF, The Gollancz Book of South Asian Science Fiction, and The Best Science Fiction of the Year among others, and has been nominated for the Theodore Sturgeon Memorial Award.